Vegas Diary
A Dish Served Cold

Charles Titus

iUniverse, Inc.
New York   Bloomington

Vegas Diary

A Dish Served Cold

iUniverse books may be ordered through booksellers or by contacting:

iUniverse
1663 Liberty Drive
Bloomington, IN 47403
www.iuniverse.com
1-800-Authors (1-800-288-4677)

ISBN: 978-0-595-53508-8 (pbk)
ISBN: 978-0-595-63626-6 (cloth)
ISBN: 978-0-595-63562-7 (ebk)

Printed in the United States of America

To Rose, who once again pushed me to take on a new challenge.

Prologue

Charlie could care less if Bruno killed Ashley. Better her than me, he thought. He sat alone in the dark, hoping that somehow he'd survive the night. Ashley would come; he'd made sure of it. Sam wanted revenge, and Bruno was his enforcer. Nobody screws with Sam.

Las Vegas is a magnet to the masses that have screwed up their lives somewhere else, and are looking to start over. Charlie Patek was drawn to Nevada in the wake of several failed businesses in southern California. The opportunities in Vegas seemed endless to him. The place attracted a thousand potential new marks a month, Charlie guessed, and the one real aptitude he had was finding a scam and a sucker, and introducing the two.

He glanced at the eight by ten picture framed in silver on his desk. He'd met Ashley Roh a few years back, and slept with her, off and on, since then. The picture was a needed touch of domesticity for the benefit of his mortgage customers.

A subtle change in temperature made Charlie look to his office door, and then beyond to the dark reception area. The drone of the air conditioning unit was unchanged, but he felt a sudden injection of desert night air in the room.

"Who's out there?" he shouted, louder than intended.

No response. Charlie wanted to move from his chair, but a sudden tightening in his gut left him immobile.

"Sam?"

The hair on Charlie's neck stiffened, and he looked to the private exit he'd installed in his office. It led directly to a stairwell and the parking lot below. From across the lot, Charlie could hear Jimmy Buffet on the juke box at Trini's, a new locals' watering hole.

Sweat, rare for Charlie in the dry air, trickled down the nape of his neck. He stared at the door to his office.

"Ashley, that you?" he called.

No response. I must be losing it, Charlie thought.

"Bruno?"

Sam Marchesi was the largest investor in Charlie's mortgage business. He had an endless supply of cash, and the word around town said it came straight from a Mexico to Vegas drug pipeline. Bruno was his bodyguard and constant companion.

Charlie's business, Patek Investments, made loans to people who couldn't afford them. They came like lambs to the slaughter and thanked him for it. Charlie took his investors' funds and loaned them to suckers who had bad credit. He loved people with bad credit. He'd loan them money, and they'd gladly pony up thousands in fees to get it. These loans were secured by the customers' real estate, typically their home.

Charlie didn't want a guy who could pay him back. He wanted one who would pay for a while and then default. Patek Investments foreclosed on the secured property, ending up with title to the guy's house. It was a sweet deal, and having done this to countless customers over the last several years, Charlie didn't like the thought of meeting one-on-one with any of them after dark.

Charlie leaned forward to grab the office keys from his desktop when a nine millimeter bullet hit the chair behind him with a soft thud. He caught the muzzle flash in the corner of his eye and was on the move.

Charlie's reflexes belied the extra forty pounds he was hauling around these days, and a rush of adrenaline made him even quicker. A lamp shattered three feet behind him when he reached the back door to his office.

He exploded on to the staircase, looking like an overweight Count Dracula dragging part of the curtain that had covered the exit door. His heart pumped in triple time as he hit the stairs. He knew his only chance was to round the corner of the building at the parking lot level before the shooter emerged.

Compared to Charlie's office, the lot was lit like a carnival. Through the down pour of a summer shower he could see the door to Trini's and safety. Charlie took the open metal stairs two and three at a time; and when he hit the asphalt lot below, shedding the remnants of his torn drape, he didn't hesitate.

Buffet's tune had ended when a twelve gauge roared from below the staircase. Charlie felt the impact of splintering brick from the corner of the building, and several pellets of unimpeded buckshot in his shoulder. The neon light from Trini's roof top sign flashed for an instant and Charlie, spinning reflexively toward the roar of the shotgun, staggered backwards into the parking lot and heard the squeal of tires on wet pavement.

Chapter One

Jack Summers was weathering a category five hangover the day he met Sarah. He'd matched knees and elbows most of the previous night with a legal secretary named Sheila. They'd hooked up at TGI Fridays after work, and though a hell raiser in the sack, he had no interest in seeing her again.

Arriving late to his office, he got an all too familiar glare from his long suffering secretary. Jack tried rushing past her desk, but she looked up saying, "You've got a full calendar today boss. Sarah Dunn from AmCon is due any minute."

He was thumbing through a stack of mail in his office when the intercom buzzed. "Miss Dunn is here to see you."

"Send her in," he said in the direction of his phone.

As Sarah entered the room, Jack forgot how bad he felt. She looked to be somewhere in her late twenties, but Jack had long ago given up trying to guess a woman's age. These days, he was lucky if he got it right within a decade. Sarah's face had a soft look about it, so lacking in the many Vegas women he'd met, with a set of startling green eyes.

She wore a tunic dress that hung from straps at her shoulders to an abrupt halt at mid-thigh. Sarah was tall; perhaps five nine or ten, with a slender, athletic build. He noticed the well defined bare arms that were the mark of the day's younger work-out set. The plain line of her dress only accentuated the curve of what were full, natural breasts.

As she took a chair opposite Jack's desk, the hemline of her dress hiked an inch or two and she simultaneously adjusted it, pulling downward with her left hand. He took note that she bore no rings on the adjusting hand, and his impression of how his morning might go brightened.

1

Jack Summers had come to Las Vegas with little more than a bad attitude. Thirty years old and looking for a fresh start, he'd moved from a suburb of Chicago. His pregnant wife of four years, Claire, had been brutally murdered in their apartment two years earlier. He'd accepted a position with the U. S. Attorney's organized crime unit out of law school, and was working late the night Claire was killed. He blamed himself for leaving her alone. The Chicago police report said it looked like a robbery gone bad, but she'd been raped and mutilated in a way that suggested her killer liked to play with knives. Jack's office looked for months for any possible connection between Claire's death and Jack's work without success.

Spending too much time with a bottle of scotch after Claire's death, Jack lost interest in his government job, and he was headed for problems with the Illinois bar when an old friend from his days as a Navy Seal talked him into moving to Las Vegas. It was a good move for Jack. Away from the everyday reminders of Claire and the loss of his unborn child that Chicago held, he'd opened a flourishing private practice on his own.

Sarah Dunn worked for AmCon Title, one of Jack's clients. He'd been put on retainer by the manager of the company and was paid a handsome sum annually to be available to represent AmCon Title if needed.

"Good morning, Ms. Dunn," Jack said. He smiled and hoped the morning's Visine drops were doing their job.

Jack had counseled several of AmCon Title's employees in the last few months. It was usually a matter of money or credit problems; questions about paying or collecting back child support; and, occasionally, a minor criminal problem that they or a family member had. Sarah Dunn didn't fit the bill on any of these.

Jack's antennas were always up when dealing with AmCon Title referrals. He needed to know the reason an employee of AmCon had come to his office. If there appeared to be the slightest adverse interest between the employee and the company, he'd stop the interview.

"Good morning," Sarah replied.

Jack willed himself to look directly at her eyes and not at the scooped neckline of her dress. Please, no conflict with this lady, Jack thought. "What can I do for you?"

Unfolding a piece of paper she took from her purse, she dropped it on Jack's desk and said, "Mr. Roxburgh said I should talk to you right away." Roxburgh was the owner of AmCon Title.

As the paper hit his desk, Jack could see the *Great Seal of the State of Nevada* crest at the top. Even upside down he could read *Office of the Attorney General* on the letterhead. It was from an investigator. He was auditing

AmCon Title's files for the Division of Insurance, and wanted to conduct a formal interview with Sarah about certain files she'd worked on.

"What's this all about?" Jack asked.

"I worked on the escrow files that are mentioned there, starting about ten months ago," she said. "The first of two files involved an acquisition loan for a company called Anasazi Properties. My boss, Ashley Roh, handled most of it. I signed up the customers. The second one closed recently for the same company and was a refinance of the first loan."

"I know who Ashley is," Jack said.

Jack knew that whether AmCon Title or any of its employees had screwed up or not, anytime you got the Attorney General's office looking over your shoulder it wasn't good news.

"Let's get a little background first," Jack said. Taking a yellow pad for notes, he asked, "You are Sarah Dunn, D-U-N-N, right?"

"Yes," she replied. She leaned back in the chair across from Jack and crossed her legs. They were stunning, and Jack tried to focus.

"Can I call you Sarah?"

"Sure."

"What's Anasazi Properties?" he asked.

"It's a land developer. I've met the owner a couple of times," she said.

"Let's start at the beginning," Jack said.

"I met the real estate agent for the sellers of some property last summer," she responded. "He was in Ashley's office with Mr. Roxburgh, and she called me in to start a file on a sale of land by an older couple."

"Did Roxburgh or Ashley know this agent?" Jack asked.

"Bill knew him," she replied. "I heard them joke about their days in the title business together."

"Go ahead. Sorry for the interruption," Jack responded.

"Well, the older man was selling fifteen acres on the west side to Anasazi Properties for one and a half million. He'd get seven hundred fifty thousand at the closing, plus a note for the balance."

"No problem so far?" Jack asked.

"Not that I could see," she replied.

"The buyer, Anasazi, was borrowing the whole purchase price from a lender, Patek Investments. Patek's a hard money lender and a regular client of ours. Anasazi used half of the loan to pay the seller, and the other half was supposed to pay loan costs and provide funds to start building houses on the property."

"Nothing out of line yet?" Jack asked.

Hesitating for a moment, Sarah replied, "It did seem kind of funny that the developer wouldn't have any of its own money in the deal, Sarah continued. "But if the numbers match the escrow instructions, I gave up a long time ago trying to figure out whether a deal seems odd to me."

Jack wondered in passing what else she'd given up on in life, and thought Sarah seemed almost apologetic as she said it.

"So, did the deal close?" Jack asked.

"Oh yes, a couple of weeks later. The seller's agent and the owner of Anasazi showed up to sign the paperwork," she said. "The owner of Anasazi was very nice. I knew he was well off, because I'd seen a copy of his financial statement in the loan file. It showed a net worth of about twenty million dollars, most of which was held in Florida and Canadian properties."

"Were there any problems closing?" Jack inquired, referring to the meeting that normally took place when loan documents and funds were exchanged.

"I didn't think so at the time," she answered. "I do remember the old couple; you know, the sellers. They came in a few weeks after the closing and the man started yelling at Ashley in her office. They seemed pretty upset. I asked Ashley what was wrong, but she told me not to worry about it."

"What happened next?" Jack asked.

"A couple of months ago, Ashley called me from home to say she was sick, and that I needed to pull the Anasazi file from her desk and do a loan closing on a refinance of the Patek Investments' loan," Sarah replied. "She said she'd already done the paperwork, and all I'd need to do was have everyone sign the loan documents. I asked her if the sellers were getting paid off, because I remembered what a scene they'd made in Ashley's office. She told me they'd been taken care of, and Ashley's paperwork showed that Patek was only owed five hundred thousand on its original loan of a million five. Ashley said that a release of the Patek security would come later."

"How much was the new loan?" Jack asked.

"It was for five million, from Sundown Mortgage," Sarah said.

Jack knew Sundown. Their reputation was of Mob connections and lots of political juice.

"And how was it distributed?" he asked.

"Well," Sarah said, trying to recall the details. "Five hundred thousand was sent to Patek Investments. Then I took out the points and closing costs and gave the owner of Anasazi the balance. It was about four million, two hundred and fifty thousand."

Jack shifted uneasily in his leather chair; his mind jack-rabbited ahead to a maze of scenarios, none of which had a happy ending.

Finally he asked, "So, there's a problem now I take it?"

Sarah's eyes had sprung that first tiny leak, a prelude to what he hoped wouldn't be a deluge, and she said, "The state's auditor told Mr. Roxburgh that Patek's deed of trust securing the first loan hasn't been released; and,

Patek Investments is claiming that they are still owed, after the payment in March, over five hundred thousand on their original loan. He also said that he contacted Sundown Mortgage, and that Anasazi Properties hadn't made any payments on the second loan."

Sarah, tears flooding her eyes, told Jack that the property also had unpaid mechanics liens for work done on the property totaling nearly six hundred thousand dollars that hadn't shown up in the title report in Ashley's file.

"Ashley is now saying she didn't tell me to close the loan without getting a release from Patek," Sarah said. Somehow, Jack wasn't surprised.

"Has anyone contacted Anasazi about this?" Jack asked.

"Ashley said she'd called his office, but he wasn't available," she replied.

Jack's hangover returned with a vengeance as his mind took in the enormity of the problem. A piece of property worth, at best, two million dollars, could now have priority debt to the tune of six million. His client would likely be on the hook for it. Best case scenario would be major disciplinary problems with the insurance division for Sarah and AmCon Title; the worst case, potential losses for his client and its underwriters in the millions of dollars. He didn't know at that moment how much worse it would get. Jack needed to buy time to review Am Con Title's files, and to talk to Bill Roxburgh.

He placed the State's letter on his desk, and handed Sarah a tissue.

"I'm sure we'll sort it all out with Mr. Roxburgh. In the meantime, I'll respond to the investigator's request," Jack said. "Tell me about yourself."

"What do you mean?" she said.

"Just start with where you're from and we'll go from there," he replied.

Glad to not be talking about the problem in front of her, Sarah launched into a description of her background. She'd come to Las Vegas with her boyfriend from Omaha, Nebraska. They found a minister to marry them after two nights in town, but her new husband turned out to have a real penchant for gambling. He ended up working sporadically during the next few months, bottom feeding on the construction business to pay their bills.

"After about a year, Jesse left," Sarah said. "I was four months pregnant at the time with my son, Adam. He's just turned five."

Reading between the lines, Jack knew Sarah's husband had left in the middle of the night, taking all of their cash with him.

Left on her own, and after several months of what Sarah called "temp" work, she'd landed at American Title Company as an entry level escrow secretary. She'd liked the work and had a natural aptitude for the business. She'd stayed with American Title for three years, and had been recruited to AmCon Title by Bill Roxburgh.

As she talked, Sarah seemed to relax.

Jack liked her. She wasn't a flake. He could tell she had a good head on her shoulders, and knew it hadn't been easy for her and her son in Las Vegas on their own. He admired her self-reliance. She wasn't looking for a sugar daddy, or even to get rich quick. She just wanted a decent career and a chance to make a good life for her son.

Jack wondered if there was a new man in Sarah's life.

"So, is there a roommate or someone you see on a regular basis that you might have told about the Anasazi files?" he asked. A real stretch, but it was the best he could do at the moment. He'd opened the door for her to talk about any new significant others and he now waited for news, good or bad.

"No," said Sarah.

"Alright then," Jack said. "I'll need your home number, in case any questions come up when I get the company files. You can give it to my secretary on the way out."

"Of course," said Sarah, "but try not to call too late, when my son's asleep."

"Absolutely," he vowed.

She stood and smiled at him. Though Jack didn't want the meeting to end, he walked Sarah to the front door of his office with the thought that maybe things weren't as bad as they appeared. Conflict or no conflict of interest, he wouldn't abandon Sarah to the wolves. As he again told her that things would work out, he was caught off guard by her last comment.

"Maybe I'm just being paranoid, Mr. Summers, but I think someone's been following me."

Chapter Two

Ashley Roh, Sarah's boss, sat alone at a bar near the high rollers room in the casino of the Rio Hotel. Only a few blocks from her office, the Rio was a convenient pause for her after work, waiting out the traffic before heading home to Green Valley in the southeast part of town.

The bar itself, a curved design maybe sixty feet long, was inlaid with marble and oozed class. She'd frequented the Impenema Bar for years, across the main casino, until she got tired of the male tourists trying to pick her up. Three hundred dollar a pop hookers were known to hang out there, and although she'd been tempted more than once to take a young member of a bachelor's party up on his offer, she never did.

At her new spot, Ashley could see both entrances to the super-charged high rollers' room; and although she'd never actually set foot in that isolated part of the casino, she longed to. Someday, she vowed, she would. Sipping a rum and Diet Coke, playing video poker, and losing, Ashley looked up occasionally from her machine to see who came and went from the plush area in front of her.

She was thinking about Charlie Patek, and how they'd met more than a year before. It was in the summer, at an AmCon Title open reception for realtors and lenders.

Ashley had expected to meet him that night, and she was pleasantly surprised at his looks. She was standing in the large conference room of her company's main office near the Strip when Patek walked in with Bill Roxburgh.

Charlie was larger than Ashley liked her men, but he was almost good-looking. Wearing a thousand dollar plus suit with a black, mock turtleneck shirt, he looked the part of a successful Vegas businessman. His only obvious flaw was his weight. You could see the strain at his belt line, below which a premature tire of too many late night dinners longed to escape. She'd read a Review Journal article about Charlie's success, however, and Ashley wasn't about to let a little extra weight bother her. She knew what she was looking for, and how to get it.

Ashley had been raised in southern California. Her parents' inquiries into her dating life consisted primarily of questions about her suitors' bottom lines. Her mother whole-heartedly approved of her association with her more affluent friends, and in particular, Shannon Mix.

Ashley had lost her virginity in the Mix home. She was just fourteen then, and well developed for her age. Standing only five foot four, she was blessed with a perfect complexion and jet black hair. She had dark eyes, and, until the last year or so, never had to watch her weight. At fourteen, her breasts were a perfect thirty-four "D."

Her first sexual experience was with Shannon's father. Ted Mix was forty-five at the time, and Shannon was having a birthday gathering for Ashley's fourteenth birthday. They'd all been to the beach that day, returning to the Mix home for a barbecue. Ashley was in a guest room's shower, washing off the day's sand, when she heard the door open. Wiping steam from the shower door, she called Shannon's name, but got no response. Ted Mix was naked and erect when he entered the shower cubicle, putting his finger to Ashley's lips in a sign of silence. He ran on the beach daily, and still had the body of a much younger man. Mix turned her, taking Ashley from behind, cupping her breasts in his hands as she braced against the shower tile. He left her without a word, and later she found an envelope full of one hundred dollar bills and a note that said "Happy Birthday" on the vanity.

Since that time, Ashley used sex to her advantage; and, though she enjoyed it enough to seek out an occasional stranger, it was primarily a means to an end. Once she realized the power she could exert to manipulate men, she knew she'd found the key to her future. She would find a suitable prospect and marry into the lifestyle her childhood friends enjoyed.

Taking a sip from her drink and feeding another twenty into the machine in front of her, Ashley mulled over her first meeting with Charlie and wondered what was screwing up her plan to become "Mrs. Patek."

Knowing Patek would be at the reception the night she met him, Ashley'd done her homework. She'd read, several times, the newspaper article that spoke of Patek's meteoric rise in the Las Vegas lending community. He looked to be well on his way to becoming one of Vegas' newest millionaires in the booming lending and real estate markets. Charlie Patek just might be one of my last shots at a comfortable retirement, Ashley thought, and I'll pull out all the stops to bag him before my looks go south.

The night she met him Ashley had watched Patek work the room with Roxburgh. When they reached Ashley, she turned her back to them.

"Excuse me," Roxburgh said, tapping Ashley on the shoulder. "I'd like you to meet one of our top escrow officers," he said, turning to Patek. "This is Ashley Roh. Ashley, Charlie Patek, with Patek Investments."

"It's nice to meet you," she said, smiling up at him.

Charlie, standing just shy of six four and nearly a foot taller than Ashley, looked down and replied, "It's my pleasure." Pausing ever so briefly at eye contact with her, Charlie's gaze dropped to the gap in Ashley's blouse, and to the exposed, top quadrant of her full breasts.

"I've heard a lot of good things about you," Charlie said.

"Oh, really?" Ashley replied.

"You've got a reputation as one of the best in town. Any truth in the rumors?" he asked.

"Best at what?" she answered.

"Well, let's just say, I heard you are very good at what you do," Charlie responded. "You may have read about our company in the Sunday Review Journal."

"No," Ashley lied. "What did it say?"

"It was just a background piece," Charlie replied. He was visibly disappointed.

Recalling that first meeting, Ashley plugged another twenty into her machine and asked the bartender for a "rum and diet."

She noticed a man sitting alone at the end of the bar, facing her at ninety degrees. He looked up at Ashley, from time to time. He was handsome, like a mature Robert Downey, Jr.; but she wasn't in the mood for company that night.

In the last year, she found herself going to the Strip hotels to gamble three and four times a week. She was, in spite of earning a very good living, constantly short of cash. She'd started letting some of her bills go overdue. And, having already been through bankruptcy once, she was toying with the idea of wiping the slate clean of credit card debt again.

"Why don't we go to my office, where we can sit?" she'd suggested to Patek.

"Lead the way," he replied.

Charlie and Ashley talked for an hour before he invited her to dinner. They covered a range of topics, and it was verbal fencing at its best. She'd flirted openly, choosing to sit on the deep couch, rather than at her desk. Charlie took one of the chairs opposite, his eyes darting at the feast as she crossed and re-crossed her legs in the short skirt.

He'd wanted to know what kind of accounts she was handling, and whether any of her customers might need his company's services. He'd asked whether she had any problem charging extra fees that might, or might not, be detailed in loan documents. She'd said she didn't. According to Ashley, if the borrower agreed to pay unusual charges, it was none of her business.

She'd been more interested in talking about Charlie that first night. Having committed the Journal article to memory, it was easy to lead Patek into talking about himself, and how far he'd come in a short time. She'd already decided he had to be making some of the serious money that Ashley was looking for. He was blatantly interested in her sexually. All she'd had to do was set the hook, and reel him in.

"Why don't we try Fiore's at the Rio?" Charlie had suggested. "I've got to check on a suite we rented there for a meeting this morning."

Fiore's Ristorante and Grille was situated away from the main casino at the Rio. World class food and service, for those who can afford it, is the reputation they enjoy.

Ashley sipped on her drink and recalled how hopeful she'd been that evening, and now nearly a year had slipped by.

The rest of that first night with Patek was a blur for Ashley. He'd ordered dinner for her with great flourish and seemed pleased when she told him her favorite drink was champagne. He'd ordered Dom Perignon, and the bottles kept coming. By the time he suggested that she accompany him to the suite, she'd wondered what took him so long.

Ashley's first view of the Strip from Patek's suite had cemented her plan to marry him. It was overwhelming, as only the combination of decadent surroundings and a billion watts of electricity can be. Floor to ceiling windows opened the suite to a light show found nowhere else in the world.

"This is fantastic," Ashley had said, moving to the window.

Charlie said nothing, but moved up behind her, pressing his erection into her back.

"Whoa, big guy, that a flashlight in your pocket?" she'd said, laughing.

"I'd like to show you," Patek had replied.

Turning to face him, she'd slid down his zipper and slipped her hand inside. She'd stayed until just before dawn, leaving a spent Patek lying naked on the bed.

As she thought of that night now, a year later, Ashley knew it was some of her best work. She'd known he would call her. The hook had been set to the bone. In fact, the ensuing months had gone so well, she couldn't for the life of her figure out why his expected proposal of marriage was yet to come.

"Tommy, one more for the road," Ashley called to the bartender, shaking herself into the present.

"I'd like to get that if I may," a man's voice interjected. It was the man from the end of the bar.

Before Ashley could protest, he shoved a hundred dollar bill across the bar.

The young bartender looked at Ashley, a question mark on his face. She relented with a nod.

"My name is Marcel," he said pleasantly. "And you are..?"

"Ashley, Ashley Roh," she replied.

Chapter Three

A year before Jack Summers met Sarah Dunn, Daryl McKenna waited at a table near the entrance to Charlie's at The Lakes bar on west Sahara. He'd been sitting like a tied puppy for nearly an hour. The anticipation of his meeting with Marcel DeMartes was driving him crazy. He could feel the heat of the desert sun sniffing its way into the darkened bar every time a new patron opened the door to the entrance vestibule. And, though the place was air conditioned, Daryl had long ago begun to sweat.

McKenna was a big man. He stood over six feet four, and these days carried an uneasy two hundred fifty plus pounds. His hair had started to disappear in his early forties, and now existed only as whitened borders above each ear and at the nape of his thick neck. He tipped his head to look at the real estate listing on the table in front of him.

Daryl grew up in Fresno, California, and although he spent a few undistinguished years in the army in his early twenties, most of his life played out in various communities of southern California. If there was anything remarkable about Daryl, it was how singularly unremarkable he was. He married a girl five years his senior when he left the army. When no children blessed their union after a number of years, they simply stopped trying.

His wife, Judy, had been working for most of their married life at secretarial or bookkeeping jobs. Daryl knocked around the real estate industry, floating in and out of sales. For ten years, he worked in the title insurance business; eventually as a title insurance salesman for Sun Coast Title in Riverside, California. It was there that he met Bill Roxburgh.

As a title marketing rep in Southern California, before the State came down hard, you practically wrote your own ticket on expenses. Daryl lived the high life like he had never seen since. He missed the days of being able to spend like it was going out of style.

McKenna played with his drink straw, twirling it continuously, and putting it to his lips from time to time. He'd given up smoking for what seemed the hundredth time last week. Now, waiting for DeMartes, he knew he'd never make it through the night without a nicotine blast to his nerves. His latest attempt at real estate sales had come on the heels of his abrupt departure from Old Republic Title.

All I need is a break, he thought.

The entrance door to Charlie's opened, and again Daryl's head snapped in that direction. It wasn't his man.

He vaguely remembered being introduced to Marcel DeMartes at a meeting of the Southern Nevada Builders Association two weeks earlier. When DeMartes had called him at home to ask for this meeting, Daryl was at a loss to remember what they'd talked about. But, when DeMartes said he was interested in developing the fifteen acres McKenna had for sale, Daryl nearly dropped the phone.

When his wife asked what was wrong, he just smiled and said, "Not a thing!"

McKenna met the owners of the property, Helen and John Kirshbaum, through his wife. Mrs. Kirshbaum had mentioned to Judy that she and her husband wanted to sell some property they'd owned for a long time near Buffalo and Westcliff on the west side of Las Vegas.

McKenna leapt at the opportunity to list the property, which he did at the inflated price of one hundred thousand dollars an acre, or one point five million. McKenna had known when he signed the Kirshbaums that the price was too high. But, he'd desperately needed the listing and felt he had a better chance of talking them down from their asking price after the property had been on the market for a while.

He'd spent much of the time waiting for DeMartes, calculating and recalculating what his commission would be under various sale scenarios. Of course, at full price, since he'd not only listed the property but also turned up a buyer, his four percent would yield a tidy sixty thousand dollars.

A smile crossed Daryl's lips as he circled and recircled the figure he'd written on the pad before him. It was a bigger pile of change than McKenna ever hoped to see headed in his direction. He'd dressed for the occasion. To McKenna, business meetings required his short-sleeved white shirt with a tie. The top button didn't quite close, but he cinched up the tie knot to give the half-hearted illusion that it did.

Where in the hell can this guy be, he wondered almost aloud. As if I've got nothing better to do!

In the parking lot, Marcel DeMartes sat patiently in his leased Mercedes SL500. The air was on full blast, and he checked his look in the rearview mirror. He'd been there about fifteen minutes, maybe longer. He knew McKenna was there and pictured him waiting inside. I should let him squirm a little longer, he thought, but didn't want to chance overheating his car. Opening the car door, he felt air sucked from his lungs as he stepped onto the softened asphalt surface.

"I'll never get used to this heat," he cursed to the empty lot.

DeMartes swung the entrance door to the bar open and tried to get his bearings in the dark interior. Momentarily blinded, he didn't see McKenna approaching with hand outstretched.

"Thought I'd missed you," McKenna said. "I was running late from another meeting on this property, and only got here a few minutes ago."

"Sorry I'm late," DeMartes said, smiling at the dark outline in front of him.

"Well, I guess it's worked out for the best, since we're both here now," McKenna replied.

"My last appointment ran over," Daryl commented as he led them into the dark bar. "I've got another buyer interested in this acreage, but he's trying to get me off the listing price. I hope we can come to terms so I can tell the jerk he shouldn't have tried to low-ball me."

Again DeMartes smiled, remarking, "I think you'll like what I have to propose. Let's sit down, shall we?"

Moving towards the table that McKenna had staked out, DeMartes took another opportunity to size up his partner-to-be.

"How have you been?" he asked McKenna as they took seats opposite each other.

"I'm doing great," Daryl said. "I've just been so busy lately. It's hard to keep on schedule. It's lucky you were held up too."

"Yes, I apologize if you had to wait long. I can't get used to the traffic out here."

"You can say that again," Daryl said.

"How's your wife, Judy, doing?" Marcel asked. "Is she still in touch with the Kirshbaums?"

DeMartes watched with satisfaction as Daryl squirmed in his seat.

How much did I tell this guy the other night, Daryl wondered. He could remember having a drink or two with DeMartes, and when he seemed interested in buying development land, Daryl couldn't resist playing the big shot by rolling out the details of his new listing.

"How about a drink?" Marcel asked.

"I'm just sipping on my first," McKenna said, pointing to his glass. "But I'll be ready by the time yours gets here."

He was already on his fourth scotch and water.

DeMartes waved at the bartender whose name turned out to be Angel. It was too early to have any floor help, so after a few minutes she walked over and took their order. She looked to be in her mid to late thirties but had kept her shape. She returned after a few minutes with another scotch for Daryl and bottled water for DeMartes. As she bent to the task of setting down their drinks, Daryl's and DeMartes' eyes moved simultaneously to her tanned breasts, half covered in a plunging v-necked tee shirt.

Daryl smiled as a co-conspirator to Marcel and said, "Outstanding!"

Ignoring the comment, Marcel took a sip from his Perrier bottle, and said, "Let me run something by you. I'll pay list price for the Kirshbaum property with some conditions. Most of my liquid assets are tied up in development land in Canada, and I can't afford to let those opportunities go. I am, however, very interested in developing the Kirshbaum property immediately."

"You wanna buy this piece with no money down?" Daryl asked.

"Yes," DeMartes replied. "I've done this before in Florida."

"You did development in Florida?" Daryl asked.

"Yes," DeMartes replied. "Let me explain. I want to borrow the full purchase price from a local lender. You'll have to help with that. I know I'll have to pay points and probably, a higher than market interest rate. I'll leave the selection of the lender up to you. I'll pay the Kirshbaums their price, but they'll have to carry back seven-fifty for two years at the same interest I'm paying the primary lender. This will free up half of the purchase price to pay the up front loan points and closing costs, and leave enough to begin development with several model homes."

"I assume you've got this listed at six or seven percent commission?" DeMartes inquired.

Without hesitating, McKenna said he had it at, "five," but only as a "favor to the sellers."

"Normally I charge more," Daryl added quickly. In truth, John Kirshbaum had easily negotiated a four percent deal.

"Of course," Marcel responded. "What I've got in mind is a development of seventy-five homes with an average sale price of two hundred and fifty thousand dollars.

I calculate, based on my research here and my experience in Florida, that we can get a good jump on the initial development and build three to four models with the seed money." After that, he explained, they would have enough sale contracts on line to allow them to get larger, "more permanent" financing in place.

Daryl for the first time allowed himself to think beyond his initial commission, and began calculating additional fees on the sale out of the homes that were built. Even at three percent, they would exceed five hundred sixty thousand.

"Have you got a marketing agent in mind for the sale outs?" Daryl asked and took a long pull on his Cutty Sark.

"How about you?" Marcel said without hesitation, sinking the hook. "You seem well qualified."

"Well, I'd have to check my other commitments," Daryl replied.

"Certainly," Marcel responded. "Of course we shouldn't enter into any formal arrangements until after the purchase from the Kirshbaums. We wouldn't want any appearance of a conflict of interest, right?"

"Absolutely not," Daryl responded, not really knowing what he meant.

As if with a trusted partner, Marcel leaned into the remaining financial details.

"I calculate the total acquisition, development and sale costs of the project at approximately sixteen million. The project should, conservatively, sell out at nineteen million. That will leave a profit of nearly three million for us; at least that's the way it worked for me in Florida," he explained.

Daryl let out a low whistle.

"I'll need your help convincing the sellers that they'd like to make a pile of interest on the money they loan me," DeMartes continued, "that, and an introduction to one of your local lenders that might be interested in this project." Marcel finished, easing back in his chair.

"What kind of interest are we talking about on the loan?" Daryl asked, jumping ahead in his mind to a meeting with John Kirshbaum.

"I think we can go as high as fourteen percent if they'll subordinate their interest to the prime lender," DeMartes said.

"What about the prime loan?" Daryl asked.

"We can afford the same level there," DeMartes said.

"How many points?" Daryl asked.

"I'd like three, but I'd go as high as five," DeMartes responded. "Why don't you run this by your clients. I'm not shopping other properties for now, and if it looks like we're in business, we can meet again when I get back from Florida in a few days," DeMartes said, ending their conversation.

He stood and shook Daryl's sweaty palm.

Daryl, lying, told DeMartes that he needed to stay for another meeting. He walked him to the door and watched as he made his way to the new Mercedes. The night was just turning to the half light of dusk as Daryl reentered the bar.

He moved to a bar seat and waved to Angel as he sat down. From this vantage point he would not only get quicker service, he'd have an improved view of Angel's cleavage. He simply couldn't believe the turn of his luck. A few weeks before, he was wondering how long he could keep the wolves from his door. Now, he had practically wrapped up a deal for a million and a half! Assuming he could make the deal work, he'd be set for the next several years, with an income that would put him back in clover.

The bar was beginning to fill with the after five crowd. Daryl knew he should be trying to contact the Kirshbaums, but he wanted to savor the moment and celebrate with a few cocktails.

I've earned it, he thought.

All those years of being the guy that didn't get the break left Daryl in a state of alcohol induced euphoria now that things were looking up. He savored the thought of telling his wife how he had already turned the big deal. The Kirshbaums could wait until morning.

They're probably already in bed, he rationalized. He'd call them in the morning and make them take DeMartes' terms.

Daryl hadn't noticed the young man who occupied a barstool a couple of chairs down from him. As he raised his glass and toasted himself, Daryl heard the man say, "Celebrating?"

"Yeah, I just closed a deal for a million five," he replied.

Over the next hour, Daryl laid out the entire transaction to the stranger. He, of course, embellished the numbers and his role in the deal. He gave the impression that he and DeMartes were actually partners in the deal, and that he would clear in the neighborhood of two million himself.

The young man, "Jesse" he called himself, seemed duly impressed by Daryl. He didn't have a lot to say, but gratefully accepted Daryl's hospitality. McKenna was running a tab, taking the liberty of pre-spending some of his soon-to-be-realized commissions.

Jesse looked like an undernourished beach bum to Daryl. But he was a good listener, and Daryl's ever-increasing slur didn't seem to bother him. When the young man finally left, he knew most of McKenna's life story and could have written the contracts on the Kirshbaum deal himself.

Daryl left Charlie's Bar shortly after Jesse. With some difficulty, he found his car and keys.

Drunk driving is a skill a man can be proud of, Daryl thought.

He found his wife asleep when he made it to their apartment, so he blissfully passed out on the couch. His last thought before oblivion was of sweet success.

Chapter Four

Daryl woke to the sound of his wife running a vacuum cleaner near the couch he'd used as a bed. His head, still thick with scotch, spun as he sat upright.

"Shut the damn thing off," Daryl screamed.

Bright sunlight spilled into the living room area of their small apartment. Daryl shook his pounding head in an attempt to clear it.

"I thought maybe you needed to be up," his wife said, "it's almost eleven."

Judy McKenna was a quiet woman; old fashioned in the way she'd always deferred to her husband. Daryl was the boss, "right or wrong," she'd tell her friends. She had a plain, drawn, look about her. Never a pretty woman, Judy would be described by most people as pleasant looking.

She made friends easily when Daryl wasn't with her. She'd worked during the last twenty years at various secretarial jobs and spent several of them doing the books for a small construction firm in California; just before Daryl drug her to Las Vegas. Life with Daryl was a challenge for Judy. They'd moved a lot, chasing from one of Daryl's jobs to the next, but she'd never complained. She remained grateful to Daryl for marrying her, and so she tolerated him. She even loved him in her own way.

"I sold the Kirshbaum property last night; the meeting ran late," Daryl mumbled, trying to justify his sojourn on the couch. Though she never really complained, Judy could always make him feel guilty.

Judy turned off the vacuum and said, "That's wonderful news, honey. When do you get paid?" Judy had seen the pile of unpaid bills on their kitchen counter.

"It shouldn't take too long to close," Daryl said. "There are a lot of details to handle on a deal this size."

"Have you got Kirshbaum's phone number handy?" he wheezed.

"It's written on the inside cover of the phone book. How much will your commission be?"

Daryl stood up from the couch with effort, licking his dried lips. He was dying of thirst, dehydrated from the scotch. As he moved toward the kitchen he said, "It should be about sixty thousand."

Judy looked at him incredulously, and he savored the surprise.

"That's not all," he said. "Looks like I'll be doing the sell-outs on almost twenty million worth of new homes. The buyer likes my work and wants me to handle the whole deal for him. Maybe we're finally going to catch a break!"

She'd heard this epitaph before, so Judy simply smiled, and hugged her husband as he passed her on his way toward the refrigerator. He reeked of alcohol.

"I'm so proud of you," she whispered, kissing the stubble on his cheek. Daryl McKenna was already a richer man than he'd ever know.

He managed to reach Helen Kirshbaum a short time later, and they scheduled a meeting at the Kirshbaum home in Sun City for three o'clock. By the time Daryl arrived he'd showered and shaved, but the odor of Cutty Sark lingered unmistakably. He sat opposite Helen and John Kirshbaum at their dining room table, trying to keep his distance.

"I've got a buyer for your property at full list price," Daryl commented. "But you'll have to carry back half the price for two years."

"I don't think we're interested," John Kirshbaum said, leaning back in his chair. "I'm looking for a cash deal."

"I understand," Daryl replied. "I didn't like the offer at first myself. But, then I thought maybe you'd like to spread out the gain on this. Your basis has gotta to be pretty low. Also, I was able to get a good interest rate on the note. The buyer wanted eight percent, but I insisted on fourteen. This will help you with capital gains and give you a guaranteed income on the carry-back of roughly two hundred twenty-five thousand over two years."

"What's our security on the carry-back?" Kirshbaum asked.

"You'll get a deed of trust, behind the primary lender, that will secure your interest," Daryl responded. "The buyer's a successful developer, so you can't lose! The property securing your note will just get more valuable." Daryl went on to explain that the buyer, whose name he couldn't divulge at this point, was a very successful builder from Florida.

John Kirshbaum had spent nearly twenty years on the Chicago police force before moving to Las Vegas in the early seventies. Now, almost twenty-five years later, he still looked at everything through the eyes of a cop.

He'd left the force in Chicago when an internal affairs investigation started getting too close for comfort. He'd been on the take for years, and there were rumors that John and a few buddies set up and killed a drug dealer as a favor to certain Italian friends of theirs. Not that another dead drug dealer in Chicago would cause any ripples. This one, however, just happened to be working undercover for the FBI. Kirshbaum decided not to wait out the investigation. Instead, he conjured up a back injury and was able to work an early retirement based on disability. The investigation fizzled when he left Chicago; out of sight, out of mind.

Kirshbaum had gone to work in security for one of the large casinos when he arrived in Las Vegas. The town was still relatively small then, and openly in the grip of certain families in the east. John's Chicago friends had helped him get the job. He'd retired with a healthy portfolio, including the acreage he was now selling. John had stayed in shape over the years, and if his six foot, one hundred eighty pound frame was disabled in any way, it wasn't obvious.

Kirshbaum liked to bully people, and Daryl McKenna looked like a prime candidate. He didn't like Daryl the minute he laid eyes on him. Looking across the table at him now, he felt like giving Daryl a good beating. Instead, he said to his wife, "Honey, will you excuse us for a few minutes?"

When Kirshbaum's wife left the room, he turned to Daryl.

"Who's the buyer?" Kirshbaum demanded. "And don't give me any bullshit about waiting for a formal offer."

Daryl, caught off guard by the threateningly direct question, blurted out the details of what he knew about Marcel DeMartes. Not wanting to jeopardize the deal, he embellished the facts only slightly.

"DeMartes is a successful land developer in Florida," Daryl said. "He's got millions in Canadian property. If his cash wasn't tied up down there he could pay outright for your property."

Trying desperately to regain some control of the situation, Daryl said, "I deal with this type of set up all the time. It's always the rich guys who can't come up with cash out of pocket."

"And I don't get any of my interest on the note until two years after we close?" Kirshbaum asked, almost as an accusation.

"Well, that was his first offer," Daryl responded. "We can counter if you want, but at this price, I don't want to scare him away."

"Alright, here's what we're going to do," Kirshbaum said, leaning across the table.

He proceeded to tell Daryl that the price and loan amount was alright, but he wanted sixteen percent interest instead of fourteen, paid in monthly installments. Finally, he wanted Daryl to cut his commission to two percent, since he hadn't really done much to earn that kind of money.

Daryl tried in vain to protest the commission cut, which would cost him thirty thousand. But it was clear that Kirshbaum wasn't going to budge. He thought again about the sale-out commissions that DeMartes was offering him, and reluctantly agreed. After all, he rationalized, the sale commission was peanuts compared to what he'd make in the next two years selling the seventy-five houses DeMartes would build.

Helen Kirshbaum entered the room at that moment, and John stood, extending his hand to Daryl, smiling.

"Looks like we've got a deal here, honey," he said, to both her and the befuddled McKenna.

"Great news!" she said to Daryl. "Say hello to your wife for us."

As he drove away, Daryl cursed Kirshbaum out loud in the car. He felt like Kirshbaum had hit him in the balls, instead of making a counter-offer. Daryl briefly considered another trip to see the luscious Angel, but the heat of the July sun poured in through the air vents of his car, and he turned towards home.

Early the following morning, Daryl made a call to Bill Roxburgh at Am Con Title.

"Hey, Bill, it's Daryl," he said to Roxburgh's greeting. "How would you like to handle a seventy-five unit subdivision, average two hundred fifty thousand?"

"Sounds good to me. What have you got?" Roxburgh responded.

"I'm putting the finishing touches on a vacant land deal for a developer from Florida," Daryl said.

He covered the layout of the deal, omitting any reference to the fact that there was no meeting of the minds at this point. He explained that his developer needed some short term acquisition and development funds, and would be willing to pay a premium. Since his considerable assets were tied up with other projects, the loan would have to come from a lender that specialized in high risk and return programs. Daryl was looking for a referral.

Roxburgh, who had started Am Con Title by catering to the hard money lenders in Las Vegas, said he thought he knew a good match for the deal. He'd been doing business with Charlie Patek's company, Patek Investments. He told McKenna that he'd arrange a meeting for Daryl's client.

A week later, Daryl sat in the reception area of Patek Investments with the man he knew as Marcel DeMartes. Patek's office on west Sahara looked cheap. It as one of a series of offices occupying a large building across the parking lot from Trini's Restaurant and Bar.

Daryl was fidgeting like a virgin bride on her wedding night. His conversation with DeMartes, earlier that day, had gone pretty well. He'd laid out Kirshbaum's counter-offer, and DeMartes hadn't seemed phased by it.

He'd told Daryl that they could probably work something out, if the primary loan could be negotiated. At least Daryl's deal still had life.

Charlie Patek kept McKenna and DeMartes waiting for more than thirty minutes by the time he emerged from his office. Dressed in suit and tie, he looked the part of a banker.

"Sorry to keep you waiting," Charlie said as he entered the reception area. "It's been kind of crazy around here lately. Has Lila been taking care of you?"

I wish, Daryl thought.

Lila was the leggy blonde receptionist who Daryl figured to be in her early twenties. She was built like a topless dancer, and good-looking in a horsy way. What Daryl didn't know was that Lila was Charlie's seventeen year old niece. Charlie liked keeping his business in the family, and he took good care of her.

"We're just fine," DeMartes said. "I'm Marcel DeMartes." He didn't bother introducing Daryl.

Charlie turned to Daryl and asked, "You must be Daryl McKenna. Bill Roxburgh told me about you." Roxburgh had described McKenna as an old acquaintance from his days at Sun Coast Title; not very bright, but harmless, was his short description.

"Yes," Daryl said, extending a hand to Charlie.

Patek ignored the proffered hand, and turned to lead DeMartes towards his office. Daryl followed, smiling at Lila as he passed her desk. He thought she smiled back, but then she seemed to have a perpetual smile on her face.

"How can I help you gentlemen?" Patek asked.

DeMartes let Daryl explain the project to Patek while he took in the lay out of Charlie's office. Everything had the feel of flea market. He figured Patek must have an interest in a used furniture store, the way the place was filled with odds and ends. He wondered what the curtain on the wall in the corner was for. It clearly didn't cover a window.

Patek interrupted with questions occasionally but gave the impression that Roxburgh had filled him in before the meeting. He already knew he'd make this loan if the price was right. He didn't really care if DeMartes had a pot to piss in. If these guys had convinced the property owner to make the deal, Charlie would be happy to charge them a bundle to make the loan. He figured the odds were good that he would end up owning the property through foreclosure when they defaulted on their payments.

Like lambs to the slaughter, Charlie thought. If DeMartes is successful, Patek reasoned, he'd make a huge return on the origination points and interest; if he failed, all the better.

"I'm going to need eighteen percent on the loan, paid monthly, and eight points up front plus closing costs," Patek said to DeMartes. "You can have the money in about a week." He was already thinking of an "A" list of investors to let in on the package. Sam Marchesi will like this deal, he thought.

Hearing the proposal, Daryl's gut wrenched. His big chance would go up in smoke. There's no way DeMartes will agree to this, he thought. Grabbing for straws, Daryl responded for DeMartes.

"That's out of the question. Way too high!"

Patek ignored him, looking to the obvious decision maker for an answer.

"Let me have Mr. McKenna call you tomorrow. I have to check some cost figures," Marcel said after a pause.

"That works for me," Charlie responded. "I hope we can do business."

As they left Patek's suite, Daryl felt like a school boy about to piss his pants. He forgot to smile at Lila on the way out. He was waiting for DeMartes to say something, but couldn't restrain himself.

"Think you can make this work?" Daryl asked.

"That depends on you, partner," DeMartes replied.

DeMartes took Daryl across the parking lot to Trini's. As they walked, he noticed the back stairs to Patek's office. That's an exit, covered by a curtain on the inside of Patek's office, DeMartes thought to himself.

It was early afternoon, and the gap between the lunch crowd and cocktail hour left the place nearly empty. Just a few gamblers leaned intently over their bar top machines. He let McKenna dangle as they walked, wondering aloud how he could handle the finance package now proposed. Finally, as they were seated at a table looking down Sahara towards the Strip, he laid out what he had in mind.

"The only way I can handle this development with my ongoing commitments in Florida and Canada, is to take you on as a partner," DeMartes announced as their waitress walked away.

"I'll need some up front capital from you; fifty thousand should do it," DeMartes said. "You can take it out of your commission on the deal. You'll act as project manager, and be responsible for getting the development off the ground floor and into build out."

"What about my real estate business?" Daryl asked, not knowing what else to say.

"We'll form a development company that will pay you a salary, say, four thousand a month," DeMartes responded. You'll handle the sale outs and earn commission. In addition, you'll get ten percent of the profit on the total subdivision. That should amount to about three hundred thousand. I'll need to be in and out of the city on a regular basis on other business. You'll run the project in Las Vegas."

Daryl scrambled over the figures in his head. It was obvious that DeMartes expected Daryl to clear enough commission from Kirshbaum to make the fifty thousand dollar investment. Daryl had told him five percent, or seventy-five thousand. However, at a two percent share, Kirshbaum left him getting only thirty thousand.

"What if I can't do this right now?" he asked Marcel, his common sense telling him to take the thirty thousand and run.

"Then we don't have a deal," Marcel replied.

"I've got some other commitments on part of the commission. Just on a short term basis," Daryl lied. "I could invest thirty thousand to begin with."

"That works for me," DeMartes agreed. "But I'll need the rest in thirty days."

"Sure, no problem," Daryl said, wondering where in the hell he'd get another twenty thousand.

Marcel made a few calculations on his bar napkin and circled the number at the bottom. He shoved the note across the table at Daryl. McKenna's face had the look of a boy about to have intercourse for the first time. He was scared, but there was no way he was backing out on almost nine hundred thousand bucks! This is a chance of a lifetime, Daryl thought. He'd control the company on a day to day basis, make a nice salary, and his mounting stack of bills would disappear. The four thousand a month would match his highest lifetime pay in the title, or real estate business. He couldn't wait to lay this on Judy.

DeMartes, watching with interest as the expression on McKenna's face revealed his decision, said, "Are we in agreement, partner?"

"Yes," Daryl said.

"Call Patek in the morning and get the ball rolling on the loan," DeMartes instructed. "Then call Bill Roxburgh and get the escrow open on this deal at Am Con Title. Place the escrow with one of their senior escrow officers, Ashley Roh." It didn't occur to Daryl to ask how Marcel knew Ashley.

Daryl sat intently taking notes on the back of the paper DeMartes had handed him, once again the pupil. Marcel ordered a scotch and water for Daryl, launching into a series of tasks that would need to be addressed by the "new operations" manager of Anasazi Properties, Ltd., a Nevada corporation which Marcel had already formed.

Chapter Five

Sam Marchesi was born in the wake of the collapsed American economy, and at the doorstep of the Great Depression. He spent his early years in Hot Springs, Arkansas, where his father did odd jobs for the Marcello crime family. Sam's father was a gambler and a drunk. By the time Sam was ten years old, he'd lived on the streets and scratched out a living running numbers and stealing.

Hot Springs, a model of corruption even then, would become the provincial southern capital of organized crime. A future president of the United States would be raised there, and the seeds of his future were already sown. Years after Sam left, that president's uncle Raymond, running slot machines for the Marcello crime family, would help launch a political career intimately tied to Las Vegas from its inception. Nevada, with its paltry electoral votes, would become a regular stop for the future president in his bid for election and reelection.

Sam killed his first man at age fifteen. He was working for Lester "Benny" Binion's organization in Dallas when a local tried to highjack the satchel of cash Sam was running between casinos. In the ensuing fight, Sam gutted him from "navel to necktie," he would boast later. Binion was the boss of the Mob's activities in the Dallas area in the early forties, so there were no arrests.

When Binion left Dallas in 1946, headed for Las Vegas, Sam tagged along. Binion opened his famous "Horseshoe" casino in 1951, and Sam hired on as a dealer. It was later rumored that Sam was directly involved in the bombing death of William Couthard, the first FBI agent assigned to Las Vegas. But, as in Dallas, the authorities refused to bring charges.

Sam moved to the Desert Inn casino when Binion left for what turned out to be a forty-two month stretch in Leavenworth prison. Morris "Moe" Dalitz, with his associates from Cleveland and Detroit, took over the operation, and Sam saw an opportunity to move up. Sam spent the ensuing years coordinating a burgeoning drug trade from Mexico to Las Vegas for his bosses back East.

He had amassed a personal fortune for himself and specialized in finding opportunities to launder his employers' immense drug profits via legitimate businesses in Las Vegas and elsewhere. A small time hustler named Charlie Patek had caught Sam's eye. He'd been bumping around Vegas for a couple of years, making some noise trying to broker private investor funds in the valley.

Marchesi had met with Patek and offered to make funds, in virtually unlimited amounts, available to Charlie's company. Sam would own no part of the operation, but made it clear that he expected *very good* returns on the money he would provide for loans. In addition, one of his corporations or designees would take title to a good share of the property that would come into Patek's hands by way of default and foreclosure. Of course, he would allow Patek a fair share of the profits. After all, Sam commented, "We're not animals."

From that first meeting, Charlie understood that it would be a bad idea to lose any of Sam's money. And, over the years since, he hadn't even come close. The various entities he used to funnel money to Charlie had also acquired a sizeable amount of residential and commercial property by foreclosing on those who were foolish enough to be late on any payments.

Charlie had known that Sam was somehow connected, but the information was never volunteered, and he knew better than to ask. Why look a gift horse in the mouth? Charlie reasoned.

He came in contact with Henry "Bruno" Stallone when he met Sam. As far as Charlie could tell, Sam never went anywhere, even to the head, without Bruno at his side. Bruno Stallone, though he'd lived in Chicago, and then Las Vegas, still sounded like he'd just stepped out of the Bronx neighborhood where he was born. He was six foot five inches tall, and had the build of a lumberjack. And, though he was probably in his forties when Charlie met him, Bruno still stood with broad, erect shoulders that tapered to a thirty-four inch waist. Looking into his eyes, if you dared, you'd think of marbles painted in flat black. There was no depth. The sport coats he wore, even in the blazing heat of the desert summers, never quite concealed the automatic weapon that hung just under his left arm.

It wasn't like Sam needed a lot of protection. Even at sixty, he gave Charlie the clear impression that he could, and would, tear your head off and shit down your neck if you crossed him.

From the start, Sam had made it clear that Charlie was to seek outside investors. As Charlie identified and attracted wealthy investors moving into Vegas, he provided Sam's friends with valuable leads. The result would be burglaries, shake-downs, telemarketing scams, and the usual high-roller hustle. Charlie's legitimate customers were fair game for Sam's cronies.

It was a time honored tradition for Sam's employers. Even Howard Hughes, the billionaire who made his fortune mismanaging government contracts, acting as a de facto arm of the CIA, and who practically bought the whole city starting in the late 1960s, would fall prey to them.

By the time Charlie called Sam to go over the details of the Anasazi Properties loan, they had each made millions. Sam was satisfied, and Charlie was living the high life. He'd just purchased a multi-million dollar estate in Spanish Trails, a fashionable suburb of Las Vegas that was home to the rich and famous who either lived there or just came to play.

Charlie'd bought his way into a spread in the newspaper by purchasing a load of advertising. As a quid pro quo, the paper had done a feature on Charlie. He was, as they put it, *going places*.

"What have you got for me?" Sam asked.

He was sitting with Charlie at a table in the coffee shop of the Barbary Coast casino, at the corner of Las Vegas Boulevard and Flamingo Avenue. It was eleven o'clock in the morning, and Bruno sat by himself at a nearby table, facing the door with his back to the wall. From his vantage point, the whole room and its entrance were in his field of vision. Sitting on one of the most valuable pieces of property on the planet, the Gaughan family had put up the Barbary Coast long before the mega-resorts which surround it arrived. Now, dwarfed by its neighbors, it was a regular spot where Sam held his morning meetings.

"I've got some guys who want a million five loan to buy and develop land on the west side," Charlie said. "The principal's a guy who claims to have done development in Florida. On paper, he's worth twenty million." Charlie looked for any sign of reaction from Sam. None came.

"What do you know about these guys?" Sam asked, leaning slightly forward in the booth.

"Not much," Charlie said, "but I checked out the property, and it's probably overpriced. If they can get some help with permits from your end, they might just make it work. If not, we take the land and go after this guy, DeMartes."

"What's in this for me?" Sam asked.

"He's going to need more money down the road to finish this project," Charlie responded. "I figure at least a couple million before the sale outs are strong enough to carry it. I called a guy I know in Orlando, and he says DeMartes's been building down there for years. Looks like he's worth what he says, so he may be good for ongoing business."

"What's the vig?" Sam asked, using his slang for interest.

"The loan will pay eighteen, plus eight points up front," Charlie answered. "It's a two year deal, but they'll need more before then."

"Want me to check the guy out?" Sam asked, settling back in the booth.

With a confidence born of past success, Charlie declined Sam's offer. He said he'd get a personal guarantee from DeMartes, plus the obvious lien on the property.

"I'll take the whole package, if they use my contractors," Sam said. "The building permits won't be no problem for this guy, and neither will the County's inspections. They got anybody lined up yet?"

Sam had several companies in construction, and figured he might as well make some more on the deal by tying his people in. He'd also know what was going on with the project. There may be other opportunities to put pressure on DeMartes with unexpected delays during the build out of the houses, he thought.

"I'll find out," Patek replied.

Sam waved at the waitress, wanting to order breakfast. They didn't hire lookers at the Barbary Coast, but once there, they tended to stick around a while. This one had served Sam for years.

"You look delicious today Margaret," Marchesi commented, patting her on the ass as she moved up next to him.

"Keep your hands off, you old goat," she replied, laughing.

Marchesi was a generous tipper, and Margaret had no problem with the ass patting. A former topless dancer, she'd turned to waitressing as gravity had wreaked its havoc over the years.

This was Charlie's signal that the meeting was over. Sam never asked Charlie to join him for breakfast, and Charlie never asked why. As Charlie stood to leave, Sam had one final question. It was actually more of a statement.

"You guarantee this deal, right?"

"Absolutely," replied Charlie, blissfully ignorant of what lie ahead. "I can control the escrow through this broad I'm screwing. With your guys on-site, I don't see any problems."

"That's not what I asked," Sam said, in a whisper. He waited for Charlie to reply, thumbing a table knife and drumming the fingers of his free hand on the table.

"Sure, as always, I guarantee your end," Charlie said.

Charlie made his way to the new Porsche he'd parked in the valet lot. Passing by the casino floor, small by Vegas standards, he waved to a familiar pit boss. Charlie's meetings with Sam, though they'd had many over the years, always left him feeling uneasy. Nothing had ever gone wrong with any of Sam's investments, but Charlie always felt slightly sick to his stomach after each meeting. Maybe it was because he didn't like dealing with someone he knew he couldn't hustle, he thought.

He left the building on the Flamingo side, Bally's Hotel rising up across the street, literally from the ashes it had become with the great fire in 1980. A summer wind was whipping super-heated air in and around the gigantic resorts, and hit him like a slap in the face. Even in the one hundred fifteen degree weather, the suckers, or "tourists" as they were politely called, packed the sidewalk.

Lambs to the slaughter, Charlie mused his favorite saying.

He'd covered two-thirds of the short walk to valet parking, near the end of the building, when an unyielding hand on his shoulder jerked him back. The stop was so sudden, Charlie felt like he'd hit a wall. It was Bruno, holding Charlie's day timer in his huge hand.

"You fogot dis," he said, glaring at Charlie and extending the scheduling book to the point of Charlie's nose.

Shaken, Charlie took the leather binder. It was the first time Charlie'd seen Bruno outside of Sam's company, and he didn't like the thought of getting an unexpected visit from the menacing giant.

He sat for a moment behind the wheel of his Porsche, collecting his thoughts, and to his surprise, trembling. The smell of new leather permeated the interior, and he waited for the air conditioner to cool it down.

"I wouldn't want to meet that asshole in a dark alley," he said out loud to himself. After a few minutes, he drove out of the covered parking garage, and on to Flamingo Avenue and the blaze of another cloudless day in Las Vegas.

Charlie relaxed as he drove through relatively light traffic to his office. Across the Strip and on to I-15 heading north, he gunned the sports car's engine and ran the gears. To the west, he saw billowing clouds of dust. His unsettling encounter with Bruno had faded by the time he exited on to Sahara Avenue going west. In minutes, he was at the office of Patek Investments. He still got a kick out of seeing his name painted on the door.

"Hey Lila, what's shaking?" he said to the buxom receptionist.

"Both of them, Uncle Charlie," she said, shrugging her shoulders seductively.

She liked to flirt with her mother's brother, and though it was all in fun, Charlie wondered what they'd look like unleashed. He grabbed a stack of phone messages and headed for his office. Picking up the headset he preferred using, he dialed the number on a message from Daryl McKenna.

"Hello," Daryl said, sounding like he'd been asleep.

"It's Charlie Patek," Charlie said.

"Oh, yes," Daryl stammered. "I wanted to let you know that Mr. DeMartes wants to make the deal."

"Okay, great," said Charlie. "We've got one more condition, which shouldn't be a problem. It's a deal-breaker if your man can't accept."

"What is it?" replied Daryl.

"We'd like you to use our subcontractors on the project," Patek said. "For this kind of money, my investors want to be sure that its quality work."

"Well," said Daryl, "I'm sure that's what we all want." He didn't have a clue what DeMartes' reaction would be.

"Good," Charlie said, "I'll get the paperwork rolling and call AmCon Title to set up the escrow on this. I've got a dynamite lady there by the name of Ashley Roh."

What a coincidence, Daryl thought. They want to use exactly the same person as Marcel.

He called DeMartes as soon as he hung up with Patek. He was surprised when he had no objection to using the investor's subcontractors as long as the costs were in line.

"You're the expert here partner, I'll leave the details to you," DeMartes said. McKenna had never remotely been referred to as an "expert" by anyone.

"I'll handle them," Daryl replied.

Charlie Patek sat in his office, putting pencil to paper on his end of the deal. Sam would make almost three hundred thousand in interest over two years, and Charlie would pick up a hundred twenty thousand up front in points. This didn't include the overcharges for loan processing he built into every deal. It was another great deal. Couldn't lose.

Later that afternoon, Sam Marchesi and Bruno were in a small warehouse on the far end of North Las Vegas. Outside was a scrap yard filled with bent and rusting shells of old automobiles. In the center of the yard, a large machine they referred to as the *crusher* dominated the yard. Its legitimate purpose was to compact old cars into hunks of metal. These would then be sold for scrap and shipped out on railroad cars. The company was owned by one of Sam's many associates. The real function of the warehouse and yard was to strip down and dispose of stolen automobiles.

Inside the warehouse, a man sat, his arms and legs held securely to the arms and legs of a wooden chair by multiple strips of duct tape. His nose had been broken, and he was bleeding from cuts about his face and neck. Bruno stood to the side of the man, his undershirt splattered with blood. Sam sat in a chair opposite. He'd been interrogating the man with two questions. Where was the man's brother; and where was the money they'd stolen from Sam's associates. The man's head listed to one side, as he slid in and out of consciousness.

"What's wrong with this goniff?" Sam said, as much to himself, as to Bruno.

Bruno made no reply. His eyes were fixed with the glaze of a carnivore on its prey.

"I'll tell you what we're going to do," Sam whispered in a guttural tone. "You screwed us. So, we're going to screw you until you tell us what we want to hear."

He nodded to Bruno, who walked to a nearby bench, and opened the Black and Decker drill case. From it, he removed a large electric drill, fitted with a screwdriver bit. Next to the drill case was a large brown bag of metal screws, four inches in length. Bruno shoved his hand in the bag, and drew out several of the black screws. With another nod from Sam, he moved to the slumping figure in the chair, quickly drilling a screw down through the man's left wrist and into the wooden arm of the chair beneath. He screamed, and the threads on the screw, having penetrated both arm and chair, oozed the mixed remnants of flesh, blood, duct tape, and particles of wood.

"Hurts, doesn't it?" Sam said, more as a statement of fact than a question. "Why don't you tell us where our money is?"

Raul and Louis Dominguez made the unpardonable mistake of robbing a liquor store owned by Sam's associates. Sam had been tipped by one of their friends in the Sheriff's office that the Dominguez brothers were the prime suspects. It took Sam less than an hour to locate Louis, hiding in a storage cabinet in the garage at his girlfriend's house. She was a dancer at one of the local all nude clubs Sam had an interest in. The girl had no option but to turn Louis in to Sam. Nobody in their right mind would risk Sam's retaliation.

Louis made no effort to reply, and Sam nodded again in Bruno's direction.

"I hope your rat bastard brother is praying for you, Louis," Sam said. "I don't think you're gonna want to kneel down for a while."

Bruno dropped to one knee in front of the sobbing Louis, and drilled another four-incher through his right kneecap. Louis wailed and passed out. This procedure was methodically repeated over the next two hours. As the bleeding and begging form in front of him lost consciousness, Sam would patiently wait, dousing him with cold water from time to time.

In the end, screws penetrating both arms, knees, his feet, and one shoulder joint, Louis gave up his brother and the money. He was waiting for Louis, with the cash, at a brothel in Pahrumph, Nevada. It was just an hour's drive from Vegas. Sam would make a quick call to the manager, who also worked for Sam indirectly, and Raul would be detained until Bruno could get there.

Louis Dominguez' life ended with a whimper as Bruno drilled a final screw down, through the top of his skull. His final remains, securely fastened to the chair that was now part of him, would become an integral part of a large hunk of scrap metal.

Sam stood up from his long afternoon's work, and stretched.

"I'm hungry Bruno," he said. "Wash up, and we'll go to the club for dinner. You can go get the other thief later."

Chapter Six

Two weeks passed since Daryl told Charlie Patek they would take his loan.

Daryl McKenna, Bill Roxburgh, and Roger Temple, one of AmCon's title officers, were meeting for drinks in the lounge of the Gold Coast Hotel and Casino.

Entering the main lounge, Daryl saw Roxburgh and Temple sitting in a booth facing the stage. It was a regular stop for them after work. If you got there right after five o'clock, you'd miss the afternoon band playing a loud combination of Dixieland and country music. The night's show, an aging soft rock group, wouldn't be starting for several hours, and the place was empty and quiet.

The three former employees of Sun Coast Title in Riverside, California liked to recall old war stories from their years together. Their recollection of the good old days changed every time, and even throughout the same night if they were drunk enough. Back in the early eighties, they were a regular three musketeers at Sun Coast Title.

Bill was manager of the title department, and Roger worked as his chief title officer. Daryl, a salesman for the company, had a lot of leeway with his expense account back then. Salesmen were encouraged to spend cash to get business in the door. For several years, the boys spent the company's money entertaining themselves instead of potential clients. They also shared common secrets of marital infidelity, gambling, and drinking. And, although never social friends in the sense that they'd include their wives, they had a lot of laughs in California. Daryl's and Bill's marriages survived those days. Roger's had not.

Roger Temple reminded Roxburgh of Woody Allen. He had a slight build and a perpetually sad look on his face. Roger got caught cheating on his wife of twenty years with a woman he'd picked up one night after work. She'd called Roger's wife, and told her their whole sleazy story. And, though he'd steadfastly denied the affair, he ended up divorced. He was now shelling out almost half his earnings for alimony; most of the rest went to support payments for his five children.

When he'd called Roxburgh several years later, looking to get out of California, Bill felt sorry for his old drinking buddy and hired him as a title officer at AmCon. The pay scale wasn't what Roger was used to, but he took the job just to put some mileage between him and his ex. These days, he was always broke. He'd cut expenses by taking on a roommate a few months back. He was a young guy who said his name was Jesse. He wasn't much trouble, and paid cash for his rent.

"It's my treat tonight, boys," Daryl said, sliding into the booth. "Tomorrow we close the Kirshbaum property sale, and you're looking at the new operations manager of Anasazi Properties, Ltd."

"How did you swing that?" Roger asked.

Since he'd already regaled Roxburgh with the tale of his good fortune over the phone, Daryl turned to Roger.

"I put the land deal together for my new partner, a multi-millionaire developer from Florida," he said. "As a part of the package, I agreed to head up his Las Vegas operations. We're starting with a little seventy-five unit project. Average price will be two hundred fifty thousand."

"Why does he need you?" Roger interjected, incredulous that any legitimate developer would let Daryl "head up" keeping the satellite toilets empty, much less the whole project.

"He said he likes my style," Daryl responded. The implication of Roger's question annoyed him. "This looks like just the beginning of a very profitable association. I'm getting a sweet per month deal, and we split the profits when the subdivision sells out."

Roxburgh asked the obvious. "How are you buying into an equity position?"

"That's the easy part," Daryl answered. "I take the thirty thousand I'm getting from the sale, and add it to twenty that Charlie Patek has agreed to lend me on the side. My investment should bring in close to a million bucks." He was embellishing on the numbers Marcel had shown him, but he wanted to impress these guys.

"How are you paying Patek back?" Roxburgh asked, knowing his reputation for ruthless collection of debts.

"I'll pay him some each month out of my salary, and the balance when I start selling out the units," Charlie responded. "He knows a sweet deal when he sees one."

"I did a date down for you on Kirshbaum. It looks good," Temple volunteered.

A date down in the title insurance business was a last minute, pre-closing check of the chain of title to see if anything had changed since a preliminary title report was done. In this case, nothing had changed. The Kirshbaums were the record title owners, free and clear.

"Is Ashley ready to close?" Daryl asked, turning to Roxburgh.

"I guess so," Bill replied, "isn't she always ready?"

The three comrades shared a chuckle over the double meaning. She'd been the subject of many a night's drunken discussion in their group. Each man, in his own mind, fantasized what it would be like to have the escrow queen in bed.

Roxburgh left the trio two hours later. He bid his drinking companions goodbye, saying he had a busy schedule in the morning, including Daryl's closing. As always, he said his wife was going to kill him. Roger and Daryl were both getting to the boisterous level of alcohol by that time.

"The guy's pussy whipped," Daryl shouted, as Bill made his way out of the lounge.

"Can't run his own garage," Roger chimed in.

The night band was getting ready to start their first set when Daryl flagged down the waitress. The Gold Coast was much like the Barbary Coast in some respects. There was a common thread of ownership, and the help tended to stay on, once hired.

Their waitress, Annie, was young by Gold Coast standards. Built more like a young boy than a Vegas cocktail waitress, she knew how to work her customers. She'd seen Daryl and the boys on several occasions and, knowing their tip would help pay her rent, she made sure the drinks kept coming at a greyhound's pace. Daryl flirted with every round, and she played him like a high roller. With every drink delivered, she'd get closer, rubbing against him suggestively.

The band had an odd mix of ages, with a bass player who didn't look old enough to drink, much less remember when the songs they played were popular. Daryl remarked that he had shoes older than the young musician. By the time they'd finished their second set, two hours later, both Daryl and Roger were drunk. They left the casino together, after Daryl made a show of leaving Annie a fifty dollar tip.

Staggering to their cars, Roger told Daryl he'd be interested if a position opened up down the road in his new development company.

"Ssuure, buddy," Daryl slurred. "I'll take care of you."

The next morning Daryl drove frantically to the closing scheduled at AmCon Title's main office. He was running late, and thanked god that Judy had shaken him out of his stupor. He was meeting Marcel there. The Kirshbaums were scheduled to be there an hour later. Daryl hadn't bothered to let them know that he'd made a deal with Marcel to work for Anasazi Properties.

Patek would be bringing in the funding check for one million five hundred thousand. DeMartes would sign Patek's loan documents at that time. Having closed one side of the deal, the Kirshbaums would show up later and sign the deed to the property, conveying it to DeMartes' company. They would receive a check for seven hundred fifty thousand and a note from Anasazi for the other half of the purchase price. Daryl would be collecting his commission check of thirty thousand. He was there, theoretically, to make sure that his clients, John and Helen Kirshbaum, got what they had bargained for at the closing.

When he arrived at AmCon's office on west Flamingo, Daryl was announced by the receptionist and escorted to Ashley's office by her assistant, a tall, strikingly pretty girl named Sarah. Marcel was already there, and his animated conversation with Ashley came to an abrupt halt as Daryl entered the room. Daryl was too hung over to notice that Marcel, reviewing the closing documents over Ashley's shoulder, had his hand on the nape of her neck.

"Good morning folks," Daryl announced, trying to sound chipper. He flopped into one of the chairs opposite Ashley. "Everything set to go?"

"I've just covered the details with Ms. Roh," said Marcel. "Looks like we're ready."

"Did you want to look over the sellers' documents while we wait for Mr. Patek?" Ashley asked. "It might save some time later."

"If you say they're alright, Ashley, they're alright with me," Daryl replied. He was in no shape to read the newspaper, much less the stack of legal documents she had in front of her.

Five minutes later, Charlie Patek showed up with a cashier's check and a promissory note, secured by a first deed of trust. By that time, Marcel had taken a seat next to Daryl, and opposite Ashley. He couldn't help but notice the distinct odor of scotch on his new partner.

Charlie winked conspiratorially to Ashley as DeMartes reviewed the loan documents in detail. When Marcel finished, Ashley called Sarah into her office.

"I'd like you to take Mr. DeMartes into the conference room and notarize his signature on the loan documents and the note to the sellers," Ashley said. "Why don't you join them, Mr. McKenna. We'll be taking the Kirshbaums in there for their signatures when they arrive."

As soon as they left the room, Charlie rounded Ashley's desk, standing behind her in a position not unlike Marcel had taken earlier. He put his hands on her shoulders and began to massage.

"Where have you been?" he said, running his fingers down the front of her blouse. "I miss you."

"I've been busy," Ashley responded, standing abruptly and breaking his hold on her. "You haven't been knocking my door down lately."

"You know, there's always another problem to handle," Charlie whispered in her ear. "I just haven't had any time lately. I'm burning the midnight oil."

"Just not with me," she said, moving away from him.

"Don't be that way, baby," Charlie cajoled. "I'll call you tonight. We'll go to Fiore's." They'd been there many times since their first meeting, and it had cost him a bundle. But with Ashley, Charlie felt it was worth every penny. He'd never met a woman who was able to keep his sexual interest for so long.

Chapter Seven

Jack woke early on the day he'd met Ashley Roh. He found he needed less sleep as he'd gotten older. His years in courtrooms made him a worrier. In the weeks leading up to and during every trial, he woke in the early morning hours, going over his interrogation of each witness again and again in his head.

There was no substitute for preparation. If you wanted to win, and Jack couldn't stand losing at anything, you had to out prepare the other side. There was always a better way to ask a question. There was always a better order in which to ask a series of questions. All of it designed to elicit a crucial response at the precise time when it counted most. There was a defining moment in the course of every trial or deposition, when you'd maneuvered the witness to give evidence essential to your case. Jack would play various scenarios in his head, reviewing alternative courses of action, dependent upon the response of a witness.

That morning, he woke thinking of a deposition he'd scheduled for ten o'clock at his office. He would depose a woman named Ashley Roh, a senior escrow officer for AmCon Title.

Jack represented a real estate broker who claimed to have been screwed out of ten thousand in commission by one of her former agents. The agent was, of course, no where to be found. Jack's theory of liability against the title company was negligent failure to follow written escrow instructions that required the commission to be paid through his client, rather than directly to the agent.

One of AmCon's escrow officers, not Ashley Roh, had taken a verbal directive in the harried moments before the deal closed to pay the agent directly. This was contrary to the prior written commission instruction. Once the agent got her commission, she left town, and failed to pay Jack's client the broker's share. Jack could have gotten an escrow officer from one of AmCon's rivals to testify that this was professional negligence by the escrow officer involved, but he liked the idea of having one of AmCon's own say the words that would condemn her employer's case.

AmCon's lawyers at the time were claiming that it was the victim. Its' employee, they claimed, had properly taken the directions on the commission pay out from the agent who brought the deal in. How were they supposed to know that she wouldn't pay her broker?

It was warm for early October. Temperatures still hovered in the mid-nineties during the day. With the sun rising over Sunrise Mountain to the east, Jack had finished a series of formal exercises in Tae Kwan Do, a form of Korean karate. Jack held a fourth degree black belt, and had practiced the art since his early twenties. In recent years, he used it as a way to keep in shape. Jack stood six foot two, and in spite of the time he spent with his ass parked behind his desk, he managed to keep his weight near two hundred pounds.

Jack had been in his new house for a few months when he met Ashley. Originally selling for over a million, the rear of the home held a spectacular view of the Strip to the north. To the west lay the Spring Mountain range and the almost surreal beauty of Red Rock Canyon. The price was a stretch for Jack, but he couldn't pass up the deal. Most of the living area was on the main floor with guest quarters accessed by a wide curving staircase occupying the lion's share of the second story. The master suite included a two story closet and a Jacuzzi tub that would accommodate four people, maybe more.

It was the pool area, secluded as it was by the layout of the house, that convinced Jack to buy the place. The pool had what was called an infinity edge. Looking at it from the house, it appeared that the water flowed over the far edge and down into the arroyo canyon behind the property. It actually dropped only a few feet, where it was filtered and returned to the main pool. There was a sunken bar, into which you could step directly up from the pool or down from the back deck. This was covered by a gazebo roof. A large hot tub spa dominated one side of the pool and created a waterfall into the main body of water.

The pool area was Jack's workout space. The great room of the house, next to the kitchen, had an exterior wall of glass. This could be pushed back, opening the entire area to the outside. It had the effect of opening a large portion of the home to the outside in good weather; making the pool and the view beyond a part of the main floor.

To one side, out of view unless you knew where to look, he'd installed a heavy bag. This was used to practice striking and kicking techniques, promoting both balance and strength. Looking closely at Jack's hands, you could see the toughening effect that regular use of the large bag created.

Jack reviewed in his mind what he knew of the morning's witness and began his ritual of stomach crunching exercises. He'd called several real estate agents who dealt with Ashley Roh. He also called a friend in the Real Estate Division to see if she had any history of misconduct or complaints from the general public. There were none. Apparently her clients loved her and respected her ability in escrow. The woman was obviously bright and would no doubt be a challenge in the deposition.

Jack arrived at his office by eight that morning. He worked to clear his desk of left over problems from the day before and, reviewing his notes again, was ready for the deposition when the participants arrived shortly before ten o'clock.

The court reporter Jack used for depositions was in her early twenties, blonde and slender with a girl next door look about her. She was good at her job and easy on the eyes.

"No hangover today, Jack?" she whispered as he took a seat next to her.

"Not today Carrie," he said.

Ashley Roh appeared next, accompanied by AmCon's lawyer and Bill Roxburgh. The attorney was young, an associate in one of the larger, well-connected Mormon firms in Vegas. Jack had seen him at the court house a few times, but doubted that he'd tried many cases on his own.

Jack found Ashley surprisingly attractive for a woman in her career. With few exceptions, senior escrow officers tended to be overweight. Ashley, while quite petite, had what appeared to be a great body. The camouflage of her lemon colored business suit made it hard to tell how great. Her hair, almost jet black, hung straight to mid-back.

The court reporter was sitting, hands poised over the keys on her computer.

"Ready to swear the witness?" she asked, looking to Summers.

Jack nodded, and turning to the young lawyer who sat opposite him at the long conference table, said, "Are we reserving objections until time of trial?"

"Yes, except form or foundation," he replied.

Jack would need to establish Ashley as an expert in the field of escrow before he could ask for her opinion on the correctness of a procedure. The reporter turned, facing Ashley, and raised her right hand.

"Please raise your right hand," she said. "Do you swear to tell the truth, the whole truth, and nothing but the truth, so help you God?"

Raising her right hand as she did, Ashley replied, "Yes."

"State, and spell your name for the record please," Jack began.

"Ashley Roh, R-O-H," she replied.

"Where do you reside, Ms. Roh?" he asked. "Or is it Mrs.?"

"Objection," the young lawyer said suddenly, as if trying out a new toy. "That's a multiple question."

Jack ignored him.

"I'm not married," she replied, extending her left hand to demonstrate the lack of a ring. "I live at 4214 South Charlotte, Henderson, Nevada."

Jack made a mental note that she lived only a few miles from him. His questioning began innocuously, asking her background history, what jobs she'd held, and when. He was qualifying her as an expert in escrow based on her experience, and at the same time looking for the names of people with whom she'd worked. If she didn't give him the answers he wanted to support his theory of the lawsuit, he'd need to discredit her later. After forty-five minutes of interrogation, it was clear that she had enough background in the escrow business to qualify as an expert.

"Should we take a short break now?" Ashley's lawyer interjected.

Jack was ready to move to an area that was the crux of his case. He didn't want to give opposing counsel a chance to talk to Ashley alone at this point.

"I've only got a few more questions. If it's alright with the witness, why don't we just finish the direct examination and then break?" Jack replied.

Ashley looked to her attorney, a puzzled look on her face. A more experienced lawyer would have insisted on taking a break at that juncture, anticipating where Jack's interrogation would be moving. It was a perfect opportunity to coach his client on how to answer the line of questioning that would follow.

"I know you're a busy lady. I'll try to get you out of here quickly," Jack said, smiling his best trust me smile.

"Let's go on," Ashley replied, returning Jack's smile and re-crossing her legs. The short skirt she was wearing hadn't escaped his attention. She had great legs.

He began by asking her to assume a set of facts that mirrored what had happened in his case. He stood and pulled down a volume of the Nevada Revised Statutes from the shelf behind him. It contained, as Jack knew, a section which mandated the duty of escrow officers to act only upon written instructions. Verbal direction was not allowed, even though in practice it was often the norm. He opened the official looking volume and laid it on the table in front of Ashley.

"You're familiar, of course, with this section of the Nevada statutes?" he asked, pointing to a provision that clearly made it illegal for an escrow officer to take verbal instructions. Jack had been carefully complimenting her as he covered her work experience. She was flattered by the attention and welcomed the mantel of expertise that he was bestowing on her. It was now all too clear why he'd done it. As an expert in Nevada escrow, she was bound, as she had earlier testified, to adhere strictly to the Nevada statutes. She'd been painted into a corner.

She'd known walking in to the deposition that her co-worker acted on verbal instruction. Her lawyer told her to say it was common practice in the industry. But, this tall, good-looking lawyer hadn't asked her that. Now, sitting a few chairs down from her boss, she was about to charge the company with violation of a State statute and probably negligence.

"Yes, I'm aware of it," she responded.

"Based then upon the facts I've asked you to assume, which include an escrow officer taking verbal instructions regarding the pay out of a commission, would you have an opinion as to whether that escrow officer violated this statute?" Jack asked.

Ashley looked to the company's attorney, but he was frantically reviewing the notes he'd been making. Jack's question hung like a drape over the room.

"Do you understand the question, Ms. Roh?" he asked.

"Yes," she replied.

"Yes, you understand it; or yes, she violated the statute, in your expert opinion?" Jack asked, ignoring his original question as to whether she had an opinion. Having finally reached that determining moment in the deposition he'd been leading up to for nearly an hour, he simply put the words in Ashley's mouth.

"I'd have to say that person, the one you've described in your hypothetical set of facts, violated the statute," she answered. Then, unexpectedly, she added, "And I'd say she was negligent."

"Whoa, wait a minute," the young lawyer interjected. "I object. That last part's not responsive to the question. He didn't ask if anyone was negligent." He was too late.

Jack ignored him. He was hardly in a position to argue that his own client couldn't volunteer information. The case was over, but this guy didn't know it yet. Jack had won. Within a week AmCon's lawyer would call, offering Jack's client a settlement of fifty percent. This too, would be ignored. Two weeks after the deposition, Jack's client received a check for ten thousand dollars, the full amount of his claim, in exchange for a dismissal of the lawsuit.

A week after he'd dismissed the lawsuit against AmCon Title, it was Jack's thirty-fourth birthday. He'd taken the day off to play golf with three old friends from Chicago.

They'd picked him up at home, as he knew it would be a night of drinking, and he planned on taking a taxi home. His buddies were staying at the Rio Hotel, west of the Strip. By six o'clock, they'd finished their round of golf and were drinking at the Ipenema bar and talking about old times. They'd all known his wife, Claire, and they shared his pain when she was killed.

Claire was killed on her twenty-fifth birthday. Jack, fresh out of law school and hired by the attorney general's office that demanded eighty to a hundred hours a week, was stuck working at the office that night. The police said it looked like someone broke in to their apartment and was still there when she came home from work. Whoever it was, they'd taken their time killing her. The investigating detective's report said it looked like she'd been partially skinned alive.

For almost two years after Claire's death, Summers wandered in and out of sobriety. His law practice was slipping, and everywhere he went reminded him of Claire. Ultimately, at the suggestion of the guys he was celebrating with at the Rio, he'd moved to Las Vegas. Though his friends remained living in the Chicago area, they made it a point to visit on Jack's birthday. They also made it a point to try and fix him up with every reasonably good looking woman they saw. They were determined to find Summers a new mate.

"Hold on a minute boys, I think we have lift off," Jack's friend, Mick, said.

He motioned towards the end of the bar where Ashley was seated, talking on a cell phone.

All heads turned, and Jack said, "I know that woman. I took her deposition a few weeks ago."

"Then go get her, buddy," Mick said, smacking him on the shoulder.

Jack was reluctant, but he'd had several beers, and the boys wouldn't take "no" for an answer. He crossed the room to where Ashley was sitting.

"Hello, Ms. Roh, nice seeing you again," he said. Ashley turned in her chair, startled out of her own thoughts.

"Well, hello Mr. Summers. What are you doing here?" she said, as if he needed any particular reason to be at the Rio on a Friday night.

"I'm celebrating with a few friends," Jack said, and pointed to the guys behind him who were gesturing wildly, a bunch of thirty-somethings transformed by several cocktails to their high school days. Mick was down on one knee, striking a pleading pose.

"We were wondering if you'd like to join us for a drink?" he asked. Ashley had planned on meeting Marcel there that night, but he'd cancelled.

"Why not," she said, gathering up her purse and phone. She'd been thinking about Jack, off and on, since the deposition.

The next several hours were filled with the Chicago boys' interrogation of Ashley. Disguised in the usual banter and flirtation of bar room small talk, they gradually drug an overview of Ashley's background out for Summers to evaluate.

Jack was attracted to her. She seemed nice, as she'd been at the deposition, but also showed a sense of humor. It was a characteristic Jack prized in people above most others. She was drinking small splits of champagne, and as the hours flew by, she relaxed into the group.

Ashley sat next to Mick, and Jack found himself wishing he'd maneuvered her a little closer to himself. Unlike the day of the deposition, Ashley was wearing a simple white silk blouse and a black skirt. He caught another glimpse of those perfectly shaped legs and wondered what the rest of the package was like.

During the first two years after Claire's death, Jack found his way into a string of strange beds. No one filled the void he felt with her gone. Claire could put up with his bullshit better than anyone. Whenever he started acting like, in her words, a "big shot attorney," she always found a way to bring him back to earth with a subtle joke. When she died, he drowned his sorrow in scotch and a series of ladies who, not for lack of trying in some cases, couldn't fill Claire's shoes.

After six years in Vegas, he'd stopped trying to replace her. He'd dated a few prospects, mostly as reluctant favors to well meaning friends. But the inevitable comparison to Claire would always sit in the back of his mind. Eventually, he'd drift away from them.

As Jack sat drinking with his friends that night at the Rio, he'd been thinking it might be time to try another relationship. Though he still loved Claire, the passage of time was making it difficult to remember the details of their life together. Besides, he hadn't been laid in months.

Around midnight, Mick stood and, motioning to the other two Chicago boys, said, "We've got an early flight out in the morning. I think we'd better hit the hay."

"It's still early, gentlemen," Jack protested.

Looking at his watch, and swaying slightly as he did so, Mick said, "Look pal, it's not even your birthday anymore."

"Can you give this drunk birthday boy a ride home?" Mick asked, turning to Ashley.

"Where do you live, Jack?" she asked. They'd been on a first name basis for over two hours.

"I live in Seven Hills," he said. "But I can take a cab."

"Don't be silly," she said. "I live in Henderson. It's no trouble."

The good-byes to the boys were not prolonged. They stood, shook hands, and left. It wasn't like leaving a co-ed group, where women take seriously the ritual of departure. Jack and Ashley were suddenly alone. They'd finished their drinks, and for the first time in the evening, Ashley turned her full attention to him.

"So, tell me about Jack Summers," she said, moving to the chair next to him.

He could smell her perfume at this range, and the proximity of her knees to his brought on a familiar stirring in his groin. As he covered a thumbnail sketch of his life for Ashley, she listened intently. Her eyes never left his, though at the point when he told her of Claire's death, she put her hand on his knee, stroking it as a mother would an injured child.

An hour later they drove in Ashley's Camaro to Jack's home. He could see she was impressed as they stopped at the guard-gated entrance. The guard gave him a familiar smile and a wink as Jack leaned across Ashley's lap from the passenger side to identify himself. The smell of her perfume was strong as his face dipped near her breasts. He wondered what the night might hold for them. They'd been talking about Jack's purchase of his house as they drove, and she asked a lot of questions about price.

"Would you like to have a peak at the house?" he asked, as they stopped at his front door.

She didn't respond at first, but sat looking at him as if something were being calculated before she could answer. For a brief moment, Jack saw the soft look of her face disappear, like a mask had suddenly fallen off. There was just a fleeting second when he felt like a deer must as the hunter lets its' arrow fly. If he hadn't been celebrating for over six hours, his inner security system would have sounded an alarm.

"I'd love to," Ashley said, breaking the pause and evaporating, like a breeze on cigarette smoke, any doubt Jack felt. She had, in that instant, reviewed her current options with Charlie Patek and Marcel DeMartes, and decided that Jack was worth the effort.

Jack took Ashley on a tour of the house, starting with the guest quarters upstairs and finishing with his master suite. She was attentive and commented on various decorator items, obviously appreciating his taste. They walked to the pool area, and Ashley took a seat at his sunken bar while Jack fixed them a nightcap. Pulling two crystal glasses from the cabinet, he poured them each a generous portion of Grand Marnier.

Taking a sip of the golden, orange flavored liquor, Ashley asked, "Is the pool heated?"

"It's about eighty degrees this time of year," he responded. "I let the spa heat up and run over to the pool. Want to take a dip?"

With the mountain of florescent light that was the Strip in the background, and a warm breeze bringing the dusky smell of the desert up and over the sparkling pool, it seemed like a great idea to Ashley. There was again a look of hesitation in Ashley's eyes, but this time it lasted barely an eye blink.

"I'll need something to wear, won't I?" she said, looking down at her blouse and skirt.

"I'll get you something," Jack said, and was on his way to the bedroom before she could comment. He was back a few minutes later with an old Izod golf shirt in hand. He'd already changed into a swimsuit, and Ashley's eyes moved the length of his muscled torso in appreciation.

"You must work out a lot," she said smiling, and turned to glance at the exercise equipment on the deck.

"I try to keep in shape," he said, returning her smile.

They swam for a while, finishing another drink in the spa. Jack felt at the same time relaxed and on edge. He was physically attracted to Ashley. The golf shirt she was wearing, once wet, clung to her large breasts and draped from there to just below mid-thigh on tanned legs. They spoke of single life in Vegas.

He said he hadn't dated much in recent years, and she told him the same. Being single in Las Vegas, for all that would seem to imply, wasn't all that great, they agreed. In the venues where you might meet someone other than co-workers, people were occupied with gambling. The singles clubs were geared to a much younger crowd than Jack liked. Ashley told him she'd had the same problems. She explained that the only reason she was in the Rio that night was to notarize some documents for a customer who cancelled their meeting at the last moment.

By three in the morning, they'd had enough of the water. Jack took her hand, pulling her from the warm spa. As she stood, the night air chilling ever so slightly, he could see her nipples were erect. They weren't the only thing with a life of their own at that instant, and he caught her glance at his crotch. He led her to the large closet in his bedroom, with its spiral staircase to the second floor.

"I've got an extra robe up here somewhere," he said, starting up the stairs.

He was two stairs up when he felt the tug on his trunks. Turning, he saw in the half light from the bedroom that Ashley had removed the shirt he'd given her. He could see tan lines above large, brown nipples. His erection was engorged in an instant, and she reached quickly to take it in her hand, pulling him downward. Jack stepped to the ground floor and swept her upward in his arms. She looked like a woman-child in his long arms, her short legs wrapped around his waist.

They kissed deeply; the mix of their heated breath and the after-taste of the liquor was heady, and he ached for penetration. Ashley pulled back, loosening his grip, and slid down his torso to her knees. She pulled his trunks down with her, releasing him. Looking up at him, now grasping the center pole of the staircase with one hand to steady himself, she opened her mouth.

Jack could hear the sound of a lawn mower in the distance when he woke. The smell in the air, of newly mown grass, took him back to the Midwest of his youth. He shook his head trying to orient himself. In a second he was back in Las Vegas and opened his eyes to see if Ashley was still in his bed. It had been quite a night.

She was gone, but her perfume hung in the air and permeated the sheets. His groin stirred again, and he headed for a cold shower. Later, when he'd cleaned up and put on his workout sweats, he found her business card by the phone.

He'd called Ashley a few days later. But the night and the moment were gone. Absent the haze of alcohol, Jack didn't find her quite as amusing. Two weeks later, he received a call from Bill Roxburgh, who wanted to put him on retainer to represent AmCon Title. It seemed a good piece of business and a reasonable excuse not to date Ashley.

Chapter Eight

The same year that the son of a strip joint owner became governor of Nevada, Jim Eccles started a company called Sundown Mortgage. He'd cut his teeth in banking at First Security, a Mormon dominated bank in Utah with ties to Las Vegas. Sam Marchesi's associates became large depositors of First Security and profitable business partners with young Eccles. When Jim wanted to start his own mortgage brokerage, he went to Sam. Sam provided start up funds and the political juice in Reno to get the charter for Sundown Mortgage.

When Marcel DeMartes told Daryl McKenna to shop more financing on their subdivision, he went to Jim Eccles.

"It looks like we'll need five million," Marcel told Daryl.

Daryl let out a low whistle, as he pondered the number. He'd been working hard to get the project up and running with Judy's help. They were down to less than a hundred thousand left from the original loan from Patek. They owed Sam's subcontractors a bundle and, though they were current with Patek Investments and Kirshbaum, the number Marcel suggested seemed impossibly high.

"Look, we've got the four models almost finished, and you've already sold two of the lots. That's like a million five in the bank for the six of them. With my equity guarantee, it shouldn't be that much of a problem," Marcel told him.

Sundown Mortgage had its main office just west of I-15 in an office building near the Palace Station Hotel and Casino. On the ninth floor, it commanded a view to the west towards Red Rock canyon and south towards Caesar's, the Bellagio, and on to the Monte Carlo and New York casinos.

Daryl sat with Marcel in the reception area, clutching a file of financial statements on Anasazi Vistas. They included his pro forma projections on the sale out of all the lots.

His big hands were sweating. If they didn't get this loan, he could see his whole financial house of cards crumbling. Jim Eccles entered the room with a smile on his face, and an outstretched hand.

"Good morning, gentlemen. I'm Jim Eccles."

Eccles was a small man, what you'd call diminutive. Standing about five foot three, with a slight build, it was a combination of his darting eyes and the way that he moved that struck most people. There was a lizard quality about him. When introductions were done they moved to a large conference room, its wall of glass commanding a view of the western valley.

"I've gone over the figures you sent me, Mr. McKenna. I think we can do business," he said, directing the comment to Marcel, who he pegged as the decision maker. "We like what you've done in Florida," Eccles added quickly.

Marcel made no comment, merely nodding to acknowledge the compliment.

"What kind of terms are you offering?" Daryl asked.

"I'll need five points in origination, or two hundred fifty thousand on five million, with an interest rate of twelve percent and the principal amortized over four years," Eccles said. "If the subdivision sells out sooner, the remaining balance is due immediately. Of course, Sundown must be placed in first position for security purposes. Your present loan must be paid or subordinated. We'll take Mr. DeMartes' personal indemnity guarantee against any existing or ongoing mechanics liens."

Daryl turned to Marcel for reaction. It seemed like a great deal to Daryl. They'd have plenty of available funds to take the project to a point where the sales would sustain it. In the meantime, they could use the proceeds to amortize the monthly payments. After what seemed an eternity to Daryl, Marcel finally spoke.

"We'll take it. How long will it take to put this together?"

"We'd like to make the loan near the end of March," Eccles responded.

Daryl's heart sank. The knot in his stomach tightened and his vision blurred. How in the hell could they make it for two more months?

"Any chance we can do it sooner?" Daryl blurted.

This prompted a look of inquiry from Eccles and something entirely different from DeMartes. Daryl could feel Marcel's glare, like a vice gripping his throat. Trying desperately to recover, Daryl mumbled, "Of course, we won't need it until then. I just thought…"

Interrupting, Marcel commented, "The time line is fine. I won't do business with a company that wouldn't do its own due diligence on a loan of this size."

Due diligence is a banking phrase that refers to the lender's investigation of a borrower to make sure they're good for the loan. In this case, Eccles was relying on Sam's indication that he'd checked DeMartes out already. The timing of the loan was Sam's suggestion. He wanted these guys, as Sam put it, a little more "strung out" on finances.

As Marcel and Daryl rode down in the elevator, Daryl felt like a rebuked child. He didn't see how they could pay their bills until the end of March, but he wasn't about to break the silence. Walking to Marcel's Mercedes, he racked his brain to try and see what Marcel's plan would be. Finally, as they reached the car, Marcel spoke.

"Sell the models to investors. You can lease them back during the build out. That should give us plenty of operating capital until the loan comes through."

"What if they don't sell?" Daryl said, getting the same look he'd received in Eccles' office.

"Look," Marcel said, sighing deeply as he did. "You're the real estate expert here, aren't you? Sales are a function of price. Lower the price until you find a quick buyer. If we don't get full price on one of the models, we'll make it up somewhere else."

With that, Daryl was dismissed. Marcel got into his car, and left Daryl standing in the lot wondering what happened. He'd gone to the meeting with DeMartes, but now was left without a ride.

Chapter Nine

Marcel had met Sarah Dunn's husband, Jesse, while sitting in a bar in West Hollywood. The money Marcel had brought from Florida was about gone. Jesse had walked in off the street, trying to hustle cash from the few mid-afternoon customers scattered throughout the dimly lit lounge.

Marcel knew the area was famous for male prostitutes, and figured that Jesse was just another one looking for a midday john. He was tall and slender to the point of being skinny. It didn't look like he'd been eating on a regular basis; and his long, dark hair was matted and tangled, like he'd been sleeping on it at odd angles for a long time.

"Where're you from?" Marcel asked.

"From the Midwest; Omaha, Nebraska," Jesse replied. "Heard of it?"

"Not really," he replied.

"It's in the middle of the country," Jesse said.

"What brings you out here?" Marcel asked.

"I'm trying to get a music gig but nothing's happening, man," he replied.

Marcel bought a round of beer, and the young man continued.

"I came out to Vegas with my girl, Sarah. We had a kid but the whole family thing bummed me out. I needed to give myself a shot in LA on my own."

"What's she doing now?" Marcel asked out of boredom.

"She works for a title and escrow company in Las Vegas; actually, for some bitch of an escrow officer," he replied.

This got Marcel's attention. He asked a lot of questions about Sarah and her boss, and by last call he'd offered Jesse a couch in his apartment to sleep on. As drunk as Jesse was by that point in time, he made it clear that he was not gay, but appreciated a spot for the night. By morning,

51

Marcel had sold Jesse on, as he put it, making a bunch of cash for a little work he needed done in Las Vegas.

Months later, Marcel sat watching Ashley pour money into the poker machine in front of her for about an hour before he approached. She was at the bar in the Rio where, because he'd been following her for weeks, he knew she'd be. When she asked for "one more for the road," he made his move.

"I'd like to get that, if I may? My name is Marcel. And you are..?"

He knew her name and quite a bit more about Ashley Roh. She introduced herself, turning slightly toward him as he slid into the barstool next to her. They spent the next hour or so getting acquainted. He told Ashley he was a land developer from Florida, looking to do some work in Las Vegas. Ever on the prowl for business, she was all ears.

"My development and acquisition work takes me all over the country, but I like to stay at the Rio when I'm in town," Marcel said. "Think we might have dinner sometime?"

Ashley hesitated only for a moment, weighing her options before she agreed.

A few days later, he called. Since that time, he'd been seeing her two, sometimes three times a month. By the time he suggested that he needed some help with a subdivision he was putting together, Ashley was quick to offer her services.

Marcel told her, after letting her prompt him several times, that he had a net worth of approximately twenty million. He always flashed a fat roll of cash, and she had no reason to doubt him.

"What I need," he explained, "is an escrow officer who can make sure some of the initial financing won't be subject to call when it comes time to refinance. I also need a clause in the seller's security requiring them to subordinate their position to any loans that might follow."

"Aren't the sellers going to object?" she asked, looking confused.

"Not if their escrow officer doesn't explain it to them," he replied, smiling like a well fed cat.

"And why wouldn't she do that?" Ashley asked, waiting for the pitch.

"Because it would be worth three thousand to her as a gratuity," Marcel responded.

"I don't think she could take such a risk for less than five, could she?" Ashley purred.

"That wouldn't be a problem," Marcel said, moving the first piece of his puzzle into place.

The risk to Ashley would be that either the seller would read her documents closely before signing and object; or would discover it later, and sue her. Either way, unless the seller could prove monetary damage, there wouldn't be much exposure. She would simply have the seller sign escrow instructions telling her to do exactly what Marcel wanted.

Months later, when the Kirshbaums came to close the sale of their property, the large stack of paperwork they signed would include instructions telling AmCon Title to prepare a promissory note for seven hundred fifty thousand. The note, by its terms, would be subordinated to any debt coming after the initial financing on Anasazi Vistas. They would be bumped back in line of priority and if the subdivision failed, they'd be the last to be paid.

With Ashley's cooperation, Marcel would be in a position to get permanent financing without worrying about paying off the Kirshbaum debt.

Chapter Ten

Three weeks after the sale of his property to Marcel's company, John Kirshbaum finally took time to read his note and deed of trust from Anasazi Properties in detail. It was then that he first noticed the position he'd been maneuvered in to. His first call was to Daryl. After several tries, he was able to track him to the office of Anasazi Properties.

"What the hell are you doing at Anasazi Properties?" Kirshbaum shouted into the phone.

"Whoa, settle down," Daryl replied, "who is this?"

"It's John Kirshbaum, asshole. I got screwed on the note you got me."

"What are you talking about?" Daryl asked, genuinely confused.

Kirshbaum explained the problem to Daryl. He also asked pointedly why his agent was now working for the company that had given him a lousy note. After a heated exchange, Daryl told him to call Ashley Roh.

Two days later Kirshbaum sat with his wife in Ashley's office.

"What seems to be the problem?" Ashley asked.

"This note you gave me puts us in last place behind any other financing these guys get," John said, the veins on his neck noticeably bulging.

"I know it does," she replied coolly, "and that's exactly how you instructed me to prepare the deal."

"I didn't 'instruct' you to do anything ma'am," John replied.

"Of course you did," she responded, sliding the signed escrow instructions across the desk in front of him. John took a minute to read them in detail. It's what he should have done at the closing. As he finished, he looked up at Ashley with a glare. He'd been had, and he knew it.

"What can we do about this?" John asked, softening his tone.

"I'm afraid, nothing," she said. "The note will be paid in accordance with its terms in two years. You shouldn't have a problem unless the subdivision fails, which I don't see happening. Mr. DeMartes is a very successful builder."

As the Kirshbaums left Ashley's office, they passed Sarah in the hall. She didn't say anything to them, but heard John say he was going to see "that weasel McKenna."

The next day, a concerned Judy McKenna stuck her head into Daryl's office and said, "Mr. Kirshbaum's here to see you. He seems upset."

"Tell him I'm not here," Daryl snapped.

Looking perplexed, Judy said, "I already told him you're here. Is something wrong, Daryl?"

Not responding, Daryl moved to the door and called to Kirshbaum, "Come on back, John."

Kirshbaum managed a smile for Judy as he passed her, entering Daryl's small office suite. The Anasazi Properties' main office wasn't much to look at. It was a ten by ten reception area that held a desk and work area for Judy, and a couple of steel framed chairs Daryl picked up at Office Depot. The carpet was worn; almost thread bare in spots. Daryl's office was only slightly larger; with room for an old desk he'd brought from home and a small conference table. The walls were covered with architectural drawings and enlarged floor plans from Anasazi Vistas. John closed the office door behind him as he entered.

"What can I do for you, John?" Daryl asked, forcing a smile. He wasn't looking forward to this meeting, after the tone of Kirshbaum's phone call.

"I wanna know what you're going to do about my note," John responded, taking a seat at the conference table.

"What do you mean?" Daryl asked.

"I mean," Kirshbaum said, "I might get screwed out of my seven hundred fifty 'Gs', and I'd like to know how you're going to fix it. By the way, when did you start working for Anasazi Properties?"

"I joined the company after we closed your sale," Daryl said. "And I don't see how you're getting screwed."

"Let me explain it to you, Mr. Expert Realtor," Kirshbaum said. "You left me unsecured on the money Anasazi owes me. If you guys borrow more money than the land's worth, I'm left with zip."

"If that's the case, Daryl responded, "and I don't know that it is, you still have nothing to worry about. You'll get paid in full."

Taking a seat at the table with Kirshbaum, Daryl continued, "Look, I can see that you're upset. There's no need to worry. Hell, you think I'd buy into this company if I thought there were any problems? My partner's got plenty of money; millions in fact. We can't go back now and change the paperwork. What difference does it make if you're paid in full anyway?"

"Paid in full is where I'm going to be, Daryl," Kirshbaum snarled. His stare hadn't left Daryl's face since he sat down.

"And you will be, John. I guarantee it," Daryl replied, his mind racing across a gulf of unknown contingencies. Why worry, Daryl thought, things are going great.

"Let me be very clear on this," Kirshbaum interjected, "I'm holding you personally responsible to see that I get every penny. If I don't, you won't live to fuck over another client."

As if to emphasize his point, the pencil Kirshbaum was holding snapped suddenly in two pieces. He opened his large hand, and let them drop to the table.

"There's no need to make threats," Daryl said, almost in a whisper.

"Take it as a promise, Daryl, not a threat," Kirshbaum responded.

Kirshbaum had left Daryl's office for several minutes before Judy walked in. He was still sitting at the conference table, staring at the wall.

"Is everything okay, honey?" she asked.

"Just working out some technical problems. Nothing to worry about," Daryl told her, not believing it himself.

Chapter Eleven

Marcel pulled into the small parking lot of Ferraro's café on west Flamingo. He was ten minutes late for his lunch with Ashley, and she didn't like to be kept waiting.

Ferraro's is a small, family owned restaurant, with several locations around Las Vegas. Specializing in Italian cuisine and elegant decor, it was an easy seventy-five dollar lunch. Marcel knew it was just what would put Ashley in a frame of mind to listen to the next part of his financing plan.

"Sorry I'm late, gorgeous," he said as he approached her. She was sitting at the bar, near the front entrance, sipping on a glass of Chardonnay and smoking one of her oversized Capri cigarettes.

"Let's eat. I'm swamped at the office," she said curtly. "You know it's month end."

Properly chastened, he followed her to a table that was waiting for them. Ordering a full bottle of the wine Ashley had been drinking, Marcel took a small black box from his side pocket and slid it across the table in Ashley's direction. She looked at him, softening her expression.

"What's this?" she asked, smiling.

"Open it, sweetheart," he responded.

"They're beautiful," she whispered, pulling one of the round diamond earrings from the box.

"Just like you," Marcel said, helping her remove the other diamond piece from its box. "They're for our five month anniversary." Marcel was surprised when he saw, for an instant, a look of genuine gratitude in her eyes.

They'd settled into lunch when Marcel brought up the subject of additional financing for Anasazi that would be hitting her desk shortly. He went through the terms, and she asked a few questions along the way.

"So, Marcel, what's going to be unusual about this one?"

"The refinance loan will leave the project too short on operating capital if we have to pay off Patek Investments. I want you to pay Patek five hundred thousand, slightly less than half of what is still owed," he replied.

"How in the hell am I going to get away with that?" Ashley asked, taking a sip of her wine. "The new lender's going to need to see a pay-off demand letter from Patek Investments, and a proceeds check that matches it. How am I supposed to handle that?"

"Do you have any blank demands from Patek?" Marcel asked, knowing from Jesse that she had a file full of them. She'd done so much business with Charlie Patek over the last eighteen months that he'd given her demand statements, signed in blank, to use in case a loan paid off while he was unavailable.

"Maybe I could get one," she replied. "What about Patek?"

"What about him," Marcel answered. "He doesn't need to know we're refinancing, does he? Just send him a check for half a million as partial payment on the loan. If he asks any questions, tell him I kicked in some more capital."

"What about his first deed of trust?" she asked, rolling over the risks of lying to Charlie in her head.

"Can't you close the deal, and tell Sundown Mortgage that a reconveyance of the first security will be provided later?" he asked. "I'll be paying it off within a couple of months at the outside anyway."

Ashley thought about what Marcel was asking. He needed more cash in the short term than his financing would provide. If she only paid Charlie five hundred thousand, Marcel would be left with slightly over four point two million. If he only needed the extra money for a couple of months, she thought, it shouldn't be a problem.

Deals were routinely closed with what was known as a recon to come on the first security deed. The second lender would have no reason to complain for at least ninety days. By then, Marcel would pay Charlie off, and Sundown would be in first position.

"Any other liens on the property, other than Kirshbaum?" she asked.

"None will show on your preliminary title report," he answered, not volunteering information on how that would occur.

"So, what you want me to do is to forge a demand for the Patek payoff and show it to Sundown Mortgage?" she asked. "That way, they'll think Patek is being paid in full and will have no reason to doubt that they'll be secured in first position?"

"Exactly," Marcel said.

Things had been going well for Ashley. Between Charlie and Marcel, neither of whom she thought suspected the other was dating her, she was entertained on a regular basis. It was like watching a horse race. It made no difference to Ashley which one she eventually landed. Either one could support her in style. In a way, she still wished the good looking lawyer, Jack Summers, was in the equation. But he'd stopped calling her when Roxburgh hired him as counsel for the company, so it was his loss.

"Any gratuity on this one?" she asked.

"Ten thousand," he replied without hesitation. "Same as last time. Cash after the closing to you. It's worth it to us to use the extra money for a while."

It was more than she'd hoped for. She smiled and nodded, accepting the devil's invitation to dance.

Chapter Twelve

Two weeks had passed since Daryl made the trip to Jim Eccles' office to set up the second loan. He sat in his office nervously thumbing through a stack of invoices from suppliers. He was waiting for Marcel, who'd called to say he would be in town that night and wanted a meeting.

Marcel had one more piece of the puzzle to orchestrate his financing deal on Anasazi Vistas. He needed the title report, which would shortly be created by AmCon Title, to omit the mechanics liens for work done by the subcontractors. These would at this point be over six hundred thousand, and take priority over the new loan from Sundown Mortgage. If they showed up in the title report, Sundown Mortgage wouldn't make the loan.

It would be a simple matter of having the title officer who prepared the report, leave the liens out. This would be explainable later, if it ever came to a fight for the property, as a title error, which was not all that uncommon in the business.

Marcel, as usual, had done his homework. His boy Jesse had been living with AmCon's title officer, Roger Temple, for several months. He'd gotten very familiar with the status of Roger's finances. Temple was one step ahead of the dogs in that regard. Between alimony and child support, if there ever was a guy who could use an infusion of cash it was Roger.

When Marcel arrived at the office of Anasazi Properties, he was an hour late. He told Daryl his plane from Minneapolis had been delayed. He'd actually been tied up making other travel plans from his motel room on the east side of Las Vegas just off the Boulder highway.

Marcel had taken up residence there almost a year before, when he first arrived from California. He paid rent by the week, always in cash. Several times a month, he would book a room at the Rio and drive his leased Mercedes across town to meet Ashley.

It was nearing six o'clock in the evening by the time he reached the Anasazi Properties' office. Judy McKenna had left for the evening, but the front door was unlocked. He shook his head in disgust at Daryl's decorating taste. Daryl was sitting at his desk, with a large stack of unpaid bills in front of him.

"Sorry I'm late, partner," Marcel said. "Goddamn airlines!"

"It's good to see you, Marcel," Daryl replied, standing. "I've just been going over the payables. Judy's worried that we may get some foreclosure notices on the mechanics liens if we don't pay soon."

"We'll have plenty to take care of those when we close the new loan," Marcel responded. "Just like Judy to worry." He gave Daryl a slap on the shoulder and winked as if to say he knew Daryl wasn't worried.

"Actually, I was wondering if you brought your indemnity agreement to cover these?" Daryl asked.

"I've got a better idea," Marcel said. "But we'll need some help from your buddy at AmCon Title."

Daryl shot back a look of confusion. He was expecting Marcel to have a signed indemnity, guaranteeing the lender payment on all outstanding mechanics liens, and an up to date financial statement. That's what had been discussed with Eccles.

"With some other deals I've got going on the East coast, I don't want Sundown nosing around my personal statement at the moment," Marcel said. "I thought maybe your title officer buddy might inadvertently miss the liens in his title report. That way, we can get the loan without laying out my other development plans for the locals." Marcel gave him a knowing wink and sat down opposite Daryl at the desk.

"Why would Roger do that?" Daryl asked, totally confused by this new wrinkle. "Because we'll make it worth his while to make a mistake," Marcel replied.

"He could lose his job," Daryl came back, almost in a whine.

"He'll take the chance for five thousand cash," Marcel said, the smile never leaving his face.

"I don't know," Daryl replied, shaking his balding head as he did.

"Look," Marcel continued, "I had to make some unexpected commitments on the coast last trip. I don't want Eccles nosing around my finances right now. It might queer our whole deal here."

A distinct chill went down Daryl's spine, and his stomach churned at the thought of Anasazi Properties failing at this point. He'd worked too hard to get the project up and running. Besides, he'd lose fifty thousand of his own money plus his and Judy's jobs.

"I suppose I could ask him," Daryl said, stating the obvious.

The next day, Daryl arranged to meet Roger Temple for lunch. They took a booth at Charlie's at the Lakes. Angel was at the bar and, although Daryl would have preferred ogling her from a seat there, they needed some privacy for the business at hand.

Taking a seat opposite Temple, Daryl got right to the point. "I need a big favor, Roger."

"What's that?" Temple asked, looking up from the salad he was working on.

"You know we've got a closing coming up on our new financing for Anasazi?" Daryl asked.

"Yeah, I haven't done the updated report yet," he replied.

"That's what I need to talk about," Daryl said, while waving at Angel to get a drink. "We need to get the loan free of the mechanics liens that you're going to see when you do your updated search. We need a little more time to pay off all of our bills. I want you to leave out the mechanics' liens you find in the date down search. I just want to put the cart ahead of the horse a little."

Roger sat back in the booth, looking with disbelief at his buddy. "I could get fired for something like that," he said.

"You won't get fired," Daryl countered immediately. "We'll use the proceeds to pay off the liens right after closing, so they'll all be released before anyone's the wiser."

"What's in it for me?" Roger asked, wondering what his old friend was up to.

Daryl offered him four thousand, figuring that he'd keep the difference for himself if Roger took the first offer. To his surprise, Temple took the bait. Roger figured that if Daryl was going to use the proceeds of the loan to pay the liens anyway, they'd be released by the time anyone noticed the error, if they ever did. He didn't think it was much of a risk, for four thousand in cash.

"You've got to swear you'll pay off the liens right after the closing, Daryl," Roger said, staring at McKenna. "It's my ass, if you don't!"

"Not a problem, buddy," Daryl said. Since his meeting with Marcel the night before, Daryl couldn't shake an uneasy feeling that was dogging him. "You'll get your money a few days after we close. I promise."

That same day, Sarah Dunn got a surprise phone call from her husband, Jesse. He wanted to meet her for lunch. She hadn't heard from him for months, when he'd called from California. Back then, he'd talked about moving back to Las Vegas. The music career wasn't going as great as he'd hoped. He asked about her new career, and how life had been treating her.

Sarah got the impression that he was desperate, and, though she still had strong feelings for him, she didn't encourage him to move back. She said her job was going well, and she thought it would be best if he stayed out of their son's life until he decided what he was going to do on a permanent basis. But it was nice talking to a familiar voice, and over the course of several calls, she told him a lot about her job, and Ashley Roh. As suddenly as his calls had begun, they'd stopped.

She met Jesse at the Blue Ox, a combination restaurant and bar located near Desert Inn and Valley View, not far from Sarah's office. Several miles to the west, Daryl was busy inviting Roger Temple to put his employer, and old friend, Bill Roxburgh, at risk.

Sarah entered the restaurant, stopping to let her eyes adjust to the dim light of the room. She could see him a moment later, sitting near the far end of the horseshoe shaped bar, drinking a beer. He was much thinner than Sarah remembered, and his long, brown hair hung in tangles. Moving closer, she could see dark circles etched under his eyes, a contrast to the pallor of his skin. She hadn't seen him for almost six years, and the passage of time hadn't been kind to him. The romantic feelings for him she'd clung to, intensified by absence, evaporated as she took a seat across from her former lover.

"Hi, sweetheart," he said, flashing a mouth full of discolored teeth. "You look great!"

He wasn't wrong. Sarah was wearing a light weight yellow sweater, over a plain brown skirt that hit her long legs several inches above the knee. Heads turned as she walked into the bar, as they did most places she went.

Sarah wondered how she could have been in love with the man sitting in front of her. They made uncomfortable small talk about old times over lunch. He told her he'd been living in Las Vegas since the previous summer, doing some work for a land developer. When Sarah asked who, he was evasive. He didn't really know all the details of the project, he told her.

"All the guy really wants is for me to keep an eye on some people for him," Jesse said. This struck Sarah as strange, and she said so. "Look," he said, "I'm not looking a gift horse in the mouth. The guy pays me two grand a month, in cash, and takes care of my rent. The rest of my time is my own."

"Why haven't you called sooner?" she asked. "You have a son, you know."

"Well, I'm not so sure this guy's totally on the up and up," he replied. "I didn't want to involve you and the kid."

"Adam," Sarah interjected. "Your son has a name. It's 'Adam'."

"Yeah, yeah, great name," Jesse replied. Sarah was hurt by his indifference, and started gathering her things to leave.

"Just a second," he said, grabbing her wrist and pulling her back to her seat. "I want you to hold this for me." He produced a wrinkled envelope from his back pocket, sliding it across the table to Sarah.

"What is it?" she asked, recoiling from the package, as if she thought it might bite her.

"It's nothing illegal," he said. "Just copies of some identification I want you to hold for me. If anything strange happens to me, open it up."

"What's going on?" she asked. "You're scaring me."

"Nothing, nothing," he replied quickly. "The first night I met this guy, I stayed at his place. I was nosing around a little and found some ID that didn't match what he'd told me his name was. So I took it with me and had copies made. Then I put the originals back. It's a sort of insurance."

"Insurance against what?" Sarah asked.

"I'm probably just being paranoid," he answered. "Just put it somewhere safe." He picked up the envelope, and grabbing her hand, closed her fingers around it. "Please, Sarah, for old time's sake," he pleaded.

She took the crumpled paper and stuffed it in her purse. She was glad he hadn't asked to see Adam. Later that night, she put the envelope in a drawer of her small desk at home and forgot about it. Within two months, Jesse's body would be discovered.

Chapter Thirteen

Anasazi Properties got its permanent financing at the end of March. The closing took place at AmCon Title's main office, and, as usual, Bill Roxburgh was there shaking hands and slapping backs. Roxburgh had an affable quality that drew people to him. He had sort of a harmless fat guy persona, leaving the impression that he was totally without guile, and therefore likeable.

The loan closing went without a hitch. Anasazi Properties netted nearly four point two million after paying points and closing costs. Jim Eccles attended the closing, verifying that Sundown Mortgage would be in first position. He was pleased to note that there were no outstanding mechanics liens showing in the chain of title. It meant that his new customers were keeping current with their bills. A quick phone call to any of Sam's subcontractors would have told him otherwise.

A payoff check for five hundred thousand was cut to Patek Investments. Charlie Patek was out of town when the closing took place, and his niece, Lila, simply deposited the check when she received it. He wouldn't discover the underpayment until more than two weeks later.

The day Charlie Patek noticed a partial payment on the Anasazi Properties loan, Daryl was sitting at his cluttered desk at the Anasazi Properties' office. He'd just gotten off the phone with their banker. His face had a chalky pallor, and he was having a hard time taking a full breath.

"What's the matter?" Judy asked, entering the room.

"The bank says we're over drawn on our account," said Daryl.

"That's impossible," Judy said quietly. "We've got nearly three and a half million in the account, even after the subcontractors' checks I sent out."

"He said that's what's causing the overdraft," Daryl whispered. "There's no money to cover the checks you wrote."

"Where's the money?" she asked, afraid to know the answer.

"He said Marcel transferred the entire balance to a bank in Florida," Daryl replied.

Judy couldn't quite get her mind around what her husband was telling her. She was used to having accounts balance. "Why would he do that?" she asked.

"I don't know," Daryl replied, "but I'd better find out in a hurry."

He reached for the phone, dialing Marcel's cell phone number. In a moment, he got a recording that prompted him to leave a message as the customer was "unavailable." He next called information to get the number for DeMartes Construction in Orlando. As Marcel had suggested many months earlier, Daryl never bothered to try to reach him at the Orlando office. He'd been told that Marcel would rarely be there, since he spent most of his time traveling. After two rings, a cheery voice answered the phone.

"Good morning, DeMartes Construction. This is Trina, how may I help you?"

"Is Marcel DeMartes in?" Daryl asked.

"He's in a meeting at the moment," the voice replied. "Can I take a message, or can his assistant help you?"

"Will he be long? This is very urgent," Daryl responded, trying to remain calm.

"I'm sorry sir, I don't have that information," she said. "Would you like to leave a message?"

Daryl paused, not knowing what to do next. He considered talking to the assistant he'd never met, but then left his name and number, asking that DeMartes call him as soon as possible. He told the Trina voice that DeMartes would know what it was about.

Judy was still standing in front of Daryl's desk, listening to the one-sided conversation. As Daryl hung up, she asked what was going on.

"Marcel's in the Orlando office," he said. "I'm sure he had a good reason for moving the money. It's probably headed back this way already. He mentioned some East coast project he is working on."

"He should have told us. I've still got a stack of bills to pay on my desk, not to mention our paychecks," Judy scolded, like a mother to a teenager who's violated curfew.

Daryl was only half listening to his wife. The implications of not having the loan funds available were staggering. Almost illogically, his first thought was of Roger. He'd planned on meeting Temple that night. He'd already written a check to cash for five thousand. He was going to stop at the bank to cash it that afternoon. He would pocket a thousand and give the remaining four to his old co-worker, assuring him that all of the mechanics liens had been paid. Now, he apparently couldn't cash a company check for five dollars, much less five thousand. And, it looked like the suppliers hadn't been paid at all.

He waited two hours before again calling Marcel in Orlando. Again Trina answered in a pleasant voice, saying that Mr. DeMartes had left the office. This time, Daryl asked to speak with the assistant.

"This is John, how can I help you?" a man's voice on the phone said when Daryl was transferred.

"This is Daryl McKenna in Las Vegas," Daryl said, as if he expected the listener to know who he was.

"Yes, Mr. McKenna, how can I help you?"

"I'm trying to reach Marcel," Daryl said. "We've got a problem with his project out here, and I need to speak with him right away."

"I'm sorry, what did you say your name was?" the confused voice asked Daryl.

"It's Marcel's partner in Las Vegas," Daryl responded, his voice one tick below a shout. "I need to talk to him right away."

"Mr. DeMartes doesn't have any 'partners', or any business ventures of any kind, in Las Vegas, sir," the man on the phone replied.

Daryl couldn't speak. The words from his phone had knocked the wind from him like a sucker punch. If the human mind is the ultimate computer, Daryl's had pumped out an error sign, unable to digest the non sequitur he'd just heard. He shook his head to clear it.

"Are you still there?" the assistant asked.

"Yes, yes, I'm here," Daryl stammered. "There's some mistake. Is this DeMartes Construction of Orlando, Florida?"

"Yes, it is," the assistant said.

"Does Marcel DeMartes run the place?" Daryl asked.

"Yes, he does," the man replied.

Daryl's mind simply couldn't get around the problem. He asked if the assistant was positive that DeMartes didn't have business in Las Vegas. Maybe he'd kept it secret from his staff?

"No," the assistant replied. "I'm his son, as well as his assistant. I'm intimately involved in all of our projects. We don't have anything close to Las Vegas, or west of the Mississippi for that matter. Are you sure you've got the right person?"

"Is there more than one Marcel DeMartes in Orlando?" Daryl asked, grasping at straws.

"I've been here my entire life," the assistant replied, "and if there is another one, I've never heard of him."

"Can I talk to your father?" Daryl asked.

"I'm afraid he's just left town on business, but he's due back in a week," the man said. "Maybe I could have him give you a call when he checks his messages?"

"Yes, please," Daryl said, pleading. "Have him call me as soon as possible."

Daryl left his office and home phone numbers and hung up the phone as Judy walked into the office. The look on his face told a story of disaster.

"Did you reach Marcel?" she asked.

"No. I think we've got a problem," Daryl said.

He quickly recounted the gist of the conversation for his wife who, midway through the tale dropped into a chair by Daryl's desk. When she'd recovered sufficiently to speak, Judy asked what they were going to do. Daryl, the color still drained from his face, answered with a single word.

"Pack."

At the same time, Charlie Patek was going through a stack of paperwork that had built up on his desk while he'd vacationed in Hawaii. He'd told Ashley that he was attending business conferences, but he'd actually flown a hot little waitress from the Rio over to meet him for a week. Half way through the pile, something caught his eye in the daily deposits.

"Lila, what the fuck is this Anasazi payment of half a million bucks?" he shouted to the outer office. His buxom niece appeared almost instantly.

"I don't know, Charlie," she answered. "We got a check in the mail, and I put it in the account."

It's a good thing this broad's got a great body to get her by, Charlie thought, as she stood wide-eyed in front of him.

"Did anyone ask for a partial reconveyance in return for the check?" Charlie asked.

Lila paused for a moment, the strain of conjuring a clear memory from more than a day in the past weighing heavily on her face.

"I don't think so," she answered, smiling and licking her lips.

"Get Ashley on the phone for me," Charlie barked at his niece. If there was one thing that could get Charlie's mind off a great set of breasts, it was the thought of losing money. In this case, a man who prided himself on the art of the con suddenly didn't like the feeling in his gut.

Chapter Fourteen

The air was thick with humidity by mid-April in Dallas. Leon Black was having a cigarette on the sidewalk outside of the "C" gates at the Dallas-Fort Worth International airport, and sweat trickled down the side of his face. It was almost noon, and his connecting flight to San Juan, Puerto Rico, wouldn't leave for more than an hour. If all went well, he'd be in his hotel on Frigate Bay, St. Kitts, in the former British West Indies by ten o'clock that night.

He'd left Vegas on American Airlines flight 1114 at seven that morning. The flight took two and a half hours, and Leon desperately needed to stretch his legs and smoke by the time they'd landed.

Leon had booked three flights. One would take Jesse through Dallas and on to Orlando. That flight was in the name of Marcel DeMartes of Orlando, Florida. The other, also connecting through Dallas and on to San Juan, was in Jesse's name. The third flight, booked separately, was in Leon's name, and took him on to St. Kitts from San Juan. They'd boarded separately, and Leon made sure they spent as little time as possible together in the airport.

Jesse had shown his own identification at the check in desk, and obtained a first class boarding card for the flight to Dallas. Leon checked in under Marcel's name, and got a boarding pass for the economy class. Prior to leaving, they switched boarding cards, with Leon taking the first class pass. Pre-9/11, in spite of the apparent tightening of security at American airports, virtually anyone could board a flight once a boarding pass had been obtained. From that point on, no one checked identification.

In Dallas, they'd followed the same procedure. To anyone checking later, it would appear that Marcel DeMartes had flown, first class, from Las Vegas to Orlando. It would also appear that Jesse had flown on to San Juan. There would be no link to Leon's separate flight to St. Kitts. They both took only carry on luggage. Once in San Juan, deplaning as Jesse, Leon checked in under his real name to St. Kitts.

Flight 606 left Dallas shortly after one o'clock in the afternoon. Leon settled back in Jesse's economy seat, dreading the nearly five hour flight to San Juan. He reached up, opening the vent to allow a stream of cool air to blow down across his face and marveled at his success. He reclined his chair, and closed his eyes as the in flight movie popped up on tiny screens that populated the ceiling above the narrow aisle. Once again, as he'd done innumerable times before, he went over the details of his plan.

Leon Black was a Navy brat. His family had moved around the United States, and several foreign countries, as he grew up. Leon's father was in security service for the Navy. Leon never really knew what his father did for a living, but in later years suspected that it had something to do with planning the overthrow of various governments in the western hemisphere. He was a demanding parent, and Leon had never felt like he could quite measure up to his father's standards.

Leon was a quick study, and, largely due to the transient nature of his youth, finally managed to earn a degree in finance from the University of North Carolina at age twenty-six. He'd spent several years as a stockbroker in the Charlotte area before moving to Florida. Born in France, during a period when his father had been stationed there, he was fluent in his mother's native tongue. He'd developed a genuine aptitude for computers while in school. In fact, his natural skills as a programmer could have earned him a very good living if he'd been willing to work. But that was always Leon's biggest fault. He looked for the shortcut in everything.

By age forty, he'd found himself working as in-house accountant for DeMartes Construction in Orlando. The job had bored Leon, but he'd been intrigued by the success of its owner, Marcel DeMartes. DeMartes, only five years Leon's senior, was a self made millionaire in the construction and development business. He'd worked hard his whole life and believed in an honest day's work for an honest day's pay. His reputation in a difficult, and often less than forthright industry, was impeccable. As the business grew, he'd seen the need to computerize his bookkeeping system and hired Leon to do the job.

Leon had quickly whipped the company's accounts into shape. It was a great disappointment to Marcel that after nearly two years an independent audit indicated someone, presumably Leon, had been siphoning funds in almost undetectable amounts into a bogus supplier account. When the final tally came back, it appeared that Leon had stolen nearly twenty thousand from DeMartes Construction. The computer scheme that made this possible was so complex that both DeMartes and the prosecuting authorities in Orlando had elected not to prosecute. They hadn't thought a jury would understand it.

Leon was fired, without explanation, and headed for California. His time with DeMartes had given Leon a taste for what real money could buy. He'd visited DeMartes' home in Naples, Florida and sailed on his yacht. It was during that first visit to Naples that DeMartes' wife had commented on how much Leon "resembled her husband" physically. He "could have been Marcel's younger brother," she'd said, "the resemblance was uncanny."

That comment sparked an idea that would lead Leon to Las Vegas. He would assume DeMartes' identity when it suited him. With the kind of credit rating this guy had, he could write his own ticket elsewhere. His computer skills served Leon well, and by the time he reached California he was 'Marcel DeMartes' and had credible identification documents to prove it.

Leon had been careful not to abuse the privilege of his new identity. And, while he freely used his new name, leasing a new Mercedes in Los Angeles, he'd made sure that nothing would trigger a detailed check into his Florida background. As the funds from his former employer began to dwindle, he'd felt it was time to make a bolder move with the help of his new persona. He'd learned how the development business worked from DeMartes. The financing end of the business was his forte. He'd worked closely with the title and escrow people at DeMartes Construction and knew what it took to get interim and permanent financing.

Leon's plan was to get his hands on millions in development funds without any intention of developing anything other than his personal fortune. As always, he'd wanted the shortcut. The pieces of the puzzle that he thought would take him to a life of leisure fell into place when he met Jesse. He needed inside knowledge of, and cooperation from, the title and escrow company that would handle his financing package. Jesse had provided him with AmCon Title. He'd needed a fall guy who was either stupid or desperate enough to act as point man for the project, and Daryl McKenna had proved to be both.

It had crossed Leon's mind more than once that he should take the initial loan proceeds, McKenna's investment, and run. But, made bold by the ease of his first success, he'd elected to wait for the sweeter pot of the permanent loan from Sundown Mortgage before disappearing. He just needed to make sure that no one could connect his assumed DeMartes identity with Leon Black.

As his flight crossed over the Caribbean Sea, miles south of the southern coastline of the United States, Leon was sure his secret was safe. When Flight 606 touched down in San Juan, the Marcel DeMartes imposter would cease to exist. The man who arrived in St. Kitts would be Leon Black, millionaire entrepreneur.

The Federation of St. Kitts and Nevis, two sister islands that lay thirteen hundred miles south east of Miami, became an independent part of the British Commonwealth in 1983. Its' checkered past spoke of blood letting and war. The two islands were discovered by Christopher Columbus in 1493, and named "St. Christopher", either after the explorer himself, or the well known patron saint of travel, no one seems to know. The larger island became "St. Kitts" under French rule, and the name remains. The British occupied the islands in 1623, and a two hundred year tug-of-war with the French ensued. The Treaty of Versailles finally placed control of the islands in British hands in the late seventeen hundreds.

Local lore whispers of how the original inhabitants, a peace-loving tribe, were conquered by the cannibalistic Caribe Indians. They, in turn, were decimated in a mass execution near Bloody Bay by the British. Left with no cheap labor to work the island's economic bedrock, sugar, the British turned to Africa. St. Kitts became a hub of the slave trade for the Caribbean and the United States. Modern St. Kitts and Nevis, with a total population of about forty-five thousand, consists primarily of the ancestors of those slaves. St. Kitts became known as the "mother" of the Caribbean, and Nevis, a forty minute boat ride to the Southeast, was its "Pearl."

It wasn't chance that brought Leon to the small nation's capital, Basseterre, that night. He'd visited the islands more than once with his father, as a young boy. The islands' economy, strongly dependent on tourism, made a stranger's face in the crowd nothing to get excited about. Since the primary language is English, he would attract no undue attention speaking his native tongue. At the same time, the islands remained a popular destination for French tourists, and his command of that language could prove useful. There were also several large international banking groups on St. Kitts, and he needed conduits for the transfer of his newly acquired funds to secure accounts in Nevis.

Stepping from the mobile staircase, and on to the tarmac of Robert Bradshaw International airport in Basseterre, Leon inhaled the familiar smell of the Caribbean night.

Sweet and moist, he thought, like sweat on a sixteen year old girl's neck at midnight. Innocence bathed in a promise of passion. A wave of euphoria rippled through him, as he waited impatiently at immigration.

"I've done it!" he marveled aloud.

Without counting Daryl's fifty thousand, much of which he'd used already to live on in Vegas, he'd managed to pull off a scam, in the Mecca of all scam artists, for more than four million dollars. With only one minor detail waiting to be taken care of in Orlando, he was home free.

Having finally made it past the slow moving immigration official, Leon swayed side to side in the back seat as his island cab, Big Blue painted in large letters on its front and sides, as it maneuvered the narrow streets of the capital city and along the south road towards Timothy Beach Resort on Frigate Bay. It was nearly eleven o'clock, Atlantic Standard Time, and he looked forward to a strong drink and a cool bed. He had a late morning meeting with Ernest Drover, principal representative of Caribbean Holdings Limited in Charlestown, Nevis, scheduled for the following day. Drover had said he would "of course be in a position to assist Mr. Black with his off-shore investments." Leon had done his homework. By the mid-1990s, Nevis had enacted several pieces of legislation aimed at attracting offshore banking and asset protection.

Two days earlier, he'd cleaned out the accounts of Anasazi Properties, wiring the funds to an account he'd opened in Orlando. It was just enough to set him up nicely, but not so much that it would be likely to set off an international manhunt even if they knew who to look for... which they didn't.

As Leon's cab slid to a halt in front of his hotel, Jesse ordered another beer in a small bar near the Orlando airport, over a thousand miles to the northwest. Jesse had spent the last several hours trying, in vain, to figure out what Marcel was up to. He'd never asked Marcel why he had two sets of identification. But he'd always got the feeling that something was going down with this guy that wasn't quite kosher. Marcel had told him to stay put in the motel, and that he would contact him the next day with instructions.

The flight in, sitting in Marcel's first class seat, wasn't too bad. He had a pretty good buzz going by the time the direct flight from Dallas landed. Marcel had also told him to keep to himself during flight. He'd done that for the most part. But there wasn't any harm in being friendly with the stewardess was there? Jesse tried several times during the flight to engage her in a conversation. He'd fantasized that she'd be based in Orlando, and would probably like to take him back to her apartment and show him what he wanted to see. It didn't work out that way, however. The attraction was a one-way street. In the end, Jesse's hopes for a night of wild sex walked out the door of the airplane in Orlando.

Half drunk from the complimentary vodkas he'd had on the flight, and another three or four beers at the motel's lounge, he thought about Sarah. He couldn't believe how good she looked when he saw her a few weeks earlier. He'd forgotten about those long legs.

Maybe I'll give her a call later, he thought. She'd probably really like to hear from me. After all, I'm the father of her kid, right?

But Jesse didn't call. If procrastination was an Olympic event, Jesse would be a multiple medal winner. He'd always had lots of plans for things he wanted to do. He just never did them. Instead, he stayed glued to his barstool until the place closed for the night. Then he stumbled in a stupor back to his room and passed out.

When the telephone rang the next afternoon, Jesse heard it like part of a dream. At first it seemed distant, as if not really something that needed his attention. Then, as he regained consciousness, it became a mind splitting sound; a jackhammer on his tender, alcohol fogged brain. He reached out, knocking the receiver to the ground. He was fully dressed and had passed out face-down on top of the bed. There was a half empty beer bottle on the night stand and, with the next blind grab for the phone, he sent it sprawling across the carpet, emptying itself as it rolled.

"Shiiiit, just a second," he screamed to the empty room and the ringing telephone. He managed to roll off the bed and landed hard on the floor next to the phone. Lifting it, he said, "Who is it?"

"Jesse, it's Marcel. Where have you been? I've been calling for two hours."

"I'm right here," he said, shaking his head to clear it. "Must be something wrong with the phone; I didn't hear a thing."

Leon woke early that morning. From the balcony off his suite he looked out on Frigate Bay, and the blue green Caribbean Sea that stretched beyond to the west. Around the point to the north lie Port Zante, with its twin T-shaped piers built to accommodate cruise liners. It was from there that he would catch a water taxi to Nevis. He could see the island clearly from his vantage point; Nevis Peak, its dormant volcano, dominating the view. Like so many of the Caribbean islands, born in the violence of volcanic eruption, Nevis lay shrouded in green and dotted with black lava.

Leon could almost pick out the Cottle Church ruins lying above Mosquito Bay, but the glare of the morning sun made his vision dance like the shimmering water that surrounded the island, and he turned away. And, although St. Kitts and Nevis were situated in a temperate climate, he felt like a steak on a grill being seared by the tropical sun. He walked slowly towards his bathroom, the cool tiles of the floor bringing a smile to his face. Almost everything seemed to make Leon smile since he'd landed the night before. He'd confirmed his meeting at Caribbean Holdings Limited and had time to clean up, take advantage of the hotel's breakfast buffet, and catch a taxi to the pier.

By ten o'clock, Leon had disembarked at Charlestown, Nevis, and walked the cobbled streets to his appointment. The morning sun was full ablaze, and though the humidity wasn't bad, he'd become used to the dry air of Las Vegas over the last year. Sweat trickled down his back as he entered the blissfully air conditioned lobby of Caribbean Holdings.

"Mr. Ernest Drover, please," Leon said, with a smile to the pretty young island receptionist.

"You must be Mr. Black. Mr. Drover is expecting you," she said. She flashed a smile, her white teeth a sharp contrast to the dark complexion of her face. "Would you like coffee or a cool drink?" Her accent was what you might expect in Oxford, not on a small volcanic island in the Caribbean.

"No, I'm fine," Leon replied, his eyes darting involuntarily to a piece of coral that hung at her cleavage. The girl caught his gaze and, though not obvious on her dark skin, she blushed.

A large man dressed in a white linen suit emerged from the back offices, diverting their attention from the awkward moment.

"Good morning, Mr. Black. I'm Ernest Drover, principal representative for Caribbean Holdings." The delivery of this introduction made Leon feel like he should congratulate or salute the man, he was so obviously pleased with himself.

"Hello, Mr. Drover, I'm Leon Black. We spoke on the phone."

"Yes, yes, of course," Drover said, extending his hand in greeting. "Shall we retire to my office? Coral, did you offer Mr. Black refreshment?"

The young girl started to speak, but Leon interrupted. "She's been most helpful." The smile and the blush were back in an instant. "Very professional job she's doing."

This seemed to satisfy Drover and he turned, leading the way towards the back office. When they reached the confines of his private office, he extended his hand, showing Leon to a chair.

"How may we be of service to you, Mr. Black?" Drover asked. Though Leon had briefly outlined his intentions over the phone, Drover wanted to start from the beginning.

"I'm going to be doing some business in the islands, Mr. Drover," Leon said. "I'd like your help in setting up an off shore corporation, with maybe a sheltered trust of some sort. Whatever you think best."

Drover paused a moment, either deciding on an appropriate response, or giving himself a chance to evaluate what the potential customer sitting across from him was up to. Finally, picking up a pen as if to make notes, he spoke.

"Of course, we can handle that for you sir," he said. "Our government has wisely seen fit in very recent times to pass legislation that will allow complete anonymity, as well as asset protection. How much of an initial funding did you have in mind?"

"About four point two million, U.S.," Leon said, the number rolling out for both men like a natural seven on the craps table.

My, what a nice little fish we've snagged today, Drover thought.

"What will this cost me?" Leon asked, getting right to the point of what both men had in mind.

Drover stalled, scribbling notes on the pad in front of him. This was no business investor, he'd decided. Black was on the run with a large amount of cash that he needed to hide. Drover had seen it before, and he could care less. The question was, how much would the traffic bear?

"Well, of course there are the legal fees, filing costs, administration charges, and maybe a few extra charges if you're in a hurry to get going," Drover said. "I'd say fifty thousand…U.S."

It was the moment of truth for Drover. If he'd overestimated Black's need for a quick, discreet place to hide money, he'd lose him now. But that was a large part of his job at Caribbean Holdings, being able to read the foreign investors who came to call. Even before Black responded, he could see from the look in Leon's eyes that he'd hooked a big fish.

"And, of course one percent of the transfer to CHL," he added, playing his hand as far as he felt he could.

They were talking a total of ninety thousand dollars, U.S., to fill out some forms and wire transfer the money in from the United States. It was a proverbial highway robbery, and both men knew it.

"If you can get the whole thing done today, I'll throw in an extra ten thousand," Leon said, after a moment of silence.

The look on Drover's face was of a man who'd just got hit in the balls. He'd done the unpardonable. He'd underestimated Black's level of desperation. But there was nothing to be done about it now.

"Can you be back here by three to sign the paperwork?" Drover asked. "We can handle the necessary documents to authorize a wire transfer of the funds this morning, and by the time they get here, we'll have the corporate and trust documents ready to authorize your deposit. I'll just need a copy of your passport."

"Certainly, maybe your receptionist could show me the island in the meantime?" Leon said with a wink.

"I'm sure she'd be more than happy to accommodate," Drover responded, thinking she'd better be 'more than happy' if she wants her job beyond lunchtime.

"Could I use your phone to call an associate in Florida?" Leon asked, reaching for the telephone on Drover's desk.

"Of course, be my guest. I'll just arrange things with your guide, 'Coral'," Drover replied.

With that he left Leon alone in the office. Leon dialed the operator, and asked to be connected with the number for Jesse's room in Orlando. After several rings, the motel operator answered, and the overseas operator gave the room information and a request for a "person to person" call for "Mr. Jesse Dunn." Several more moments passed, and the operator relayed that there was "no answer in Mr. Dunn's' room." Leon said he would try later and hung up.

Where is that son of a bitch, he wondered as he left Drover's office.

Drover was leaning over the young receptionist's desk having an animated conversation with her as Leon entered the lobby. They both stopped talking as he approached. Drover turned to Leon, a forced smile on his face.

"Mr. Black, this is Coral Jones," he said. "She'll be more than happy to show you our island while your documents are being prepared, wouldn't you Coral?" The tone was more of a threat than an invitation, and Leon could see the reluctance in the girl's eyes.

"I'm very pleased to meet you, Ms. Jones," he said, extending his hand to take hers. As he did, she stood to her full height. Much taller than Leon had thought, maybe five eight or nine. "I don't want to inconvenience you, but I'm new to the area, and it would be most helpful if you could spend some time with me over lunch giving me background on your lovely island." It was the most genuine tone Leon could muster, and the girl seemed to relax a bit.

"I'll be happy to show you around, Mr. Black," Coral said. "An extended lunch would be lovely."

The emphasis on extended seemed to let Drover know that not only would she be back when she felt like it, but that he'd owe her for the favor.

"Yes, of course, Coral. Let's get Mr. Black back here by three, please. We've some important transactions to finalize," Drover responded, letting her know he'd gotten the point.

"Just let me gather a few things, Mr. Black. I'll meet you out front," she said, moving towards an open hallway off the lobby.

"I'll see you at three o'clock then," Drover said, turning his gaze from the departing backside of Coral to Leon. "Enjoy your look at our native treasures."

The irony of the comment was not lost on Leon as he moved to the front door.

Coral Jones was twenty-three years old, tall and slender. For Leon, her look was about as far from that of Ashley Roh as you could get. She was noticeably taller, and her breasts, while firm and full, weren't nearly the size he'd become accustomed to while bedding Ashley. Coral's complexion, black and smooth, had a luminescent quality to it; as if there were white ancestors in her bloodline. Leon chuckled to himself as he lit a cigarette, waiting for his guide to emerge from Caribbean Holdings. He'd love to see the look on Ashley's face when she found out the rich lover she'd been cultivating for so long wasn't coming back. It served the bitch right.

In a moment, Coral emerged from the building purse in hand. They had lunch at Unella's by the Sea, overlooking the ferry dock where boats unloaded supplies for the island and the water taxis came and went with their cargo of tourists and natives. Coral seemed nervous at first, but Leon felt he had all the time in the world to work on this piece of the island. He was the perfect gentleman, and gradually she opened up. After lunch she walked him up the hill, past Chapel Street, to the Museum of Nevis History and the ruins of the old fort overlooking the harbor.

By quarter to three, they were back at Caribbean Holdings. The afternoon's heat didn't seem to bother Coral, but Leon was glad he'd worn cotton slacks. Sweat dripped from his temples as he entered the cool lobby.

"There you are," announced Drover, as they entered. "I was afraid Coral had kidnapped our newest favored customer."

"Quite the contrary," Leon replied, "she's been most informative. A real asset to your organization, I think."

Again she blushed and smiled, but this time Leon saw more of a look of gratitude than embarrassment.

"Are we ready to proceed?" Leon asked, turning to Drover.

"Yes," Drover replied. "If you'll step into my office, I think you'll find everything is in order."

Leon asked if he might first use a private phone to call his associate, and was ushered into an empty office. Following the morning's routine, he finally heard Jesse's voice on the phone. It sounded as if he'd dropped the phone, before answering. After hearing Jesse's excuse about the "phone not working," he told Jesse to stay where he was.

"I'll be there day after tomorrow to pay you off," Marcel said. "We're not going back to Vegas."

"Why the hell not?" Jesse asked. "What about all of our stuff?"

"I'll replace whatever you need," Leon snapped back. "I want you to wait for me in Orlando. I'll send someone to collect your belongings in Vegas later."

He hung up abruptly and joined Drover in his office.

"Everything alright?" Drover asked as Leon took a seat.

"Hard to find good help," Leon replied with a smirk. "This one's about out of a job."

"Well, I hope you're not too inconvenienced," Drover said, smiling.

They spent the next hour going over the documentation for Leon's new off shore corporation. A trust had been created, into which Drover had deposited four point two million dollars, U.S., and a draft made payable to

Caribbean Holdings Limited for one hundred thousand had been prepared, drawn upon the trust. Leon signed on various lines through the stack of papers, including the draft.

As he pushed Drover's check across the desk he asked, "I assume I can count on your complete discretion?"

"Absolutely, Mr. Black," Drover answered. "Our laws, as well as my fiduciary obligation to you require it. I assume you'll want to take a few days to consider your investment opportunities for the balance?"

"Yes, thank you," Leon answered. "I'll get back to you in a week or so on that. In the meantime, I'll be earning interest in accordance with the trust agreement?"

"Absolutely," replied Drover, and stood to again shake Leon's hand. "Welcome to our islands."

Leon paused briefly to again thank Coral for her help, and to ask if they might have dinner some evening. She smiled and gave him a local phone number on one of the company's generic business cards.

He left the building and walking the short distance down Main Street, he made his way to the ferry dock. He caught the five o'clock ferry to St. Kitts, and was back in his suite at the Timothy Beach Resort by shortly after six. He showered quickly, and walked to the main lounge. Ordering a tumbler of "Grey Goose on the rocks," he pondered the fate of the last piece of unfinished business in his plan, Jesse. He would take care of that problem tomorrow and live like a king in an island paradise for the rest of his life. Maybe there'd be a place for the beautiful Coral in that life. Not bad, for an underachieving Navy brat, he thought.

That evening, Jesse sat at the motel bar in Orlando, sipping his third beer, hoping to erase the previous night's hangover. He'd been trying in vain to strike up a conversation with the waitress, who apparently wanted nothing to do with a skinny, long haired patron, with dark circles under both eyes.

Jesse didn't like the fact that Marcel wanted him to leave all his personal stuff in Vegas. It pissed him off that he wasn't included in the details of whatever Marcel was up to. He'd pretty much already decided that he wouldn't wait for Marcel to get there in two days. He still had over two thousand in cash that Marcel had given him.

Maybe it's time to dump this gig, he thought, and go see Sarah. Who knows, he mused, maybe we can get back together. After all, shouldn't I be able to see my own kid?

After two more beers, Jesse called the airlines and made flight reservations for Las Vegas in the morning. Not too early, eleven o'clock. I can make that, and still have a good time tonight, he thought.

The next morning, Leon's plane touched down at the Orlando airport at ten thirty in the morning. He'd caught the red eye out of St. Kitts to Miami, and then on to Orlando. He'd hoped to surprise Jesse, who wouldn't be expecting him until the next day. If he'd been five minutes earlier, he would have passed Jesse in the concourse on his way to boarding a flight to Las Vegas.

Chapter Fifteen

By the time Leon deplaned in Orlando, almost three thousand miles to the west Jack Summers entered a conference room at the Nevada Division of Insurance's office in Carson City. It was early morning in Nevada. Jack had taken a late flight to Reno the night before, driving a rental to the capital city that morning.

He'd been summoned there to represent AmCon Title and several of its employees at an "informal conference." The stated purpose of the meeting was "to determine if cause existed to bring formal charges" against AmCon Title, along with some key personnel, for "fraud, improper supervision, negligence," and a host of other statutory violations, as a result of a complaint made to the Division by John Kirshbaum and others.

Seated at the table were John Kirshbaum, Charlie Patek, Jim Eccles, and Fred Snead, a deputy attorney general. Jack knew Snead. Town idiot came to mind. Word had it that his daddy was a ranking judge in the state, and that he kept his position as a political favor. Jack had seen his type before. The practice of law was full of them. God knows how this guy passed the bar exam, but Jack had always suspected that the tentacles of daddy's influence probably extended well beyond the attorney general's office.

Fred Snead, moronic son of the honorable Samuel Snead, was one dangerous son of a bitch in Jack's estimation. Kirshbaum sat at the far end of the rectangular conference table, jaw clinched tight, looking like he'd like to beat someone to a pulp. Patek, dressed in a pin-stripped blue business suit, sat to the left with an unopened file in front of him. Eccles sat across the table from Patek and next to Snead. Snead and Eccles were conferring privately when Summers entered the room, but all conversation stopped when he arrived.

Jack had suggested the meeting in a letter to the Division after his first visit with Sarah. He'd reviewed the closing documents from both the initial loan, and the subsequent refinancing by Suncoast Mortgage. It was his suggestion that the principal players meet with Snead to determine if a formal charge could be avoided.

"Good morning," Jack said affably as he walked to the remaining open chair, opposite Kirshbaum. "Thank you all for agreeing to come."

Jack knew that the meeting would not be taking place but for an instruction from Eccles to Snead. While not personally acquainted with the well-known mortgage broker, Snead knew Eccles' reputation for having both political and Mob clout. Dull-witted as he might be, Snead would know from his own family ties that he needed to defer to a man like Eccles and the people he represented.

As he unloaded documents from his briefcase, Jack took charge of the meeting.

"It seems that we've uncovered what appears to be a rather isolated comedy of errors on this Anasazi Properties project," he said.

Kirshbaum was immediately on his feet. In spite of the eight foot table between them, Jack instinctively moved to a defensive position, and balanced his weight for an attack. The move would be obvious only to the trained eye of an expert in martial arts, but the subtle change would allow him to handle anything coming in his direction.

"Errors my ass!" Kirshbaum shouted. "Your clients are a bunch of crooks, and I want them in jail."

Snead, seated to Kirshbaum's left, attempted to put his hand on the ex-cop's arm in restraint, but was thrown aside with what appeared to be little effort. Jack made a mental note that the ex-cop should be taken seriously if he did more than threaten at this point.

"Please, Mr. Kirshbaum," Snead cajoled, "we're here to get the facts and proceed accordingly. I can assure you that if there's been any criminal activity, we'll prosecute to the full extent of the law."

Jack, in an effort to make Snead agree to the informal meeting, had promised to make both Ashley and Sarah available for questioning the following day should they not be able to reach a resolution of the charges immediately. They were scheduled to meet with him later that day, in Reno, to prepare.

"I don't think we're here to either make threats, or engage in unsubstantiated accusations," Jack said as he took his chair and opened his briefcase on the table in front of him.

Just inside the case, sheathed in a leather side pocket, was a perfectly balanced throwing knife. Jack kept it sharp as a razor and used it as a letter opener. It was an old friend from his Navy Seal days, and he could have pinned Kirshbaum to his chair with the flick of his wrist. The thought briefly crossed his mind, and he smiled.

"What's so funny?" Kirshbaum demanded, continuing to glare across the table.

"Nothing," Jack replied, removing a large stack of files from the case and placing it on the table. All eyes at the table moved reflexively to this new addition. "On the contrary, I don't think there's anything funny about threatening to put my clients out of business; one which they've worked long and hard to build, without first hearing all the facts."

Jack glanced in Eccle's direction with the last comment, and the lizard squirmed perceptibly. Jack continued.

"I've prepared copies of what I feel are the key documents in this dispute for each of you, and I propose that we go over them together. There have clearly been some mistakes made in these transactions and, when we finish, I have some solutions I'd like to discuss with you."

Jack was presenting a united defense for AmCon, Ashley, Roger Temple, Bill Roxburgh and Sarah. Since no formal action had been taken to this point, he felt it was a better strategy to have them all stand together in defense of the claims of wrongdoing. He also knew, all too well, that very soon each would need their own counsel if the matter wasn't concluded quickly. The finger pointing had already begun. It would escalate as charges and counter, or cross, charges were made. It was going to get ugly.

As Jack went through the file in front of him, he took a moment to explain each document's significance in the over-all problem. He started, taking the position that the mere existence of an oversight, or simple mistake, would not constitute legally actionable fraud. He wanted to let Snead know what the parameters of their discussion would be. If Snead thought there was sufficient evidence to prove active fraud, whether criminal or otherwise, they might just as well end the meeting now. Jack made it clear that if there was to be a quick resolution, it would have to be on some much less onerous grounds.

Seeing no strong reaction from Snead or Eccles, Jack pushed forward. Patek had said nothing since Jack's arrival, and Kirshbaum sulked quietly in his chair. When Summers finished describing each of the individual documents in front of the group, he pushed back from the table and stood. After so many years in a courtroom, he felt more at ease thinking on his feet.

"Here's the bottom line as I see it. Mr. Kirshbaum, let's start with you. You've loaned seven hundred fifty thousand dollars to a man you met only once, and from whom you got a deed of trust that may or may not protect you in the end. If you've lost your money because you failed to read what you signed, I can give you a library full of case law that says you're out of luck. Personally, I'd be trying to locate Mr. McKenna, your agent, if I were you. Has anyone seen Mr. McKenna lately? No, I didn't think so."

The group sat in silence, so Jack continued.

"It was clearly not the duty of AmCon Title, or any of its employees, to make sure your backside was covered. We were presented with a set of instructions by your man that we duly committed to writing and you signed, telling us to structure the deal the way we did. As a disinterested third party, we had no choice but to stay disinterested. I dare say Mr. Snead would probably have us up on charges if we'd stuck our proverbial nose in the deal and told you not to sign!"

As he finished, Jack made it clear that he had dismissed Kirshbaum out of hand. The man had been burned by his own greed and, as he looked around the table, he saw little disagreement.

He then turned to Patek, who had been furiously taking notes but now stopped, and said, "You claim to have been short changed on your pay-off, in spite of the fact that you made a small fortune in points on the front end of this deal. And if what you say is true, then maybe you haven't made quite the pile of dough you thought you would out of this. On the other hand, you still appear to be first in line to get paid if this property goes to foreclosure. And, from what I've been able to find out, you should be made whole in the end. That a fair statement?"

Patek said nothing and, pausing briefly to take a sip from the water glass in front of him, Jack continued.

"Why would Ms. Dunn fabricate the existence of a pay off demand which was only half the size it, according to you, should have been? I don't see her motivation. Do you think she was in cahoots with McKenna or DeMartes? Frankly, the little I've known her, she doesn't seem the type. Isn't it more likely that your assistant, in your absence, might have made a mistake in sending the wrong pay off information?"

Charlie involuntarily shifted in his chair as he thought of his buxom niece. I'll kill the bitch was the expression on his face.

"Of course," Jack went on, "should you continue to press any claim against my clients in this regard, I'm afraid I would insist that all of your pay off demands for say, the last ten years, be examined in detail to determine if there were any irregularities… pattern of conduct, so to speak."

Jack's comment had its intended effect. The look on Patek's face was one of sheer terror. The last thing he wanted was a full scale investigation of his files!

"I'm not sure those would be relevant to this deal," Charlie sputtered, at a loss for words.

"Well, I'm very confident that I can make a strong argument that they are relevant," Jack shot back. "In fact, I believe that, under the circumstances, an in depth review of all of your loan files would not be beyond our liberal discovery rules. Who knows what relevant information might turn up?"

Jack knew he had Patek where he would need him - by the proverbial balls. It was fairly common knowledge in the Las Vegas legal world that Patek ran what was tantamount to a loan sharking business. There was no way he could let anyone nose around in his affairs. More importantly, Charlie would know that it was suicide to invite an investigation of many of his investors' interests. This was especially true of Sam.

When Patek failed to respond further, Jack took the initiative again. He turned his focus on the Mormon broker sitting next to Snead. He knew that Eccles was not only his shrewdest opponent at the table, but also the most dangerous. It was his mortgage company that stood to lose the most in this fiasco, and Jack had a fairly good idea who Eccles' investors would be. They probably wouldn't show up at the annual stockholders' meeting, but you'd recognize where the power lay all the same.

"Mr. Eccles," Jack began, "could you indulge us by describing the due diligence process you followed in screening your loan to Mr. DeMartes? Surely you have a rather extensive background and identification check made on someone to whom you're going to lend millions of dollars. I would imagine you have some internal policies that require it, don't you? I mean, in your position as a fiduciary, you would have an absolute duty to check out your borrowers before closing on a deal. Right?"

As Jack anticipated, Eccles didn't respond. This was not a man to be easily backed into a corner. His statement was really more designed to confuse the dim-witted assistant district attorney, than to elicit a response from Eccles. Jack did, however, catch just the slightest shift in Eccles steady glare when he'd mentioned "due diligence."

My god, Jack thought, could it be that he hadn't checked out DeMartes? Could he have handed over millions of dollars of the Mob's money without having him investigated?

He was momentarily at a loss for words as he took in the enormity of Eccles' problem, and Snead jumped in to fill the void.

"Mr. Summers, you're casting a lot of blame around the table today, but it's your clients who we're here to discuss," Snead said.

"I apologize if it seemed as though I was casting blame, Mr. Snead," Jack responded. "I was merely attempting to clarify each party's position in this unfortunate matter. I am wondering, however, why the focus of our meeting isn't on locating Mr. McKenna and Mr. DeMartes rather than rattling sabers at my clients."

What followed was a round table discussion of where in the hell McKenna and DeMartes had gone. Snead was no help. There wasn't enough evidence to initiate criminal proceedings against them. Kirshbaum's only input was to the effect that his wife had been trying to reach Judy McKenna for a couple of weeks, without success. Kirshbaum had gone to their apartment, but it was empty - "no furniture, no nothing." It became painfully obvious that no one had the slightest idea where either man had gone. What's more, no one had a clue as to DeMartes' true identity.

It wasn't more than a few days after Daryl McKenna had called Florida, trying to reach DeMartes, that Patek had gone through a similar scenario with the real Marcel DeMartes' son on the phone. Wisely, he informed Sam of the problem immediately. Sam dispatched a couple of the Mob's attorneys from Miami to personally call on DeMartes Construction and find out what was going on. They met with DeMartes, who gladly posed for photographs and provided more than ample identification verifying that he was who he said he was. These were faxed to Sam, who had Bruno deliver them to Patek.

Patek opened the folder in front of him and, retrieving the stack of papers and photos, spread them on the conference table.

"This is the real Marcel DeMartes," Charlie said. "Apparently, the man who presented himself in Vegas under that name is a phony. We don't know who he is. We do know that he seems to be gone."

Turning to Snead, Jack said, "I think that we have more than enough evidence of fraud here on the part of McKenna and whoever his real partner was, to start a criminal investigation of these parties. I suggest that you do so immediately. We'll have ample time to sort out any civil liability among the parties represented at this table later."

Jack was hoping to buy some time for AmCon Title by diverting the thrust of the investigation away from the fledgling title company and its employees at this point. His major fear, as he'd already discussed with Roxburgh, was that Snead would rush to get a protective order to shut down the company's operations. If they did that, it would be the end of AmCon Title no matter how the evidence developed later or who played what role in this fiasco.

Silence sat like an uncomfortable first date on the assembled group. Each man weighed his options. Summers scanned the small hearing room that they were using for their conference. It was quintessential government issue.

The ex-cop spoke first. He'd been knocked down by Jack's comments, but was by no means out of the fight.

"I think he's right. We need warrants issued for the arrest of McKenna and his partner. But it don't stop there. I think this guy's clients were in on the scam, and we need to bring them in for questioning too. I'll get the truth out of them."

You could see the blood rise in Kirshbaum's face as he spit out the last words. Jack could easily envision what Kirshbaum had in mind for the questioning of his clients. It would be a regular Chicago style bad cop and more bad cop grilling. He would keep his clients as far from this man as possible.

"I don't think it would hurt to try and locate these guys," Charlie interjected. He was still thinking about how he could open his files to the discovery that Jack had alluded to without getting himself killed.

Snead was next to jump on the bandwagon. "You've agreed to make your clients available for questioning, and I insist that you do so," he said, shooting a side glance to Eccles.

The mortgage broker had said nothing to this point. He sat staring intensely at Jack, weighing his adversary. When he spoke, it was in a low monotone, as if he'd been practicing the line. "If I may ask, Mr. Summers, what is your intention with regard to making your clients available to us?" Jack was certain that he anticipated his response.

"At this point, I quite clearly represent AmCon Title," Jack replied. "Which of its employees I ultimately end up representing will, to some extent, be determined by the facts of this matter as it develops. And, of course, by what position the State takes at this stage."

He had already decided that he must advise Sarah, Ashley and Temple that they would need to seek separate counsel for further formal representation. The potential for conflict of interest was simply too great. Bill Roxburgh was, for the moment, so closely aligned with the interest of the corporation that he would continue to act as his lawyer. It was essentially a lawyer's typical non-answer of the direct question, and Eccles pressed on.

"Could we at least speak with some or all of them regarding the whereabouts of McKenna and/or DeMartes?" Eccles asked.

"I will be happy to discuss it with them this evening," Jack replied. "If one or more is willing to talk to you, I'll let Mr. Snead's office know and present them here tomorrow for inquiry if you'd like."

It was a verbal jousting contest. Each man tried to determine the boundaries beyond which the other would not cross. Eccles was smart enough to know that Jack wouldn't allow unfettered access to his group at this point. Jack felt it was in AmCon Title's best interest to investigate avenues of cooperation with Eccles that could lead to a resolution of the matter outside of Snead's hands.

When Eccles didn't respond, Jack continued.

"I will, of course, make Bill Roxburgh available to you for questioning regarding the whereabouts of the Anasazi principals. I will also recommend that the others provide whatever level of information they feel comfortable with in this regard. I can tell you candidly that I will first suggest that they consult with an independent attorney before they do so. However, if they have helpful information they're willing to divulge, we'll of course pass it on."

As he finished speaking, Jack began gathering up the paperwork that was spread before him on the table. He was ready to leave. As he stood, Snead bolted from his chair, the State's mouthpiece ready for battle.

"Wait just a doggoned minute! We had an agreement that your people would be here to answer questions about this matter, and I'm going to hold you to it!"

Jack paused before responding, letting Snead's sword dangle without challenge. He pulled a copy of a letter from his briefcase.

"If you'll review my letter confirming our understanding of the ground rules for this meeting," Jack said, "you'll see that I, quote, 'agree to make my clients available for questioning in any area which I believe would be reasonably related to issues that might be resolved concerning the allegations made by the complainants', close quote. Since we have yet to determine what, if any, 'issues might be resolved', I don't feel obligated to produce anyone. However, if it may be suggested that there is an avenue to pursue resolution here, well short of criminal or administrative sanctions, I'm happy to cooperate. And, so are my clients, AmCon Title and Bill Roxburgh."

Jack now had briefcase in hand and was shoving his chair back from the table when Eccles responded before Snead could say anything further.

"Speaking for Sundown Mortgage, our primary concern is the quick recovery of our money," Eccles said. "If your group can assist us in this regard, we will withdraw our formal complaint."

It was exactly what Jack had hoped for. He'd come to the meeting to test the waters. Eccles had given him and AmCon Title a way out of the quagmire. Find DeMartes and McKenna, and go in peace. Well, maybe not quite that simple, but at least it may be some road to recovery. He was certain that Eccles controlled Snead. Patek could be held off, not only because he feared investigation himself, but because Jack guessed he reported to about the same bosses as Eccles. Kirshbaum would be left to stew about a claim that would be put on the back shelf until Snead got further marching orders.

Snead looked like a man who'd had the wind knocked out of him. He was ready to go to battle. He wanted to show everyone how he could bring this company to its knees!

Jack resisted the urge to smile as he said, "I will be here with Mr. Roxburgh at nine tomorrow morning. I will also urge the full cooperation of the other AmCon Title employees in locating the apparent perpetrators of this scam, to the extent their counsel will allow." With that, he turned and left the room.

It was uncharacteristically cool in northern Nevada for the time of year. As Jack pushed through the exit doors, he felt a rush of the north wind on his face and a trace of moisture in the air. He would use the hour long drive back to Reno to collect his thoughts, and begin the all too familiar process of building a strategy of defense for his clients.

Chapter Sixteen

Back on the main highway, Jack glanced in his rearview mirror and caught a glimpse of a dark colored Chevy Blazer that followed him up the inclining road out of Carson City, headed north. He couldn't make out the driver's face, but he was clearly a very large man; broad at the shoulders, and well over six feet tall.

As he cleared the top of the pass, the line of vision between his rental and the Blazer was momentarily broken. Jack pulled his vehicle to a stop on the shoulder, waiting for the Blazer to crest the hill. Seconds later, it did. He caught a clear view of the other driver as he passed. Apparently taken by surprise that Jack had pulled over, he stared squarely at Jack as he passed, hitting his brakes for a second, and then quickly releasing them. The Blazer continued into the valley that lay between Carson City and Reno, and Jack pulled out behind it. Somewhere, sometime, he'd seen the other driver. Jack would spend much of the remainder of the trip trying to place the man. Just south of Reno, Jack lost the Blazer in traffic.

Exiting the freeway at his hotel's exit, Jack reflected on his meeting that morning. Clearly Eccles was the man to be reckoned with. Control the situation with him, and AmCon Title would be fine regardless of who screwed the Anasazi deal. He thought briefly of Sarah and smiled. He could save the day for her in this mess and be her hero. Who knows what might develop after the case was cleared up? He had arranged for individual fact finding meetings with each of the principal players from the company at his hotel that night in Reno. He would first convene a joint dinner to discuss generally the ground rules of the process to come with everyone present. This would include Bill Roxburgh, Ashley, Roger

Temple and Sarah. Each had made their way to Reno earlier in the day and would be waiting at the Pepper Tree.

The Pepper Tree Hotel Casino was a favorite of Jack's. Centrally located, with easy access to the freeway and the airport, it hosted one of the finest restaurants in Reno. The Crystal Room was divided into several levels with semi-private dining areas available. It proved to be an effective place to entertain and prepare clients on many previous trips. Set carefully apart from the casino, the restaurant took you immediately out of the casino atmosphere that made up most of the first floor of the hotel.

The suites were also to Jack's liking. Larger than your run of the mill casino hotel room, they provided spacious conference tables and, in some cases, a separate bar and Jacuzzi. It was the kind of place Jack would choose for recreation as well as work.

He continued to go over the part each participant he would interview had played in the case. He'd thoroughly reviewed the paperwork connected with both Anasazi Property closings and was starting to mentally fill in some gaps with logic bred of experience.

Forty minutes after leaving the capital, he turned his rented vehicle into the entrance of the Pepper Tree. The light showers he'd driven through in the mountain pass were gone, and the sun glared in his face as he pulled into covered parking garage.

The guest parking area at the Pepper Tree was a dark refuge from the bright sunlight, like driving into a cave, as Jack pulled his rental car into a parking stall. Turning off the engine, he sat waiting, letting his eyes adjust to the contrast with the outside light. At nearly seven o'clock in the evening, the light of a June night in Reno was still a blaze compared to the illumination provided by the garage overheads. After a moment, he stepped from his car. Bending forward, he reached for the loaded briefcase on the front passenger seat.

The small hairs on the back of his neck told him he had company. Before he could react, he felt the silenced muzzle of a hand gun press against the base of his skull. The touch of the cool cylinder was familiar. He hadn't seen Bruno and his companion, a flunky from Reno, waiting in the darkened garage.

Pressing the barrel of the automatic further into Jack's neck, Bruno whispered in a low, almost guttural tone, "Move slow. This can go easy or hard. You pick."

Jack straightened, dropping his briefcase back into the driver's seat. He felt, rather than saw, the size of the man behind him. There was someone else near too, but his eyes hadn't fully adjusted to the darkness, and he couldn't place his exact position.

"Turn slowly, and move to the Blazer at the end of the row," Bruno grunted.

As he turned, Bruno took a step back, and Jack faced his captor from the front. He immediately recognized him as the driver of the car that followed him out of Carson City. They must have known where Jack was headed.

Bruno's large hand, dwarfing the weapon he held, dropped to Jack's mid-section. Smart move, Jack thought. Aim at a wider target. He's done this before.

The two men paused, each taking measure of the other. Jack could just make out the flat, black eyes of a man who wouldn't think twice about killing him. There was movement from behind Jack and two powerful arms encircled him, pinning his own against his sides like he'd been dumped in a small barrel. At the same instant, Bruno moved forward, swinging his free hand into Jack's solar plexus.

Air shot from his lungs, and Jack thanked those countless hours on his abs' torture track at home for his ability to withstand the blow without passing out. Sucking air with a deep gasp, he lunged forward at Bruno, pulling the beast behind him forward abruptly. As expected, the man behind him reacted violently, pulling back against Jack's move.

In an instant born of years honing his reflexes, Jack reversed his ground, moving with the restraining man's weight. He drove them backwards and, as his assailant struck the concrete pillar behind them, it was his turn to empty his lungs. The vice grip he held on Jack relaxed for a moment, and Summers dropped to one knee in a modified front stance. It was a move he'd practiced a thousand times in karate training. He heard the familiar puff of air as the silenced gun discharged. Jack could feel the hot blast as its bullet passed above his head, catching the man behind him squarely in the chest. It was exactly the space he had occupied a second earlier.

Again, the second attacker expelled breath and staggered. Bruno moved toward him in the dark of the garage, apparently not knowing whether to fire again, and Jack launched a snake like forward punch at Bruno's groin. The forward punch used a twisting motion, with the opposite hand and arm moving in the other direction. The effect is to dramatically increase both the speed and power of the striking hand. The leverage was perfect, and his target was at eye level. Jack had used this same offensive punch in training exhibitions to break through six inches of hardened boards with ease. It was a real crowd-pleaser.

Now, as the leading knuckles of his right hand struck the meat of Bruno's soft groin area, the large man dropped to the floor. He was unconscious before his head hit the garage deck with a satisfying crack.

In one continuous motion, the reversal of his punch gave Jack the momentum he needed to turn on his knee, swinging his other leg into the ankles of the man behind him. His attacker was already off balance, and

Jack's move put him airborne, as his feet flew out from under him. He landed like a side of beef; his unbroken fall ending as his shoulder and head struck pavement, producing the unmistakable sound of his collarbone breaking with the contact.

Jack was instinctively on his feet and moving to where he'd heard Bruno's gun drop. He still couldn't see clearly in the dim light, and as he stepped forward, his foot caught the pistol, sending it sliding across the floor. It could be a valuable piece of leverage, Jack thought, but there was little time to look for it now. He had no idea if these guys had company nearby, and didn't want to find out.

Bruno was groaning softly, and Jack grinned reflexively as he thought of the effect his attack would have had on soft tissue. It would be a while before this Italian stallion serviced anyone.

He retrieved his briefcase from the open car seat, and closed the door, locking it with his remote key. He stepped over the motionless body of the man who'd grabbed him from behind. Jack guessed he was either dead already or would be soon. A wash of dark liquid spread across his chest where the bullet had hit him. Rounding the back of his car, Jack caught a glimpse of the blackened weapon lying near the rear tire of the vehicle parked next to his. He quickly removed his suit coat and, using the sleeve as a glove, picked up the gun and folded the coat over his arm. The only set of prints on what was likely a murder weapon would be from the big man with the swollen balls behind him on the ground.

Moments before he reached the lighted entrance to the casino, with its security cameras in full view, Jack used his cell phone to dial the front desk of the hotel. He made an anonymous report about a fight taking place in the garage. Hotel security passed him on the dead run as he entered the main lobby of the casino, headed for the hotel's elevators.

Bruno's eyes snapped open and he struggled to orient himself. He lay curled in a fetal position on the cool garage floor. As he straightened, pulling himself to one knee, the pain in his groin hit him like a sucker punch and he fell to all fours. Slowly, the recognition of what happened came back.

It was supposed to be a simple snatch of the lawyer. Sam had told him to grab the guy and find out what he knew about the imposter, DeMartes.

"Don't kill him," Sam had said, "just find out what he knows and make sure he cooperates when he finds out more."

Now, looking at the corpse of their Reno man laying in a growing pool of blood, he realized how wrong things had gone. Sam wouldn't be happy. Bruno had been with Sam long enough to know that making him unhappy was like slapping a rattlesnake.

He could hear the sounds of the hotel's security personnel entering the garage, and there was no time to look for his weapon. Forcing himself upright, he moved quickly toward his parked vehicle. He'd only enough time to quietly slip inside and lay across the front seats when the guards came upon the body. He would be stuck there until an opportunity presented itself to leave the premises. It gave him time to think about what he should do next. He could hear the muffled shouts of the guards to call for the police. The throbbing in his groin became a dull pain, and the swelling in his balls grew steadily worse. He tried to focus on a plan of action, but all that came to mind was the face of the lawyer. It would be a face he'd see again. Soon, he vowed in the darkness. Soon I'll have your balls, Mr. Lawyer.

Hotel and casino guests continued to enter the garage area and, when word of the corpse spread, they came in droves. Everyone wanted to see what was going on. Before the police arrived, closing down the garage completely, Bruno seized the opportunity to start his car and slip away with other exiting guests. He was worried about his gun. If the police found it, it would only be a matter of time before they'd check for prints. His were on file in several locations back East. Eventually they would lead the inquiry to him. Sam would figure a way out of this mess. He always did.

On the fourth floor of the hotel, Jack entered his room about the time Bruno left the garage. He moved quickly to the bathroom, laying Bruno's weapon, with its long black silencer extending from the barrel, carefully on the counter. He made sure that he didn't touch any part of the weapon himself, and was sure he hadn't wiped away much of what would surely be clear fingerprints. Reaching for his shave kit, he removed a large plastic bag. He was in the habit of putting his shampoo and cologne in it when he traveled. It was a solid way to insure against the adverse effect of any leaks. Now, removing the contents, and using a hand towel to pick the weapon up by its barrel, he slipped it into the empty plastic bag and sealed it. If he had any insurance against another meeting with the large man and his swollen balls, this could be it.

Chapter Seventeen

Jack moved to the ornate sink in the suite's bathroom, a typically overdone vestige of casino accommodation, and bent splashing cold water in his face. He'd been in tighter spots in the past, but not recently. His adrenaline levels were still spiking as he stripped and turned the shower on hot. Just as he stepped in, he heard a knock at the suite's door. Again his stomach tightened, and he fought a natural instinct to hide.

"Who is it?" he shouted from the bathroom door.

"It's Ashley," came a subdued reply.

The breath that Jack had been involuntarily holding escaped, slow and deliberate. He couldn't help but be relieved. Wrapping a towel around his naked torso, he returned to the shower and turned off the now steaming flow of water.

"I'll be right there," he yelled in the direction of the door.

He thought briefly of looking for some item of clothing to throw on, but moved instead to the door, looking quickly through the peep hole and then stepping back. She was clearly alone.

As he swung the door open, Jack said with a wry smile, "I'm afraid I'm not dressed for company."

Moving through the open door, Ashley smiled and took an obviously deliberate look up the length of his body, from toe to head. As their eyes met, she whispered, "Let me be the judge of that."

"We weren't supposed to meet until eight o'clock in the restaurant," Jack replied, ignoring her comment.

"I know, but I was anxious to see you," she said. "It's been a while."

"Yes, I know," he responded lamely. "I felt it would be best that we not get involved, since I represent your employer. That's especially true, given our present situation."

He felt defenseless, clad in the hotel's none too large towel. The sight of her caused an involuntary quickening in his groin. She was wearing a mini skirt and high heels. Great legs for a short woman, he thought again.

"Do you have anything to drink in here?" she asked, changing the subject. "I got in early and hate to wait alone at the bar downstairs. It doesn't seem proper."

Jack had a mental flashback to their one night together, and "proper" didn't come to mind.

"I'm sorry, I don't," he said, ignoring the suite's mini-bar.

He was moving backward, toward the door of the bathroom with its bagged murder weapon in clear view on the counter. As Ashley reached his bed, Jack pulled the bathroom door closed.

He returned to the door of the suite, and pulling it open, said, "I need to shower and prepare for our meeting later. Maybe Bill, or some of the others got in early too."

Before Ashley could reply, he saw her eyes swing to the open doorway behind him. He turned, half expecting Swollen Balls to be standing there. Instead, Sarah stood with her mouth half open, suitcase in hand. Her green eyes darted alternately back and forth between Ashley, lounging with her short skirt hiked to her ass cheeks, and Jack, speechless for once in his hotel towel.

"I'm sorry," she said, breaking the silence. "I just got here, and I was trying to find my room."

After what Jack was sure could have been one of the longest pregnant pauses in history, he finally was able to blurt a non-response.

"Oh, Ashley just came looking for you. She wants to have a drink with someone while I finish getting ready for our dinner meeting."

Again, there was a lull, with Jack assessing the damage this would cause to any chance he might later have with Sarah. Ashley provided no help, just smiling from the bed.

Sarah finally spoke, her eyes continuing to compute the input in front of her. "Sure, just let me drop off my suitcase. I think I'm right next door."

As Sarah moved to the door of the next room, Ashley walked past a still flustered Jack Summers and out the door. As she passed, brushing ever so slightly the towel covering a soldier that had gone at ease with the tension of the previous moment, she whispered, "How convenient...right next door."

Jack closed the door behind her, turning the deadbolt. "Shit!" was all he could vocalize as he returned to the shower and preparation for dinner.

Two hours later, Jack entered the lounge area of the Crystal Room. He paused, allowing his eyes to adjust from the bright lights of the casino floor. Although he was fairly certain that the goon from the garage wouldn't make another move at the hotel, Jack had been on edge since their encounter. Sweeping the room with his eyes, he saw the AmCon Title group seated at a large round table in the rear. Bill Roxburgh was standing, waving his short arms, and looking something like the Pillsbury Dough Boy, drowning in a dark pool.

"Hey there, Counselor," Roxburgh said, smiling as Jack approached. "I saved a chair for you."

Jack accepted the invitation, and slipped into the open chair next to Roxburgh. To Roxburgh's right sat Roger Temple, then Ashley, and finally, directly to Jack's left, Sarah. He caught a faint breath of her perfume as he drew his chair up to the table, and a brief glimpse of long, magnificent legs, as she shifted to allow him more room. Jack hadn't spoken with Sarah, except for their brief encounter upstairs that afternoon, since their initial meeting in his office.

"Did you hear about the murder in the hotel today?" Roxburgh asked.

"What are you talking about?" Jack replied, maintaining a blank look.

"Somebody got killed in the hotel garage this afternoon," Roxburgh continued. "Didn't you hear?"

"Sorry, I guess I've been working in my room since I got back from Carson City," Jack replied. "What happened?"

"The Bell captain told me some local thug got shot in the garage late this afternoon," Roxburgh said. "You must have just missed the action. He said they think it's some kind of drug thing gone bad. You know these casinos. They don't like to advertise bad news."

His comment reminded Jack of his first trip to the Pepper Tree. He'd arrived about noon on a weekday, just in town for a series of quick depositions. As he exited his cab, hotel security was rolling a cart with a closed body bag out one of the front entrances to a waiting limousine. Dozens of people were walking in and out of the casino without so much as a glance at the mini drama. When Jack asked at the front desk, he received a terse reply. "Heart attack." The flashback sent a chill through Jack, a mental image of what could have happened to him in the garage that afternoon. Would he have been a "heart attack?"

Jack kept the pre-dinner conversation light. Roxburgh made all of the perfunctory re-introductions around the table, but Jack explained that he'd had some contact with each of the parties in the past. An hour later, as they waited for dessert to be delivered, Summers returned the group to the matter at hand.

"I'd like to spend some time with each of you, individually, tonight," he said. "Kind of a general fact finding session, really. My meeting at the capitol this morning tells me that there may be a way out of this mess, short of State involvement, and maybe even litigation. However, there are no guarantees. If we can't resolve the problems with Anasazi Properties informally, it may be necessary for each of you to retain independent counsel. There's a fairly large conflict of interest possible here."

Temple spoke first. "We've got to hire lawyers? Who's gonna pay for this?"

"I'll be discussing that with Mr. Roxburgh," Jack answered. "It may be that the company will defer some of the initial costs until we get a little farther down the road. What I'd like to do now is have an informal, off the record, discussion with each of you to fill in some gaps in the paper work I've reviewed on this. If you don't want to do this, and would feel more comfortable retaining your own attorney immediately, that is your choice. No hard feelings, and I can assure you that the company will not hold that against you."

He looked to Roxburgh for mandatory assent to this last statement and received a confused nod.

"Are we going to be sued individually on this?" Ashley interjected. "I'm not paying for somebody else's mistakes!"

"It's difficult to say at the present time," Jack responded, "exactly which, if any of you, would be joined in either private or State actions under the present circumstances. Obviously, it's in everyone's best interests to resolve this quickly and informally, if we can. I believe that the complaining parties are more interested in covering their potential losses as soon as possible, than in exacting any pounds of flesh from you."

"So, you just want to meet with each of us privately to gather facts tonight?" Roxburgh commented.

There was a moment of silence as each person at the table reflected on their own thoughts. Sarah broke the moment. "I don't have any problem telling you what I know, Mr. Summers." She was looking directly at him, and as their eyes met, Jack forced a smile.

"Good," he replied. "As you may have heard through the company grapevine by now, the principal of Anasazi Properties, Marcel DeMartes, was a phony. It would appear that he, along with his partner, McKenna, and maybe others unknown at this time, have perpetrated a rather extensive scam on you."

As he laid out the last statement, Jack carefully judged the reaction on each member of the party's face. Temple looked visibly ill, his complexion draining, with a noticeable general slump in the shoulders. Ashley, reacted very little, Jack thought. He caught what he saw to be a momentary fire in her eyes at the news, and then her mask of indifference reappeared. He had already relayed this information to Roxburgh, so there was no noticeable change in his appearance. Sarah sat speechless, for a moment.

"I checked his identification. It all looked in order," Sarah volunteered.

"I'm sure it did, Sarah," Jack responded. "These guys obviously knew what they were doing."

"Well, let's get started right after dessert," said Roxburgh.

Jack had each of them write their name and room number on a small pad of paper he produced. He explained that he would be meeting with Bill first, and would then call each of them to come to his suite for a brief interview. This would give them time to collect their thoughts, and to decide, privately, if they wished to proceed informally at the present time.

Two hours later, Jack sat alone in his room. He'd completed his interviews with Roxburgh and Temple. He'd recounted the gist of the morning's meeting to Roxburgh, explaining the position he took on AmCon Title's behalf in detail.

It didn't appear to Jack that Roxburgh knew much of anything that could be helpful at the present time. He didn't know anything about the counterfeit DeMartes, other than what McKenna had told him. And that wasn't much. He'd told Jack that he'd known McKenna for many years, dating back to their employment at Sun Coast Title in California. He'd described McKenna as kind of a harmless loser, who didn't seem smart enough to pull off a deal like Anasazi Properties. He hadn't been able to contact him for several weeks now and heard that he'd left town.

Jack told him that the two of them would return to Carson City in the morning as promised. They wouldn't be able to provide much information, but it was important to appear to be cooperative at this juncture. He got the general impression that Roxburgh wasn't hiding anything from him.

Roger Temple was another story. Jack's interview with him had been brief. After giving his general background information about past employment experience, and the fact that he was divorced, Roger had volunteered little. He'd admitted to having known McKenna for a long time, but said they weren't very close. When Jack tried to tie him down in connection with the overlooked mechanics liens in the Anasazi Properties file, he'd become defensive. He'd said there was no way that, given the volume of business AmCon's title officers were expected to churn out every day, mistakes could be avoided. If he'd overlooked a few liens, then it was probably a computer error in the central title plant.

When Jack had pressed him on the details of how this might occur to the extent of liens in excess of six hundred thousand dollars, he'd clamed up. He'd told him that maybe he should be getting his own lawyer if he was going to be accused of any wrongdoing.

Roger Temple is afraid of more than losing his job, Jack thought. What's his role in this puzzle, he wondered.

When Jack called Ashley's room, it rang several times before she answered.

"Hello." The voice was soft and low.

"It's Jack Summers," he said. "Ready for our interview?"

"Oh, sure," she replied. "I thought you'd forgotten me. Just give me a few minutes." She kept him waiting twenty minutes before he heard the soft knock on his door. Jack had been dreading this particular sit down. Everything in the paperwork smelled to him like someone on the inside was involved. He refused to believe that it could be Sarah.

"Sorry I kept you waiting," Ashley purred as she entered his room. "I was getting ready for bed when you called."

She was wearing low sandals, as opposed to her normal spiked heels. Beyond that, she wore a red silk robe that fell from her shoulders to about four inches above the knee. It was tied loosely with a silk belt at the waist. As she reached his bed, she turned, taking a seat on the edge. This new position hiked the hemline on her exquisitely proportioned legs and caused the front of the robe to spread at her bust line. He caught a quick glimpse of what appeared to be a sheer nightgown straining at her cleavage before looking quickly away. He headed straight for the conference table and took a chair.

"Why don't we work over here, Ashley," Jack said, not really as a request.

As she moved to the conference table, taking a seat opposite him, he kept his eyes on the paperwork in front of him. With her seated in the chair, at least he'd only have to deal with the constant motion of her cleavage, swaying just above table height.

"Am I your last interview?" she asked coyly.

"No," Jack replied quickly, without elaboration. The disappointment in her eyes was unmistakable.

He then launched into a subtle interrogation of Ashley, covering all aspects of both Anasazi Properties transactions. He wanted to know the exact extent of her involvement in the process. More importantly, he wanted to know if she had any prior relationship with McKenna or the DeMartes imposter. He was also interested in how many deals she'd handled that involved Patek's company or Sundown Mortgage. Finally, he questioned her about the Kirshbaums, and whether they complained to her about how they were treated at AmCon Title.

Summers kept his style and tone conversational. It wouldn't do him any good to put her on the defensive at this point. Given their brief, but intimate history together, Jack fought the urge to take it easy on her. If she were going to try and use their night together to influence him, she was barking at the wrong dog. But, all in all, he felt her performance that night was pretty good given the circumstances. She exhibited what seemed to be genuine concern for the fate of AmCon Title and her fellow employees. She was, however, adamant that Sarah's responsibility included review of all final paperwork.

Ashley told Jack that she knew Charlie Patek professionally from several deals in the past year. She denied any social interaction with him, although she admitted seeing him at industry functions.

As far as DeMartes was concerned, she said she had never laid eyes on him until he'd been at AmCon Title for the first closing. The Kirshbaums, she said, had come to her office to complain that they didn't get a proper Deed of Trust securing their note. She told him, as she had them, that it wasn't her place to invent the deals ... only to record them. She didn't have time to second guess the way realtors made their contracts. If it came to her without a security condition, or in this case one that could be subordinated, that's how the deal was closed. Apparently, that's what happened here.

As Jack wound down their conversation, taking no intimidating notes, he quickly reviewed the covered areas in his mind.

"I guess that's it for now, Ashley," he said. "I'll let you get to bed."

She smiled at his comment, and leaned back in her chair, raising her feet up to the seat level. In this position, most of her bare thighs were visible. As she leaned back, the belt on her robe loosened and slid back. What lay beneath was a sheer, short pajama top. Jack could see her large, brown nipples lying erect beneath the light material.

"Which side would you like me on?" she whispered.

"Sorry, Ashley. Not tonight. This is strictly business, and I've got more work to do," Jack said. "Thanks for all your help."

When she'd gone, he moved to the bar and poured scotch over a handful of ice cubes into a short glass. Sipping the glass to half empty, he leaned on the bar and cleared his mind of the dismissal of Ashley from his room. He knew that his last session waited for him just beyond the adjoining door to the suite next to his.

Sarah. He'd thought of her almost on a daily basis since their first meeting, but this would be their first time alone together in weeks. Moving to the door that joined their suites, he knocked softly. A moment later, he heard her voice.

"Yes?" she said.

"It's Jack Summers, Sarah. I thought that since our rooms adjoin, it might be easier at this hour for you to simply open the door and come in for our interview."

"Give me a moment," she said.

Jack moved quickly to the conference table. As he heard the bolt click open on the door that separated their rooms, his mind pictured her entering in Ashley's outfit, the red silk robe hanging loosely open in front. But then she was in the doorway, dressed as she had been at dinner. She wore a dark gray, loose fitting dress. It was belted at the waist, and the skirt pleated from there to above here knees. All business, but stunning.

"I apologize for keeping you up so late," Jack said. "My other interviews ran a little longer than I thought."

"I heard Ashley leave," she said. "I didn't mean to eavesdrop, but the walls are pretty thin. I've been reading a book, since I talked to my son."

"How is he?" Jack asked.

"He's fine," she replied. "He's with a school friend's family until tomorrow night. I didn't know how long this would take. We've never spent a night apart."

"Again, let me apologize for this inconvenience," Jack said. "There was no way to know whether I'd need you here tomorrow or not." She hadn't really entered his room at that point. Hovering in the open passageway, she waited for an invitation.

"Please, join me here," Jack invited, motioning her to the open chair opposite him. To Jack it seemed as if she moved in slow motion. He caught every detail of her walk across the suite. She seemed to float, her shoulders and breasts erect. Her skirt swayed softly, like water grass in a night breeze.

During the next hour, Jack and Sarah rekindled the feeling of mutual trust they'd struck in his office. He asked her details about her involvement with the Anasazi Properties files, and she answered honestly.

There's nothing disingenuous here, Jack thought. It was one of the most difficult interrogations he'd ever conducted. It took all of his considerable powers of concentration to listen to the content of her answers, rather than the simple melody of her voice.

"I guess that's about it, for now," Jack said, pushing himself back from the table. "Only two more items."

"What are they?" Sarah asked, a question mark on her face.

"You mentioned that you thought someone was following you at our last meeting. Any more of these suspicions?" he asked.

"No. I guess I was just feeling paranoid," she replied. "I felt much better after I left your office. I feel like I've got a friend on my side."

"You do, Sarah," he said, managing a smile.

"What was the second item?" she asked.

Jack hesitated, not wanting to blow any future he might have with Sarah by seeming unprofessional. "It's been a very long day for both of us," he said. "Your plane won't leave until tomorrow afternoon, but I must be out of here early to Carson City with Bill. I thought maybe you'd join me in a nightcap. It sometimes helps me to sleep."

If there were any doubt in Sarah's mind, it didn't show. She said she'd love to have something to help her sleep too.

An hour later, Sarah was back in her suite, and Jack lay motionless in the dark in his king-sized bed listening to her breathing in the room next door. She'd said she didn't want to act like a big baby, but that she would sleep better if she could leave the door open between their suites. She wasn't accustomed to sleeping alone, without her son.

Jack listened as she prepared for bed, whispering "Goodnight" to him. Moments later she was asleep. It was a luxury Jack couldn't enjoy until almost an hour before dawn. As he left his room, he looked through the open door into Sarah's. She slept quietly, as she had all night. Her covers now askew, he held his breath as he took in the length of her, covered in flannel pajamas.

He pulled the adjoining door closed silently, bolting it from his side.

Chapter Eighteen

The trip back to Carson City with Bill Roxburgh the next day held no surprises. Jack gave him a thumbnail sketch of his conversations from the previous night with Temple, Ashley and Sarah. He liked to keep such summaries strictly factual, without interjecting at this stage of the case, his personal feelings about the veracity, or lack thereof, of the witnesses.

They met for an hour at Snead's offices once again, and the exercise proved to be another mental jousting match with Jim Eccles and Snead. Jack assured them that AmCon Title would extend its complete cooperation in the matter, all geared towards an attempt to locate the perpetrators of what appeared to be a rather straightforward case of fraud. He suggested that they pool their efforts in the task of locating the counterfeit DeMartes, and his sidekick, Daryl McKenna. He explained that Roxburgh had known McKenna for several years and would look to mutual acquaintances to find him as soon as possible.

Jack concluded the meeting by suggesting that they meet again in a week in Las Vegas, with or without Snead's presence, to share information. This would, of course, be premised on their mutual agreement to leave the State investigation and all other litigation in a holding pattern. Reluctantly, all parties agreed, even Kirshbaum. Just before leaving the group, Jack turned to Eccles.

"Did you hear about the shooting at my hotel in Reno last night?" he asked.

"Nasty business," Eccles replied, not asking which hotel.

"Yes, very disturbing," Jack responded, staring directly at Eccles. "Makes it hard to concentrate on getting your money back with such things going on around us. I hope nothing like that happens again."

Eccles didn't respond, so Jack left the room with a final comment. "I heard they haven't found the murder weapon."

As Jack pulled his rental car back into the Reno airport, he told Roxburgh that he needed to take a later flight back to Vegas because of some business that had surfaced in Reno unexpectedly. Roxburgh retrieved his luggage, toddling away into the terminal, and Jack hit the speed dial on his cell phone.

"This is Mac, speak now or forever hold you peace," the answering party barked.

"It's Jack. I need a favor."

"Anything for you, buddy," Mac replied, "as long as it involves you giving me more strokes on the golf course."

Mike McCormick, "Mac" to his friends, was one of Jack's closest friends in Las Vegas. In his late fifties, Mac had retired as an agent for the Federal Bureau of Investigation four years previously. Since then, he acted as head of security operations for a local casino group. They owned several smaller hotel and casino properties, including the Pepper Tree in Reno.

"Why don't I just mail you a check to save time?" Jack replied. Jack and Mac were in the habit of betting on their rounds of golf together, and although the amounts weren't really significant, the competition was fierce.

"What is it you need?" Mac chuckled. "I know it's not a golf lesson."

"You have a regular daily flight down from Reno, don't you?" Jack knew that a private jet flew from Reno to Las Vegas, presumably laden with cash from the previous day's take at the Pepper Tree.

"Yeah, it leaves about five o'clock. Why, you thinking of robbing me?"

"You should be so lucky, Mac," Jack responded. "Maybe you'd have to actually work for a change."

Jack explained that he needed a ride back in a setting "more private" than a commercial flight would afford him.

"I can arrange that," Mac said, without further question.

Their relationship had evolved over the course of several years of golfing together. Jack met Mac while looking for a pick up round at the Tournament Players course in Summerlin on the west side of the valley. Paired with Mac, and a couple of the guys he worked with, their constant competition and common background investigating the mob had forged a bond of mutual respect and trust. They both felt that you could tell more about a man's character in a few rounds of golf together than you could in years of social or other business contact.

Jack asked Mac to meet him at Jack's office an hour after the casino's private jet had flown him, and several million dollars, back to Vegas. He was waiting at his desk when Mac stuck his head in the door.

"What's up, buddy?" Mac inquired as he flopped into one of the high backed leather client chairs in front of Jack's desk.

"How about a cocktail, Mac?" Jack said. "You might need one."

"As I always say, come to Papa," Mac quipped.

Jack moved to the private wet bar which he'd opened upon his arrival. He grabbed a glass tumbler, dumped in a handful of ice and covered it with scotch. Handing the drink to Mac, Jack took a seat opposite him behind his large mahogany desk. Mac gulped half the contents of his drink in one swallow and eased back into the soft leather chair.

"This isn't about Saturday's golf game, right?" Mac said, smiling.

Jack leaned forward, sliding a check that he'd made payable to Mac for twenty dollars across the desk.

"This is about confidentiality, Mac. I'm hiring you as my investigator. This makes it official." An investigator's duty of confidentiality requires that he not share any information about his clients or their business outside the parameters of his own staff.

Mac looked down at the check and said nothing for a moment. He knew that Summers wouldn't have asked for the accommodation of a plane ride from Reno, nor would he be worried about a paper trail of "confidentiality," if something serious weren't afoot. Jack said nothing, allowing Mac to weigh his options. He could see the wheels spinning in Mac's head. After a few moments, Mac came to a decision.

"Okay, fire away, Boss," he said.

Jack began to methodically fill Mac in on the background of the DeMartes scam. He left out little detail, preferring to give Mac too much information, rather than not enough. He even gave him a quick rundown of each of the players. As he finished, Jack opened his desk drawer, and grabbing the plastic bag with Bruno's gun, slid it across the desk.

"Want to quit your new job yet?" Jack asked.

"Nice piece of hardware, pal," Mac replied. "Care to tell me where you got the silencer on this?"

"I picked this up at your hotel in Reno late yesterday," Jack said. "A big Italian guy shot his friend with it in the garage."

"Holy shit!" Mac whispered, letting out a slow breath. He didn't reach for the weapon, just let it set between them on the polished dark wood of the desk. "Care to give me a little more detail on how this evidence of a homicide got in your possession?"

"Only if you're in for the full Monty, so to speak," Jack answered.

"I guess if I trust you on the course, when my money's on the line, I'll have to do it here," Mac volunteered.

Jack recounted the only details that he'd previously omitted. He described his ride back after the meeting in Carson City, and his surprise visit in the parking garage. Mac jokingly said that the hotel wouldn't be paying any claims for improper security at their facility, if that's what Jack had in mind.

"I'd like you to hold on to this for a while," Jack said. "When I think the timing's right, you can say you found it, or someone turned it in anonymously. I may need it as insurance, or leverage."

Again Mac sat quietly for a few minutes, looking around Jack's plush office. It wasn't what you'd call enormous, just comfortably large. Bookcases covered one entire wall, with the built in bar filling out another. The remaining space consisted of floor to ceiling windows looking across the Strip to the North, West, and South.

"I'll only ask you this once," Mac said, quietly. "You've got a pretty solid deal going here. Nice practice, good clients. Sure you want to step into the gutter with the likes of Sam Marchesi and his associates?"

Jack smiled and nodded, saying, "I really don't have a choice at this point."

"Okay, pardner," Mac said finally. "I hope she's worth it."

Jack hadn't mentioned his attraction to Sarah, or his personal vow to keep her out of harm's way. But Mac was no rookie. His years in law enforcement, and most particularly the investigation of organized crime, gave him an edge when it came to reading between the lines.

Jack outlined his plan of action. He would need Mac's connections to help locate and identify the DeMartes phony, as well as McKenna. The sooner they got a line on locating the missing four million plus, the better chance he had of extricating his client from its current problem.

Mac felt that the money was probably long gone already. His experience with this type of scam was that the perpetrator already had a plan of escape set up when he took the final mark. The money was most likely already out of the country. There were two possibilities, however. Either they were so greedy that they wanted to stick around for an even bigger sting, or they'd get sloppy in moving the money. The former would mean they'd resurface in Vegas. The latter meant that Mac's contacts might be able to trace the funds.

"If we find the cash, who's gonna ask this crook to give it back?" Mac asked.

"I'll let you know when we get there," Jack replied. "Just find the money, or the guy, as quickly as you can."

Mac finished his scotch and left. Jack sat facing the Las Vegas skyline, pondering his next move. He glanced at the antique clock on his credenza, a gift from an appreciative client. It was nearly ten o'clock. He picked up the phone, and dialed Sarah's number. After several rings, she answered.

"Hello."

"Sarah, its Jack Summers. Sorry to be calling so late. I just wanted to make sure you'd gotten back alright."

"Oh, sure, Mr. Summers," she said, sleep in her voice. "I was getting ready for bed. Our flight was right on time, and I just got Adam to sleep. Is there anything wrong?"

Jack visualized her sitting in her apartment, head to toe in her flannel pajamas, and he felt a twinge of guilt for having called her. But the sound of her voice, low and soft, as if he were in the bedroom with her, caused him to flush.

"No, nothing's wrong. But I'd like to meet with you in a couple of days, if that's alright. You know, to discuss the case," he said feebly.

"Of course. Any time you like," she said. "Just let me know. I look forward to seeing you again."

"Alright then," Jack stammered. "I'll call you in a couple of days."

He leaned forward, resting the phone in its cradle with a satisfying click. Did she say she "looked forward" to seeing me again!

Roughly a mile to the west, in a small office situated above an all nude strip club, Sam Marchesi sat listening to Bruno's explanation of what happened in Reno. Bruno knew better than to lie to Marchesi. He didn't have a problem shading the truth, however. The way he saw it, it was their dead associate's own fault that he got killed. If he'd done his part of the job right, it would have been a simple snatch of the lawyer.

When Bruno finished, Sam sat quietly without responding. He looked around the dingy office as he considered their options. The room, used occasionally by Sam, overlooked the main floor of the club through a one way mirror on the wall. From there, you could watch the suckers slobbering over naked dancers on the main stage. On a tripod next to the window stood a video camera with a zoom lens. This was used to record not only the employees, but also to eavesdrop on and record the more private lap dances that occurred from time to time involving local politicians and other men of wealth or influence.

The club had file drawers full of potentially embarrassing, and therefore influential, tapes. The opposite side of the office was filled with a large casting couch. Even in the dim light, Sam could see the fabric was awash with stains from past employment interviews. He'd used it himself on many occasions in the past when a new dancer came on board.

Nothing like a fresh, young face in your crotch, he mused.

He was worried about how the Anasazi Properties deal was unraveling. This lawyer, Summers, could be a problem. His sources in Reno told him that the police hadn't recovered Bruno's piece. If they did, it would only be a matter of time before the trail on the shooting led back to Bruno, and then

Sam. If the police and hotel security didn't have it, it made sense that the lawyer did. If so, he'd have to be dealt with. Listening to Bruno's account, Sam's instincts told him that Summers was a guy to be worried about.

"I want you to put a tail on this guy," Sam said. "Don't touch him at this point. I want to know what he's doing, and who he's doing it with. Let's find out his Achilles heel, his weakness. What makes him tick. We're going to have to come to an understanding with him at some point. We need our boys to find the real estate schlep, McKenna, and this phony DeMartes, pronto. If we get to the money first, then we can have our cake and eat it too."

Bruno wasn't exactly clear on what Sam had in mind, but he understood the basics. He'd call some of their friends and get them tracking these guys right away. In the meantime, he'd keep an eye on the lawyer himself. He'd been sitting on bags of ice for hours since his return to Vegas. His balls were still double their normal size and a horrific black and purple color.

That son of a bitch will pay, big time, he relished.

Sam made no direct threat to Bruno. Both men knew what was at stake. Over four million dollars of Sam's money had disappeared, and Bruno didn't like to think about what might happen if he didn't get it back.

There was a knock on the door. Sam was finished with Bruno for the moment, so he had him answer it on his way out.

A tall, slender blonde, with a pair of Las Vegas' finest store bought boobs, stood naked in the doorway. She looked to be about twenty years old, but who could tell these days, Sam thought. He motioned for her to come in. As Bruno closed the door behind him, the blonde rounded the desk to where Sam was sitting. She smiled down at him.

"Feeling a little tense today, Mr. Marchesi?' she purred coyly.

"Just get to work baby," was Sam's reply. The young girl knelt in front of him, unzipping his pants.

Chapter Nineteen

Charlie Patek had been summoned to Sam Marchesi's office on Industrial Avenue. The invitation was extended to him by Jim Eccles during the plane ride back from Reno, after their second meeting with Roxburgh and Summers in Carson City.

Charlie didn't like the way things were going. It hadn't been his idea to involve the Department of Insurance at this stage. That fool, Kirshbaum, had filed a complaint with Snead's office. Snead, in Charlie's opinion an even bigger buffoon than Kirshbaum, had started the ball rolling. This left Charlie, and Sundown Mortgage, with little choice but to go along. Charlie hadn't talked to Ashley yet, but was scheduled to see her later that night at her house.

When Charlie discovered that Patek Investments had been short changed on their pay off, he was furious. He'd been trying to contact Ashley ever since. It wasn't like her to make this kind of mistake, and Charlie didn't like what his gut was telling him.

What's that bitch been up to, he wondered.

Charlie had just enough time to drive from McCarran airport to his home in Spanish Trails on west Tropicana, shower, and change clothes before heading back to Sam's office. He gunned the engine of his new Porsche, and ran the gears quickly as he accelerated through the guard station, tires squealing as he hit Tropicana headed east.

Fifteen minutes later, he pulled into the parking lot off Industrial Avenue, parking near the private entrance in the rear. He'd only been to Sam's office once before. That had been for a boys' night out gathering to celebrate the lucrative take-over of a large piece of raw land in the Southwest part of the valley. Some unhappy borrowers had over extended themselves, and Sam, through Charlie's efforts, ended up with the land. It sat in the much sought after corridor next to the soon to be built I-215 loop around the west side of the city.

Charlie pushed the electronic security button on his car, and climbed the back stairs to Sam's office. Even though he was meeting with Sam, he felt uneasy leaving his new toy parked in that part of town.

At the top of the stairs, Charlie met a large doorman, dressed incongruously in a dark suit with the temperature still in triple digits. The guard patted Charlie down in a way that suggested he could do it in his sleep. When he'd satisfied himself that Charlie was not armed, he knocked on the door, and quickly opened it.

Jim Eccles was seated with his back to the door talking to Sam, who rocked back in the overstuffed chair behind his desk. Their conversation stopped abruptly as Charlie entered the room.

"Charlie. C'mon in," Sam bellowed as Patek appeared in the doorway. "Of course you know Jim Eccles. Jimbo and I were just discussing our mutual problem with this Anasazi development."

Sam struck Charlie as being a lot more cordial than he was used to.

"I wanted to ask you about that Sam," Charlie said, taking the other chair opposite Marchesi at the desk. "Why was I cut out of the second loan?"

"You should feel lucky, Charlie," Sam replied. "Jimbo here is stuck for four large." Eccles shifted uneasily in his chair. It was true, Charlie wouldn't want to be in his shoes.

"I'm still out over five hundred grand," Charlie interjected. "How am I covered on that?"

"Relax, Charlie," Sam said. "We're all reasonable businessmen here. I propose that we locate Jimbo's money by tracking this goniff who stiffed him. If we get to him before anybody else, we take back the money on the side, and nobody's the wiser. Then, Jim's company forecloses on the project and we get the money and the property."

"What about me?" Charlie queried, not seeing how this helped him.

"Seems like you're a victim of escrow fraud to me, Charlie," Sam said. "I'll go to this Roxburgh character and, in the words of my favorite writer, 'make him an offer he can't refuse'. Jim gets the money and the project. You and I get controlling interest in the title company for a lousy half million. It's worth at least two million as a going concern. Seems like a sweet deal to me."

"Roxburgh won't go for that," Charlie blurted, still not grasping Sam's logic.

"He will, my friend; because if he doesn't, your lawsuit will put him out of business," Sam replied. "Better to keep a slice of the pie, than no pie at all. You just make sure your girlfriend, Ashley, plays ball with us. She testifies that Roxburgh's company screwed up, and we're home free."

"How are we going to find the money?" asked Charlie, the bigger picture now coming into focus.

"I've got Jimbo and some of our security associates working on that," he replied. "We'll find these guys and the dough."

Charlie thought about Sam's plan for a minute. It seemed to make sense for everybody. He'd already made a bundle on the costs of the first loan. Now he'd have a chance to control AmCon Title, which is what he'd been lusting after for some time. All he had to do was make Ashley play ball. That shouldn't be too tough. After all, he was convinced that she was somehow in the middle of this mess anyway.

"And Roxburgh's lawyer and the other escrow officer? What about them?" Charlie asked, knowing the answer before he heard it.

"Let me take care of those details," Sam said smiling. "The mouthpiece could be a problem, but he's unfortunately rubbed Bruno the wrong way. Usually people who do that, don't stick around very long."

"Where is Bruno, tonight?" Charlie asked. He was Sam's constant companion.

"I've got him running some errands for me." Sam's reply sent a chill up Charlie's spine. He'd hate to be the object of one of Bruno's errands.

Sam turned his attention to Eccles.

"You've got the most to lose here, Jimbo," Sam commented, with what Eccles took as a menacing tone. There was no need to remind him that it was Sam's money they were talking about. "What have you found out?"

"Our people have surveillance on everyone involved," Eccles answered. "We've bugged the title company and the lawyer's office. Should get something soon, I would think. The girl's got a kid that could provide some leverage, if we need it. If she's involved with our mystery man in this, we'll hear about it. I'm checking on the title officer, Temple. He's up to his eyeballs in debt and is a likely candidate to have a part in this. No big deposits in his bank, though. But he might have been paid in cash.

Ashley Roh made an unusual deposit right about the time Charlie closed on his loan. We'll need to keep an eye on her. So far, nothing on the imposter. But we've got the line out on him across the country. He'll surface somewhere. That kind of money tends to burn a hole in your pocket."

"What about the mouthpiece?" Sam asked.

"Summers is a little tougher nut to crack'" Eccles said. "He's a widower who keeps to himself. No current broads, and no family in Vegas. Word is that he's an 'ex-Navy Seal'. It might explain why Bruno ran into a problem. Based on our meetings in Carson City, I'd say he's a smart son-of-a-bitch. He's well respected within the courtroom crowd. He's got one of those newer homes in Seven Hills, overlooking the city, and a mortgage that he's got no problem handling. Off hand, I'd say he's not the type who will cooperate, unless severely motivated."

"That's our specialty," Sam quipped. "Reasoning with smart guys."

Sam spent another half hour going over the details of how he proposed to handle their problem. He emphasized that it was important to keep the number of people involved to a minimum. He ended by saying that he knew he could "count on" both Patek and Eccles to be "stand up" guys when he called on them to solve any unexpected delays or hitches in carrying out their plan. Left with no apparent options, both men eagerly agreed.

As the meeting ended, three young dancers, clad only in G-strings, entered the office.

"I thought you might enjoy some entertainment after the day you've had," Sam said, rising to greet the ladies.

The bodyguard who had frisked Charlie was standing in the doorway.

"Henry, get these guys a cocktail," Sam said.

Charlie stood, apologizing to Sam. He explained that he'd arranged to meet with Ashley Roh. His workday wasn't over yet.

"No rest for the wicked," Sam responded, slapping him on the back and laughing. "Go get me something useful."

Chapter Twenty

Charlie took a deep breath, leaning back in his Porsche. He let the air escape slowly, like a tent drops when you take out the center pole. Marchesi made him nervous. He liked the sound of Sam's plan to take over AmCon Title. It was a prize he'd coveted. If he had controlling interest in a title and escrow company, a lot of the unhandy details of his projects could be swept under the table. He'd keep Roxburgh around as a front, if he cooperated. If not, there was no shortage of title schleps hanging around Las Vegas who could do the job.

He eased the sports car out into southbound traffic, putting distance between himself and Marchesi. He was trying desperately to figure out how Sam was going to fuck him on the deal. He was convinced that he would. It was just a matter of time. Charlie lit a cigarette as he entered freeway traffic, headed for Ashley's house. It would take him about fifteen minutes to get there, barring any traffic problems. Plenty of time to get his head ready for her.

When Charlie pulled into Ashley's driveway, the front porch light came on. She'd been waiting for him. By now it was nearly ten o'clock. A long day, and miles to go before I sleep, he mused.

Ringing the door chime, Charlie flicked the remainder of a cigarette into Ashley's lawn. He knew it would drive her crazy. A moment later, she swung open the front door. She was dressed in a T-shirt; one he'd given her months earlier. In large letters across the chest it said, "Property of Patek Investments." Charlie smiled reflexively.

"You took your sweet time getting here honey," Ashley said as a greeting. "I was beginning to worry."

That's a laugh, Charlie thought.

"Sorry gorgeous, I got back late from Reno," he said.

Ashley smiled up at him. In bare feet, the top of her head hit him just below his breast bone. She pulled him through the door, grabbing his crotch and squeezing gently.

"I've missed you, big guy," she purred.

"That why you're not returning my calls?" Charlie responded.

"That's not true," she replied, a hurt look on her face.

Ashley turned, heading for the mini-bar that sat in a small alcove off of her living room. It wasn't a large home, but it suited Ashley well. She'd decorated it in predominantly black and white. Not done expensively, but a notch above starter home furnishings.

She poured him a glass of vodka over ice, and walked back across the room to where Charlie had taken a seat. Watching her walk, Charlie could see that she was naked beneath the shirt. She handed him the drink, sliding into his lap.

"Tell me what you're in such a fuss about, Charlie," she said. "Maybe I can make it all better."

Charlie took a long pull on the iced vodka, the familiar burn hitting his stomach. He reflected a moment on the woman with whom he'd shared so may nights of sexual pleasure. He shifted his weight, as if to set the drink on the side table next to him. She smiled up at him seductively, anticipating his hands on her breasts.

Instead, whipping his arm, he swung the half full tumbler into the side of Ashley's head with an explosion of ice, glass and vodka. The blow knocked Ashley from Charlie's lap, and several feet across the living room floor. She landed like a rag doll on the carpet, T-shirt soaked in vodka and hiked above one large, bare breast. Blood poured from a cut on the side of her face, extending needy fingers into the white carpet. She was dazed, but not out.

Ashley let out a low moan as Charlie drug her, by a handful of her long black hair, into the kitchen.

"We need to have a serious talk, sweetie," Charlie said, huffing from the effort of moving her. "As you may have guessed, I'm not happy with you at the moment."

Charlie heaved Ashley into one of her kitchen chairs, blood still covering the side of her face. She was crying, unable, or unwilling, to speak. Saliva dribbled from her open mouth, cascading with her blood onto the Patek Investments shirt. Finally, as if summoning her wits from deep within, she lashed out at him.

"What-the-fuck are you doing, you asshole!" she sobbed.

"Getting your attention, my dear," Charlie replied cheerily. "Apparently my phones calls don't work; especially when I'm missing half a million bucks in one of your escrows."

From an apparent state of helplessness, Ashley sprang, a cat with its tail on fire, for a rack of kitchen knives a few feet away. But she was too slow for Charlie. For a big man, he was quick. He caught her in the solar plexus as she lunged forward, and sent her whip-lashing back into the chair.

"So much for small talk," Charlie grimaced, clutching the back of her shirt with one large hand, while the back of the other snapped across Ashley's cheek.

Pulling the leather belt from his pants, Charlie doubled it over, and for the next several minutes, beat Ashley without mercy. He concentrated on the upper legs and torso. She begged and screamed, trying to escape his grasp. He was too strong. The T-shirt tore, but didn't give. He shoved her forward, causing her to sprawl face first on the floor.

Charlie's rage was fueled by the twin Hydras of jealousy and fear. Her obvious betrayal of him with DeMartes burned a hole in his gut. The thought of Sam's reprisal, should they not retrieve the stolen funds, was motivation enough for Charlie to do anything.

She rolled back and forth, arms raised in an attempt to protect her face. His initial barrage was such that, after a few minutes, he needed only to snap the belt on the countertop to elicit an immediate jerking response from the sobbing Ashley, who lay in a fetal position on the floor.

Over the course of the next hour, Charlie heard all about her meetings with DeMartes, the initial pay-off to screw Kirshbaum, and the promised money for misleading Sundown Mortgage about the real status of the title to the Anasazi property. The only details she was able to omit, were those of her sexual encounters with DeMartes. She feared that if she told Charlie this, in his present state, he would kill her.

Later, Charlie lifted and carried her to the bedroom. There, he wiped the blood from her face with a wet towel. The cut on the side of her head, where the glass had broken, was not large. Like most head wounds, it looked worse than it was.

What a waste, Charlie thought as he closed the front door behind him.

He knew that any future with Ashley had probably ended. He'd miss their times together. But for Charlie, if the dog bites you once, you don't give it a second opportunity. He couldn't trust her, but she'd do what she was told. It was that simple.

Charlie lowered the driver's side window on his car as he turned west on Warm Springs, headed home.

"What a fucking day," he said aloud to himself. It was then, for the first time, that he noticed his hand was bleeding at the knuckle. The plasma, looking almost black in the moonlight, had trickled onto the Porsche's leather interior.

"Shit!" he cursed, and accelerated to the west.

Ashley spent the remainder of the night, drifting in and out of consciousness. By first light, when the reality of her condition forced her awake, she tried to rise from the bed. The pillow she'd been resting on was covered in dried blood. The hair on the side of her head matted together, as if she'd fallen asleep in some sticky bowl of food. Her first attempt at sitting caused searing pain to shoot down her back and thighs. Looking down at her naked torso, she could see the raised welts on her legs, stomach and breasts. The pain in her back told her that the damage there was probably even worse. Lying back, she tried to clear her head. She was in trouble like she'd never seen before and needed help.

At six thirty, the cell telephone that Jack had brought outside with him rang. He was in the middle of finishing the final set of crunches on his torso track, relishing the familiar burn on his abdominals. He'd risen early, mentally reviewing the events of the last two days in Carson City and Reno. He was scheduled to be in court at nine, and wanted to find out if Mac had turned up anything for him since their conversation the night before. He knew that his friend would have started the ball rolling, even though it was late when he'd left Jack's office. Half expecting to hear Mac's voice, he grabbed the phone, still breathing heavily.

"Jack?" Ashley said, before he could speak. "It's Ashley. I need to talk to you."

"Sure, Ashley. I can meet you at your office this afternoon," he replied.

"No, I'm not going in today," she said. "I need you to come to my house as soon as you can."

Jack's mind raced ahead, trying to figure out what she was up to. He told her he had to be in court all morning, but that he could meet with her that afternoon. From the sound of her voice, it was obvious that she was upset.

"If it's about the Anasazi Properties deal, maybe we should wait until I can see you in the office," Jack replied, his trial lawyer's guts telling him not to meet with her alone at her home.

"This can't wait, Jack," she said plaintively. "I'm in trouble."

"Alright," he said, after a moment's hesitation. "I'll be there by two."

Returning to his workout, Jack tried to figure out what Ashley had in mind. His conflict of interest guardian angel was yapping overtime in his ear. What was it that couldn't wait? Was Ashley about to confess some expanded role in this deal? Was she somehow involved with DeMartes? More importantly, did she know how to find him?

In the end, it was Jack's curiosity that made refusing her request a non-option for him. He'd spent his entire adult life trying to ferret out the truth in situations where people really didn't want to hear it. If Ashley could help him along, then he couldn't resist.

By the time Jack knocked on Ashley's door, later that afternoon, he'd heard from Mac that the money trail led to an island called "Nevis" in the British West Indies. He didn't know who'd received it there, but that's where the wires led them. The financial institution was called "Caribbean Holdings Limited." Mac had obviously used his FBI connections. He'd laughed when he related the beginner's mistake that the DeMartes phony had made.

"He should have bought bearer bonds, or taken cash," Mac quipped. He never understood how what seemed to be some of the smartest guys in the world, made the dumbest mistakes. Mac concluded by telling him "he'd better get to the money fast," because Marchesi's sources would be "almost as good as his."

When Ashley answered the door, she was wearing dark glasses and a robe that covered her from the neck down.

"Are you alright, Ashley?" was all Jack could think to say.

She stepped toward him, wrapping her arms around his waist. Jack didn't know how to react. He ended up leaving his hands at his sides, standing in the afternoon heat with Ashley clinging to him like a child. After a few moments of uncomfortable silence, she backed away, leading him into the chilled interior of the house. Taking a seat on the living room couch, she finally broke the silence.

"I know you're not my personal lawyer, Jack," she said. "But I think of you as a friend, and after the times we shared, maybe something more than a friend."

Jack said nothing. He'd taken a seat opposite her on a separate chair. He was about to say that, of course, they were "friends" and hoped they always could be, but Ashley stood up abruptly, and removed her eyeglasses. He could see that the left side of her face was swollen and starting to discolor. Her eyes were bloodshot, as if she'd been weeping. Before he could ask what happened to her, she untied the belt on her robe, letting it slide off her shoulders to the floor. Jack audibly gasped at the sight of her naked body. It looked like someone had horse whipped her. She was bruises, neck to knees. As she turned, he could see that the backside was even worse.

"Who did this?" was all Jack could muster at the sight in front of him.

She was crying now, tears rolling off her face and on to her battered chest. It was obvious to Jack that she wanted to tell him in the worst way, but seemed to hesitate.

"I don't want the police involved," she said quietly.

Warning bells were going off in Jack's head like a three alarm fire. If this had something to do with the Anasazi Properties case, he was walking down a road to ruin. If her present state was the result of some involvement in the deal that she hadn't already revealed, his client, AmCon Title, would be at direct odds with her. He weighed his options in the moment it took her to pull the robe back over her shoulders, tying it in front.

"If this is the result of some role you played in the Anasazi Properties deal, this isn't the time or place to tell me about it," Jack said. "You will need separate counsel, immediately. As much as I'd like to help you, I think you should report this to the police. Anyone who would do such a thing is capable of much more, and your life could be in danger. If it's unrelated, then please tell me; I'll do anything I can to help you."

Her answer was on her face. She said nothing.

Jack shook his head. He'd already guessed that she was involved. The lawyer in him said to turn tail and run. The man in him stepped forward, cradling her in his arms as she wept.

When the worst of the sobbing subsided, he asked if she knew where to find the man who had impersonated DeMartes. She said she didn't, and hadn't seen or heard from him. Jack told her to call him immediately if he contacted her, and after writing down several names of attorneys who could represent her, he left. Backing out of Ashley's driveway, it crossed his mind that maybe the escrow queen wasn't so tough after all.

Chapter Twenty One

Daryl McKenna shook himself into consciousness. The haze of a three week drunk sat on his brain, a steam engine wheezing its way up a steep grade. As his eyes slowly focused, he realized it was his wife, Judy, saying something to him.

"We need to talk, honey," she said. "What are we doing here?"

When Daryl had realized that DeMartes wasn't coming back with their money, he'd quickly packed their belongings and stored them in Las Vegas. He and Judy fled, getting as far as a Motel 6 in Victorville, a town off the I-15 that baked in the high desert of California, situated half way between Las Vegas and Los Angeles. His dream of riches had evaporated once again. Now, considering the mountain of debt he'd left in Las Vegas, he felt like a trapped rat. He was effectively banned from the only industry he'd ever known. He couldn't think past the bottle of vodka that had been his constant companion.

"What are you talking about?" Daryl slurred.

"We can't just go on hiding here indefinitely," Judy replied, being uncharacteristically direct. "You need to call Bill, and get this thing straightened out. It's not your fault if DeMartes took the money."

Daryl had neglected to tell Judy about his role in bribing Roger Temple.

"What's Bill gonna do. He'll probably have me arrested!" Daryl said.

"No, he won't," Judy responded. "He's your friend. Maybe he can help us figure a way out of this mess."

Daryl considered this for a moment. Maybe she was right. After all, he rationalized in the tradition of the classic alcoholic, none of this is really my fault. If I call Bill, maybe I can salvage something. I didn't do anything wrong. Hell, I'm just as much of a victim as anybody. I'm getting screwed out of a million bucks! The more he thought about it, maybe he could somehow be the hero, and blow the lid off this whole scam. There might even be some kind of reward in it for him!

"I'll clean up and give him a call," Daryl said to his long suffering wife. She smiled and ruffled his thinning hair.

An hour later, Daryl dialed the number for AmCon Title, asking for Bill Roxburgh. He didn't notice anything unusual as the recording device clicked on at a remote location near the Strip. AmCon Title employed the same security company, owned by associates of Sam Marchesi, as did the building that housed Jack's office. It was one of a number of legitimate businesses that Sam's friends had taken over in the last ten years.

What a laugh, Sam had thought when they'd muscled their way into owning the company. We run the security company. Pick and choose who gets hit. Easy access to innumerable businesses, both during and after hours. It was sheer genius. As soon as Sam had gotten word of what happened in Reno, he'd told Eccles to have both offices electronically bugged. The boys had become ever-increasingly high tech in response to the government's surveillance of them. What's good for the goose, is good for the gander, Sam liked to say.

"Bill, it's Daryl," Daryl announced when Roxburgh identified himself.

"Daryl, where the hell are you?" Roxburgh asked.

"I'm not in Vegas, if that's what you're asking," Daryl responded. "Look, I don't know what you're thinking at this point, but I didn't have anything to do with Anasazi Properties not paying its bills. I'm a victim too!"

Pausing for a second, Roxburgh replied.

"You probably are, Daryl. Best thing you can do now is get your ass back here. I'll put you in touch with our lawyer, Jack Summers. I'm sure he can straighten this out. Where's this DeMartes character? You know that's not his name?"

"I guessed as much," Daryl said quietly. "I'm in a Motel 6 in Victorville. Tell Summers I'll be up to talk to him in a couple of days."

Roxburgh congratulated him on making the right decision, and dialed Jack's number as soon as they hung up. Yet another voice activated recording device silently spun into action as he was connected with Jack's office. He was told that Mr. Summers was in court, but that he would return the call as soon as possible.

"I'm going back to Vegas," Daryl said to Judy, who had been eavesdropping on his side of the conversation.

"That's a good idea, Daryl," she replied, once again giving him credit for an idea she'd put in his head.

Within two hours of Daryl's phone call to Roxburgh, a black SUV left the parking lot of the strip club on Industrial Avenue, turning south. A young hood from Chicago drove, and in the passenger seat sat Bruno. There was little conversation. Each man was lost in his own thoughts. Sam made it clear that he wanted answers from McKenna. "When you've exhausted the resource, make it disappear," were his instructions.

At dusk, as the sun settled behind the mountains to the west, the black vehicle pulled into the parking lot of the Motel 6, just off of I-15. They parked with a vantage point commanding the bulk of the rooms. The lot began filling in with the nondescript cars of weary traveling salesmen and vacationers headed west. When Daryl and Judy opened the door to their room, stepping out into the still super heated night, they didn't notice the SUV, or its occupants. They were headed to Kentucky Fried Chicken for supper, and Daryl was sober for a change.

A little after ten o'clock, Daryl woke in the dark. The reality of his situation came to him slowly. His hands and feet were bound behind him. Some type of bag covered his head, leaving him in blackness, and he felt a wave of nausea. His mouth tasted of dried vomit. He realized that he was in some type of vehicle, and from the sound of it, they were on a rough, probably gravel surface. He could hear Judy sobbing nearby.

"What's happening?" Daryl croaked, his bindings straining against his throat as he moved.

"Shut up!" was the response. Daryl felt a sharp pain and saw a bright flash as the pistol grip slammed into the side of his head.

The snatch of Daryl and Judy had been simple. Bruno had a description of him from Charlie Patek. They knew which motel they'd find him in. It was painfully easy to scope out the cars with Las Vegas plates, and wait for Daryl to appear. Once he did, Bruno simply waited for them to return to their room. Bruno and his companion were waiting for them.

They'd loaded their targets in the back of the SUV, properly trussed and hooded, and driven east on I-15. Just past the Air Force base, they turned north on a private road. It led about fifteen miles into the desert and low mountains. The property was owned by one of Sam's companies, and Bruno had been there before. There was a small, unused hunting shack near the end of the road. The nearest neighbor would be more than thirty miles distant.

Depositing his cargo on the floor of the shack, Bruno instructed Dean, his new helper from Chicago, to drive a mile or so cross country into the desert, and dig a hole big enough to hold their guests. When Dean returned to the shack, he was covered with the dust of his work.

"Damn, that ground's hard," he said as he entered the room. "I had to use the pick and pry bar!"

He saw Daryl first. He was tied, in a standing position, to the center support beam of the shack. His hood was off, and Dean could see blood streaming from lacerations on his forehead and lower lip. His eyes were fixed on something across the room. Following Daryl's gaze, Dean saw what appeared to be the naked form of the woman, bound in a bent position over the edge of a large wooden table. Her arms were stretched forward, and her legs, spread the width of the table, were bound to the table legs below.

Dean stopped in his tracks. He'd grown up hard on the streets of Chicago, but the sight of this middle-aged woman tied in the most undignified position he could imagine, made him flinch.

Bruno sat in a chair just to the side of the table, his shirt and pants off, thumbing the blade of a long knife with an eight inch curved blade. The kind you'd use to bone a fish. Dean could see blood on his knuckles, apparently the cause of McKenna's facial problem.

"I was just asking our friend here, where's our money," Bruno stated in a matter of fact tone. "He says he don't know; can you believe it!"

Dean hadn't worked with Bruno before. He only knew him by reputation. "Psycho" was the term that usually came to mind, when people thought of Bruno. Sam ruled his roost with an iron hand, and Bruno was the reason you never crossed him.

"I just told him his old lady was a bum lay," Bruno growled. "He started crying when I stuck it in her ass. This upsets me. He doesn't like to share information, or this hag. Maybe he'd like to fuck her himself."

Extending the knife in Dean's direction he laughed, saying, "Here, cut off his cock and shove it in her. He can fuck her from across the room."

There was no change in Bruno's expression or eyes as he held the knife out to Dean. He might as well have been ordering a Ham and Swiss sandwich. Dean didn't move. Judy began to moan softly for her husband's help.

"What's the matter, kid, getting a little squeamish on me?" Bruno asked, menacingly.

With that, Bruno moved to the table, and with a flick of his wrist ran the blade down the length of Judy's exposed spine. The razor sharp blade didn't cut deep, but her skin filleted open, blood pouring from broken subcutaneous vessels.

After midnight, the screams and whimpers from inside the shack finally stopped. Dean had gone outside to throw up when Bruno started peeling the skin off of Judy McKenna's back with his knife. He'd told Daryl that he was going to "skin her alive" unless he found out where DeMartes and the four million were.

Daryl continued to sob that he didn't know, and begged for mercy. Almost immediately, he had recounted every detail he ever knew about the Anasazi deal. He volunteered anything he could think of about each of the parties involved, start to finish; but Bruno was unrelenting. He enjoyed his work.

When Bruno emerged from the shack, his torso covered in blood, he said simply, "Guess they weren't much help."

A chill enveloped Dean as the monster smiled down on him from the porch. Dean wrapped the mangled torsos of Daryl and Judy McKenna into a large tarp he'd brought in the SUV, and deposited them in the hole he'd dug in the desert. There was a full moon, and a light breeze that almost cooled the night air. Dean threw the last shovel full of dirt and sand on the makeshift grave. After a day or two of the desert wind, the McKennas' final resting place would disappear forever.

When Bruno and Dean returned to Las Vegas, just before dawn, they drove directly to the scrap yard where Sam had interrogated Louis Dominguez. They pulled the SUV behind the warehouse, where it would be burned and then crushed later that morning. Any last forensic remains of the McKennas would disappear like their grave.

Chapter Twenty Two

The morning's squall came to a dripping end, as Leon arrived at Jesse's hotel in Orlando. He parked the rented Ford Taurus near the side entrance, and slipped in without encountering anyone. In and out quickly, he told himself. One last detail to clean up.

Leon had never killed anyone, but he knew it was the only way to be sure he'd covered his trail. How hard could it be, anyway? He felt again for the knife in his pocket.

This won't be that hard, he reassured himself for the hundredth time.

He approached Jesse's room and stood quietly for a minute listening. He could hear the sound of the television, but nothing else.

The son-of-a-bitch is probably still asleep, he thought.

Leon knocked softly. He wanted to be gone quickly. Hopefully he wouldn't run into anyone who might later recognize him. There was only the sound of the television, no movement. Pausing a minute he knocked loudly, calling out to Jesse. Still no answer.

Just then, a housekeeper rounded the corner at the far end of the hall. Leon turned his back to her, continuing to knock on the door. No response. He was about to walk away, keeping his back to the hotel employee when she tapped him on the shoulder, saying, "Vacant. Senor leaves this morning."

Caught off guard by the unexpected news, Leon turned to find a middle-aged Cuban woman smiling up at him.

"He's checked out?" Leon asked, incredulous.

"Si, this morning early. To airport in cab," she replied.

Leon thanked the maid, and headed for the parking lot. This was an unanticipated wrinkle.

Where the hell is that piece of shit? he wondered to himself.

At the car, Leon stopped. The tropical sun burned a hole in the cloud cover over Orlando, and sweat darkened his shirt. He walked directly to the hotel lobby, approaching the registration desk where a slender, dark haired Latin beauty stood, punching information into a computer.

"Excuse me," Leon said, mustering his most charming smile. "My little brother checked out of room 224 this morning. He just called to tell me that he'd misplaced his copy of the room charges. I wonder if I might get another copy for him, if it's not too much trouble?"

She hesitated for only a second. The good looking middle aged man in front of her looked honest enough. Returning his smile, she ran her fingers quickly across the computer's keyboard, and a fresh new copy of Jesse's room charges brought a nearby printer to life. Leon quickly scanned the pages as she handed them to him.

There's what I need, he thought.

Jesse had made two calls to Las Vegas from his room the day before, and one to American Airlines. The prick's headed back to Vegas, Leon concluded, running over his options. Do I go back for him, or let it go?

"Thank you so much," he said to the desk clerk. "It's just what my brother needed."

Leon dropped the knife he was carrying in a trash can as he returned to his car, and headed for the airport.

Chapter Twenty Three

When Jesse's plane landed in Las Vegas, he took a cab to Roger Temple's apartment. He would gather his stuff and planned to go to Sarah's place. After all, they had a kid together. Why shouldn't they all live together like a family? Besides, he had nowhere else to go at that point. DeMartes, or whatever his name was, had obviously finished with him. Nice gig while it lasted, he mused.

Jesse raced through the apartment, stuffing his clothes and anything else he thought might be of some value in a large duffel bag. Roger was due home from work soon, and Jesse was in no mood for any confrontations about past rent or property division.

At that moment, he heard the key turning in the front door and Roger was catapulted into the living room, landing unceremoniously on the coffee table and sliding to the floor. He was followed immediately by two large men dressed in suits. Jesse's first thought was that they were bill collectors of some kind. God knows, they called Roger often enough. But then he noticed that the smaller of the two had a pistol drawn, pointed at Jesse's midsection. He had the index finger of his other hand in front of his mouth, in a quieting motion.

"We're looking for DeMartes," Bruno snarled at Roger, still sitting on the floor. "Tell me where I can find him, and you and I won't have a problem. You don't want to have a problem with me, do you?"

Bruno's question didn't appear to register with Roger at first, and he made no response. Then, as Bruno moved toward him, Roger found his voice.

"How would I know where he is?" he blurted, shuffling backwards like a crab until he hit the television stand on the far wall. "I've never even met the guy."

"That's the wrong answer, buddy," Bruno said matter-of-factly.

He side-stepped in Jesse's direction and hit him squarely in the face, flattening his nose. The pop of his cartilage cracking sounded something like a cork being pulled from a bottle of wine. The blow knocked Jesse into the wall behind him; blood, like an open tap, running down his chin.

"I'm gong to hurt your boyfriend here first," Bruno said to Roger with relish, "then I'm going to hurt you. Tell me where to find DeMartes, and we go away. It's simple."

Roger started to protest again that he didn't have a clue where this DeMartes guy was, and that he'd never even met him. Jesse, having slid to the floor, interrupted.

"He went to San Juan. I was supposed to meet him in Orlando tomorrow, but I changed my mind."

Roger's jaw dropped open. He stared at Jesse in disbelief. How the hell did this kid know who DeMartes was, much less where to find him? At least he'd given this beast what he was looking for. Maybe they'd leave him alone now, Roger thought.

Over the course of the next ten minutes, Bruno grilled Jesse about his history with the guy called DeMartes. Jesse saw no reason whatsoever not to tell his Italian interrogator everything he knew about Leon. He related their meeting in California, and how he later was paid to keep an eye on Roger. At that, Temple started to speak, but was silenced by a look from the other intruder whose gun was now leveled at Roger. He explained how they'd switched airplanes in Dallas, with Jesse continuing on to Orlando, and Leon taking his seat to San Juan.

As Jesse ran out of information to volunteer, Bruno pulled a cell phone from his coat pocket and hit a speed dial number. A few seconds later, he told the listener on the other end, "The guy's supposed to be in Orlando tomorrow morning. He's gonna meet a guy checked in as Jesse Dunn."

Bruno repeated the essentials of what Jesse had told him about Leon. Jesse left out only the fact that he had given two sets of identification he'd taken and copied from Leon's room to Sarah. Even a shit-heel like Jesse knew enough to keep this thug away from Sarah.

"What you want I should do here?" Bruno asked, finishing. He smiled at the response and ended the conversation. "Time to go," Bruno said, looking in Roger's direction. Roger breathed a sigh of relief. They got what they came for, and now they'll leave, he thought. He could deal with Jesse when they were alone. Bruno slid his hand beneath his coat, pulling a small handgun from the waistband. Walking slowly across the room, he could see the fear freeze in Roger's eyes. Bruno told Dean to take a look outside, and his companion moved to the door, opening it quickly and scanning the area.

"Looks good," was all he said as he turned back into the room.

Bruno grabbed Roger by the collar, lifting him with little effort, and pulled him across the room towards Jesse. As he did so, he scooped up a small pillow from one of the chairs. When they reached a point several feet in front of where Jesse sat, Bruno looked down and said, "Why'd you shoot this guy?"

Both Roger and Jesse were still trying to figure out what their antagonist was talking about when Bruno pressed the pillow and the gun into Roger's face and fired one shot through his forehead. Pieces of brain and skull sprayed like a shotgun blast from the back of Roger's head, and Bruno loosened his grip, letting Temple's body hit the floor. The muffled report from the small gun would have sounded like television noise outside of the room. Jesse sat, as if nailed to the floor, staring at Roger's now lifeless body.

"You been very helpful pal," Bruno said, looking down at Jesse. "So I'm giving you a break."

He pulled a syringe from his side pocket and faced Jesse. "I'm gonna send you on a little trip," he whispered. "You won't remember any of this. Roll up your sleeve."

Jesse readily complied. Hope for somehow surviving this night filled the void in his head. Taking three tries to find a vein, Bruno pumped enough heroin into Jesse to kill ten men. As his eyes began to glaze with the euphoric rush of the drug, Bruno placed the small revolver in Jesse's hand. He'd carefully wiped it clean of his own prints. The last thing Jesse heard before losing consciousness was Bruno telling him to fire the gun into the couch, leaving ample gunpowder discharge on his hand. He did as he was told.

Satisfied with his work, Bruno left quietly with Dean in tow. No one saw them exit Roger's apartment. Minutes later, a neighbor who hadn't had the nerve to look outside, called 911 to report a gunshot.

Leon's flight arrived in Vegas two hours after Bruno dispatched Jesse and Roger. He retrieved his leased Mercedes from its storage garage near the airport, and drove straight to Roger Temple's apartment. As he turned onto the street where Temple's apartment was located, he first saw the police and media lights flashing. The sun had been down for some time, and the police and news vehicles gave the street a carnival appearance. Leon parked, walking casually towards the scene, a neighbor, just out for a stroll.

When he reached earshot of an on camera reporter he could hear "Stacy" with Channel 3 News reporting that "more drug violence had struck the valley, just east of the Strip." Two men had been discovered dead in their apartment, one "shot in an apparent argument over drugs," and the other, from an "overdose." Police had not yet determined what kind of drug was involved, but they suspected heroin. Names were being withheld, pending notification of next of kin, but Leon could see that it was Temple's apartment. As the reporter signed off, lowering her microphone, he heard her say that "the deceased men lived together" in the apartment.

That was all Leon needed to hear. Retracing his route, he drove towards the airport. He'd leave the car in long term parking since he had no intention of ever returning to Las Vegas. Police would find it a week later, tracing it as a leased vehicle in the name of Marcel DeMartes.

Chapter Twenty Four

"Is this Sarah Dunn?" the voice on Sarah's phone questioned.

"Yes," Sarah replied.

"This is Las Vegas Metro detective Alan Smith, Ms. Dunn. Do you know a Jesse Dunn?"

"Yes," Sarah said, expecting to hear that Jesse'd been arrested. "He's my estranged husband."

"We found your name and phone number in his wallet. When was the last time you saw him?" Smith asked.

"Several weeks ago, I met him for lunch," she responded, wondering what kind of trouble Jesse had gotten into.

"He was found dead in his apartment, tonight," Smith said. "I'm sorry."

Sarah's face drained of color. She didn't know how to respond. How could Jesse be dead? The detective broke the silence by telling her that he'd died of a drug overdose. The finality of death hit Sarah like a sledge hammer. She began weeping softly for the man who she'd once loved, the father of her child. A flood of memories from their good times together washed across her. She cried as much for her son, Adam, who would never know his father, as she did for her own lost youth.

"I'll be over within the hour to get some background on your husband," Smith told her and hung up.

Sarah stood, holding the phone in disbelief, until the drone of the disconnect signal brought her back to reality. Trying to clear her head, Sarah picked up the phone again, and dialed the one person in Las Vegas she felt she could trust to help her. After a couple of rings, Jack answered.

"Mr. Summers, it's Sarah," she blurted out before he could speak. Her voice told him she was upset. "Jesse's been killed."

It took Jack a minute to assimilate the statement. Then it dawned on him that she was talking about her husband. "What happened, Sarah?" he asked.

"A policeman just called to tell me he'd 'died of a drug overdose'," she responded. "It's on Channel 3 right now. The detective is coming to my house. I don't know what to do."

Jack reassured her as best he could. He explained that this was all routine, and that she just needed to relax. He then said, getting directions from her, that he'd be there in fifteen minutes. Twelve minutes later, Jack pulled up to Sarah's apartment. More than a few traffic ordinances had been ignored along the way. He'd been with Sarah, going over the gist of her conversation with detective Smith, for about twenty minutes when Smith knocked on her door. As he entered, he gave Jack a questioning look. He recognized him from the courtroom.

"Out kinda late tonight, aren't we, counselor?" Smith said, extending his open identification to Sarah.

"She's a client and a friend," Summers replied. "I'm just here for moral support."

Looking at the long legged beauty in front of him, Smith wondered just how close a "friend" this was. He proceeded to recount what they knew, in a nutshell, about Jesse's death. He said that the initial finding was a probable argument over drugs, with Jesse shooting Temple, either as a result of an overdose or immediately preceding one.

Jack knew better than to ask many questions. Smith wouldn't give him the details of an on-going investigation. The detective took notes as Sarah explained Jesse's background to him. She told him how they'd moved to Las Vegas, but that Jesse had spent most of his time in California. She said he'd called her, and they'd met a few weeks earlier. Jesse told her that he'd been working for a real estate developer for about a year, but she didn't know who. She also didn't know if he was involved in any illegal drugs, but that he wasn't when they were together.

Jack sat, cross-legged, in a chair across the room from Sarah and Smith. While she talked, he took the opportunity to look around her small apartment. It appeared to be a two bedroom layout, and she'd told him that Adam was asleep in one of them. Decorated in simple taste, the place looked like he'd imagined it would. The decor spoke of a woman who chose carefully, stretching a dollar, but not skimping to sacrifice style. His Claire would have probably decorated the place in the same way.

"Did you know his roommate, Roger Temple?" Smith interjected as Sarah finished Jesse's history. The mention of Temple's name brought Summers upright in his chair. Sarah looked to be in shock.

"Is this the Roger Temple who works for AmCon Title?" Jack blurted out in disbelief.

"Looks like it was. But he won't be in for work tomorrow. Got a hole in his forehead, apparently courtesy of her husband," Smith said nodding toward Sarah. "Why, do you know him?"

Jack was on his feet, explaining that they both did. He described his representation of AmCon Title, and recalled for Smith an outline of their recent trip to Reno. When he'd finished, Smith shook his head and said, "Odd coincidence, don't you think?"

"I take it that you didn't know your husband was living with your co-worker, Mrs. Dunn?" Smith asked Sarah, trying to figure out if there was something sinister in this turn of events.

"No, I'm sorry," was her reply. "Like I told you, I've only seen him once since he got back from California. But he called yesterday to say that he wanted to see Adam. Frankly, I didn't take it seriously. He wasn't very dependable."

Jack's mind raced ahead as Smith interrogated Sarah. What was the connection between Temple and Jesse? Could this really have been a coincidence? Jack didn't believe in them. He wanted to ask Sarah several more questions, but kept quiet. Better to wait until Smith had left. He did so soon afterwards. Leaving his card with Sarah, Smith said he would "be in touch" if any further questions developed.

As soon as Smith left them alone, Jack asked Sarah if she could recall anything that might give them the identity of the developer who was paying Jesse. He had his suspicions. It had to be the DeMartes imposter. It was then, for the first time since Jesse had handed it to her, that Sarah thought of the envelope Jesse gave her at lunch. She walked to the drawer where she'd placed it weeks before, and pulled out the sealed envelope. She handed it to Jack, and said that Jesse had asked her to keep it for him.

He tore the crumpled envelope open, spilling the contents onto her kitchen table. There were copies of two separate sets of picture identification. The same picture was incorporated in each, but one described a Leon Black of Orlando, Florida. The other, which Sarah stared at, transfixed, described Marcel DeMartes.

Jack wasn't surprised when Sarah said, "That's him, Jack. That's Mr. DeMartes from the Anasazi Properties deal."

Jesse had reached out from death to identify Leon Black as the man who stole over four million from Sam Marchesi. If Marchesi has this information, he'll be tracking Leon Black right now, Jack thought.

Were Jesse and Temple's deaths an unconnected coincidence? Jack didn't believe it. No, Marchesi was after the money. If he got to it before Jack, Jack's client would be ruined. What concerned him more, were Marchesi's methods. Having seen Ashley's condition earlier that day, and knowing what happened to Jesse and Temple, Jack was sure Sarah would be the next person Marchesi reached out to for information.

Though it was late, Sarah and Jack spent the next couple of hours talking quietly in her apartment. The first time she excused herself to check on her son, Jack stepped out onto the balcony off Sarah's living room. He needed a cigarette, and hadn't seen any ashtrays inside. The night air was still hot, and he sucked it in as he inhaled smoke.

He'd noticed the dark colored van parked, sitting opposite Sarah's apartment when he arrived. The glow of a cigarette, like a pinhole in a dark sheet, partially illuminated the occupant of the driver's seat.

They're already watching her, he thought as he reentered her apartment, feeling the relief of cooled air on his face.

"Is everything alright?" she asked.

"Sure," Jack mustered. "Trying to quit the cigarettes, but after a long day my resolve dissolves."

She smiled at him, her eyes lighting the room. She'd lowered the lighting while he was outside. Was it an invitation?

"Sarah, do you trust me?" he asked.

She nodded in response.

"Then have a seat, and I'll tell you what I think we need to do," Jack said.

He proceeded to tell her how sorry he was about Jesse. He could see from her reaction that she was more worried about Adam than herself and what had happened to Jesse. He asked if she knew a close friend who could watch Adam for her for a few days.

She could tell he was all business, and after considering it, said she had a friend on the floor below. She was a nurse who was currently off work on partial disability. The nurse had offered to take Adam in the past.

Jack explained that it was essential to not only AmCon Title's best interests, but also to hers and Ashley's that they locate Leon Black immediately. He felt that it was the only way to maintain any leverage with Marchesi, although he didn't say this to Sarah. He asked if she had a current passport, and when she said she did, he told her he wanted her to take a trip with him to find Black.

"Where are we going?" she asked.

"I'd rather tell you tomorrow," Jack responded, thinking for the first time that the man in the van outside may be listening in on their conversation. "Just pack for a few days, warm weather."

Inside the van, the driver turned, commenting to his companion that it "sounds like they're headed for Orlando."

Looking into Jack's eyes, Sarah knew he would take care of her. She said she'd go down and ask her friend first thing in the morning. It was only a few hours away.

"Good," Jack said. "If you don't mind, I'll camp here in your living room for the rest of the night, and we can make arrangements to leave early. I'll contact Roxburgh and clear the trip for you." Her look of relief, at having Jack stay with her after what happened to Jesse, was obvious.

Jack spent what remained of the night going over the day's events, and what needed to happen to get Sarah out of this mess. He stepped outside only once, noting that the van had not moved. Sarah retired to her bedroom, leaving the door ajar. It was the second night they'd spent together, chastely separated by a few feet and an open door. The early rising summer Las Vegas sun had just started to break the horizon when he entered her room, gently shaking Sarah from the rhythmic breath of sleep.

While Sarah deposited Adam with her neighbor for safe-keeping, Jack made a brief call to the Las Vegas police. He reported a suspicious van in the apartment's parking area. By the time Sarah had thrown together a small suitcase, the occupants of the van were busy explaining to a patrol officer exactly what they were doing. Jack couldn't resist a smile in the direction of the van's driver as Jack and Sarah drove away in Jack's car. Stopping briefly at Jack's house to gather clothes, a briefcase, and passport, they were on their way to McCarran airport.

Jack called Bill Roxburgh from his car, giving his client a capsulized version of the events from the previous day. He told him that Ashley would most likely not return to work yet; that Jack needed to borrow Sarah in an effort to locate the DeMartes imposter; and that Roger Temple had made the late news. Roxburgh had seen the report on Temple.

"What the hell's going on, Jack?" Roxburgh asked, his company crumbling around him.

"I'll fill you in when I get back," Jack said. "Right now I'm following a hunch, hopefully leading to the money DeMartes took. If I can get it back, I can probably negotiate you out of this mess."

Jack elected not to tell Roxburgh his destination, only that he and Sarah should be back in a few days. He finished by telling Roxburgh, "Watch your back, our opponents are connected to some very bad people. They're definitely playing hardball."

Roxburgh related to Jack his telephone conversation with Daryl McKenna. He said McKenna was supposed to be in to talk to him. Summers told him to keep Daryl in Las Vegas if he showed up. He felt certain that it was Leon Black who'd be the key to the missing cash.

Sarah and Jack took the first available flight out of Las Vegas headed east to a major hub. The luck of the draw would take them through St. Louis, and on to Miami, San Juan, and finally, St. Kitts. When they'd been in the air for an hour, Jack told Sarah their destination. She didn't question him. Her only comment before falling asleep was "I'm in your hands."

Chapter Twenty Five

Sarah was standing in a large hotel suite, facing a four posted king-sized bed made of dark mahogany, and covered with a feather-stuffed comforter. The air filled with the scent of tropical flowers, and a warm breeze moved sheer curtains that hung partially opened to a balcony overlooking the ocean. The room, lit only by candlelight, seemed to glow, warm and safe. She felt Jack's breath on the back of her neck, as his strong arms encircled her from behind. The red silk pajamas she wore, felt cool against her skin. Her blouse was unbuttoned and, hanging partially open from her shoulders, revealed rounded breasts that stood upright against the smooth fabric. Her nipples, the color of coffee and cream since the birth of her son, were fully erect. He kissed the nape of her neck gently and, without a word, slid the pajama top off her tanned shoulders.

She felt a flood of warmth in her belly, nerves dancing across her torso as Jack let his hands slide tenderly down her breasts and stomach. She turned, facing him, ready to give herself to him completely. He wore only white boxer shorts, and Sarah let her hand roam inside the waistband. They kissed deeply, sharing the taste and smell of each other, as Jack led her to the bed. Drifting back and down, as if floating, she lay across the bed in anticipation. He stood for a moment surveying the length of her. She felt the pleasure of his eyes as he took her in. "I love you," she whispered quietly, as he pulled the remaining portion of her pajamas gently from her legs.

Then she was drowning, clawing for the surface of the water in darkness. She woke with a start when she hit the surface, and realized she'd been dreaming. Jack and Sarah were somewhere over the eastern Caribbean, headed for St. Kitts. As she woke, she saw that she'd been laying, her head nestled against Jack's shoulder. He seemed to be dozing, facing the window. Sarah's face was flushed, and she felt again the warming sensation in her belly. It was late afternoon, and they'd been on the move since early morning. When she finally shook the sleep from her head, she smiled, embarrassed by the intensity of her dream, and confused by its implications. She'd had no lovers but Jesse, and at twenty-eight, her hormones were in overdrive.

Somewhere over Missouri, Jack had explained his hunch that they might find Leon Black in Nevis. Without revealing Mac's involvement, he'd said the embezzled funds had been tracked to that small island. The picture identification that revealed Black's real name wasn't all that clear. Jack needed Sarah to identify him.

"The money is the key," he'd explained. "Find it, and we may get out of this mess yet."

Jack had been to St. Kitts several times, years earlier, at first as a Navy Seal, when he'd taken shore leave there. Now, late afternoon still hovering on turquoise water below, he could see St. Kitts, the "Mother" of the Caribbean on the horizon, with its sister island, Nevis, lying just beyond.

Though he and Sarah had been fortunate with last minute connections, they'd still lost four time zones heading east from Las Vegas. He'd managed to sleep in fitful intervals during the day, catching up on his loss from the night before. Sarah, too, had slept intermittently since he explained to her why they had to leave her child and board a plane, traveling thousands of miles on the spur of the moment.

She'd accepted his explanation without objection, and her trust in him was obvious. The simple pleasure of having her sleep peacefully, resting against his shoulder, recalled for Jack some happier times in his life. Times less lonely, perhaps, he mused. The short time that he and Claire were able to spend together, came back to him like a flash flood from one of Las Vegas' unexpected summer showers.

"It's beautiful," Sarah whispered, leaning across him and craning to see out the small window. Jack inhaled a heady mixture of Sarah's perfume and the smell of her hair at close proximity, and tried to focus on what problems lie ahead for them.

"Yes," he responded, "but I doubt we'll have much time for sight-seeing." He regretted his comment immediately, as a flash of the rebuked child crossed Sarah's eyes. "What I mean is we're going to be pretty busy finding this Leon Black. But, of course we'll get to see some of the island in the process." It seemed to satisfy her, and she smiled broadly at him.

Once through customs, they caught an island cab to the hotel that Jack had asked his secretary, Stella, to book. He'd called her on the way to the airport, asking her to book two rooms at the City Resort in St. Kitts for them. Jack selected the small resort, situated on a bluff at the west end of the main street in Basseterre, for its convenience to the hub of the city, and its commanding view of the port.

The City Resort catered to businessmen moving through the Caribbean, and a few tourists who wanted to remain in closer proximity to the airport than the outlying, larger plantation resorts would afford them. It was simple, and by French standards would be considered clean, with its suites cascading down the hillside from the main lobby. The entire exterior of the structure was painted a bright blue, with contrasting white trim; an eye sore anywhere but in the islands. Small terraces jutted out from each room, overlooking both the city and the ocean. You could see Nevis in the distance, a forty minute ride by water taxi.

The woman at a small registration desk in the hotel's lobby had the look of a native. Her accent was a curious cross between French, and the slow moving, almost lyrical English slang of that part of the world. She fussed over her registration cards as Summers took in his surroundings. The lobby wasn't much larger than his living room back in Vegas, but was open to the outside, and tastefully decorated in bright colors contrasting against dark, mahogany trim and furniture.

Sarah, for her part, looked the part of a child in the toy department of Macy's at Christmas. From the moment they'd left the plane, she was lost in the sights and smells of the tropical island. St. Kitts, like so many of the islands of the Caribbean, was a mixture of volcanic rain forest and sprawling sugar plantations, all rolling down to the abrupt coastline of the ocean. Unlike many of the islands farther to the west and south, the topography of the bulk of St. Kitts allowed for few natural beaches. Most of the island, except for the southeast peninsula, came to a rocky and precipitous halt at the sea. Robert Bradshaw International airport found itself nestled in a cradle of land that spilled more gradually down to the island's main port. A temporary pier served as the primary docking point now, the massive docking facility for cruise ships having fallen victim to one of the many hurricanes that changed the face of the island from time to time.

"Is there some problem with our reservation?" Jack asked politely, after the receptionist had completed her third shuffle of the three by five cards which were the apparent extent of the hotel's reservation log.

"You said you'd reserved two suites?" the receptionist queried with a smile.

"Yes. Two suites, both under the name of Summers," Jack replied.

"I'm sorry, Mr. Summers," she said, "the day girl has situated you in our Queen's Suite. It has a large master bedroom, with a small, second bedroom directly off the common area of the suite on the opposite side. It was the only vacancy we had, I'm afraid. Will you and Mrs. Summers be expecting someone else?" She smiled and looked alternately back and forth between Sarah and Jack. "It's a lovely accommodation, really."

There was a momentary pause as Jack looked at Sarah apologetically.

"No," Sarah said finally, "that will be fine. But it's Ms. Dunn and Mr. Summers."

To Jack, she whispered that "this is getting to be a habit with us," and smiled.

The diminutive receptionist looked relieved, and rang a bell on the desk, summoning an elderly porter.

It's a good thing we don't have much luggage, Jack thought as the hotel's employee listed under the weight of Sarah's single suitcase. Jack insisted on carrying his own luggage. The porter led them through a maze of hallways, at times going up stairs, and then ultimately down what Jack guessed to be one level, to the double doors marked Queen's Suite.

The interior walls of the hotel were covered in stucco, in varying degrees of decay; painted a kaleidoscope of yellows, oranges, and blues. Jack was pleasantly surprised when, with a flourish, the aging porter swung open double doors to the main living area of the suite. Like the hotel's lobby, the trim and crown molding of the suite was done in dark, mahogany wood. It contrasted against the pale yellow of the rooms, much like the cool blast of the air-conditioned room felt a world apart from the humidity of the open air lobby and passageways.

"Should I unpack for you?" the porter asked, looking to Jack.

"No, that won't be necessary," Jack replied, handing him a twenty dollar bill, and wishing he'd thought to pick up some change when they'd switched planes in Atlanta.

The old man smiled, revealing dark gaps where several teeth should have resided. He bowed quickly and backed from the room, pulling the doors closed as he left.

"Just made his day," Jack commented.

When he turned back to the room, he could see that Sarah had already discovered the balcony off of the living room. She'd pushed back the curtains, allowing the view of the ocean, with Nevis on the horizon, to become part of their suite.

"It's incredible!" she said, as he joined her on the balcony. "I've never seen anything so beautiful." The look of wonder in her eyes took Jack by surprise. He'd traveled extensively, both during and since his Navy years, and had long ago lost the sense of excitement that a place like St. Kitts could bring a person with Sarah's limited experience. They stood side by side in silence, taking in the vista as twilight settled on the harbor below.

Leaning into the tropical breeze, Jack recalled his previous trips to St. Kitts. Having seen the island for the first time while in the Navy, he'd returned a few times on vacation with Claire. The last trip brought him there the year after Claire died. He'd spent two weeks at Mary's Pub, without a sober minute to show for it. Except for the now abandoned concrete moorings of the destroyed cruise-liner dock, the island hadn't changed much in ten years.

Jack moved Sarah's suitcase into the master bedroom. It was a spacious affair, with its own balcony commanding the same view as the living room. His own small case was deposited in the second bedroom, with access only to the interior living quarters and a small bathroom and shower. Servants quarters, Jack mused, just what the lawyer deserves.

They both settled into their respective space, Jack showering quickly and changing into white linen slacks, coupled with what passed these days as his only island shirt. He looked the part of a typical American tourist.

Jack could hear through the open door to her bedroom that Sarah was still showering as he made himself a drink at the suite's small bar. In lieu of his normal scotch and water, he poured a generous splash of rum on ice, topping it with a just enough Coke to give it a little color. He dialed for the international operator, and moments later heard Mac's booming voice telling him to "speak or forever hold your peace."

"Mac, it's Jack," he said.

"Jacko, my main man," Mac shouted into the phone. "You been watching the news? One of AmCon Title's employees turned up dead. It was the title officer, Roger Temple."

"I heard, Mac," Jack responded. "The escrow officer, Ashley Roh, got roughed up yesterday by one of the players in this deal. I'm in St. Kitts with Sarah Dunn right now. I'm hoping to find the guy who impersonated Marcel DeMartes. His name is Leon Black, and he's recently from Orlando, Florida. Think you could run his name through your system, and get me some background?"

The system to which Jack referred was a sophisticated computer network that would allow Mac's casino employers to develop a fairly detailed profile on almost anyone who, Mac liked to joke, "farted" in the United States, and most of the remainder of the civilized world. It was essential that the house maintain its edge by knowing who came to try and win their money.

"I can do that. Where do I reach you?" Mac replied.

"I'm at the City Hotel in Basseterre," Jack said.

Jack gave him the main desk's fax number, asking that he send the information as soon as possible.

"It should only take a couple of hours," Mac said. "Are you sure you know what you're getting into?" Jack's silence was enough response for Mac. "Don't let your little head do the thinking for your big head," Mac commented before hanging up.

Jack was still smiling at the comment, when Sarah entered the room. She was wrapped up in one of the hotel's white, cotton robes, drying her hair.

"Everything alright? What's so funny?" she asked.

"Just spoke with a friend in Las Vegas," Jack replied. "He'll get us some more information on Leon Black by morning. Can I get you a drink?"

Sarah said she'd have what he was having, and returned to her room to dress. He guessed she'd wanted to see how he'd dressed, before selecting her outfit. It was one of those feminine wiles that Claire had used on him in their years together. When Sarah reentered the room, she was wearing a pale yellow sun dress; a wrap around piece that tied with a wide belt at her waist. The contrast with her Las Vegas tan and auburn hair was stunning.

"You look lovely," Jack said candidly, and she blushed at the compliment. Handing her the rum and Coke he'd made for her, he said, "Why don't you call and check on Adam."

He could see the look of relief in her eyes. She'd been wanting to, but didn't want to be a bother, and wasn't sure how to make the international call. With Jack's help, she made the call and spoke softly for several minutes, first with her neighbor, then with her son. The tone of her voice changed perceptibly as she talked with Adam, as only a mother's could, sending comfort and reassurance across the miles that separated them. Hanging up the phone, she smiled broadly at Jack.

"Everything's fine," she said.

"We should get some food before it gets too late," Jack suggested, and Sarah agreed.

Jack had the front desk call for a cab, and a short time later they were headed west, along the coast road towards Old Town. Old Town is the site of one of St. Kitts' original plantation settlements, and had served as its capital prior to Basseterre. On their left, the expanse of the Caribbean spread to the west and south, dark now but for the moonlight highlighting gentle surf on the rocky coast. To the right side of the cab, Mt. Liamuiga, the island's dormant volcano, rose ominously to dominate the skyline. A little farther down the ever-winding two lane road would be Brimstone Hill, the site of a now abandoned English fort. Situated eight hundred feet above the shoreline, it stood as a silent reminder of the island's violent past.

During the heyday of the sugar barons, the fort, known as the "Gibraltar of the West Indies," had commanded a large portion of the trade routes, and protected the valuable sugar interests of Mother England.

Jack directed the cab driver to a locals' restaurant he knew was nestled along the south shore. From the outside, it had the look of what you'd see in a big city slum. Odds and ends of corrugated metal formed a makeshift wall that shielded the dining area from the highway. The restaurant boasted an ocean view from an array of wooden picnic style tables. On one end was a counter. Behind that, there were several half-barrel grills, sizzling with an array of fresh whole lobster and red snapper.

The native fisherman caught their fare daily, cooking the feast each night for a loyal following of locals. It wasn't the kind of place you'd find in a tourist brochure. Jack escorted Sarah to an open table and walked to the counter, ordering a combination of lobster and fish, garnished with fresh corn and black beans. He grabbed two bottles of Heineken, and joined Sarah.

"Not very fancy, but the food's the best you can get here," he said as he slid into the seat opposite her.

The two of them stuck out in the local crowd like a sore thumb, but no one seemed to notice. A large table behind them held a sprawling family of islanders, dressed for and celebrating the birthday of a young girl.

"It's perfect," Sarah said. "The smell here is delicious. I'm suddenly starving."

An hour later, they were heading back towards Basseterre, and Jack asked Sarah if she wanted to make one more stop before they returned to the hotel. During the course of dinner, he'd recalled for her his previous visit to St. Kitts and Nevis. This led into a discussion of his Navy days, and then, at Sarah's insistence, to Claire. She now knew a thumbnail sketch of his history, much as he knew hers.

He directed the cab to one of the small streets that run off of the Circus, a central hub in downtown Basseterre. It was so named as a tribute to Piccadilly Circus in London, and is dominated by the Berkeley Memorial Clock, a clock tower at the center of its round-about. As the cab rounded a sharp corner on the narrow passageway, Jack saw the familiar sign, swinging in the night breeze above the door of Mary's Pub. The pub's owners were British ex-patriots, Tony and Mary Dunhill. Now in their sixties, they'd come to St. Kitts in the late seventies. A pair of free spirits, even by the standards of those days, Jack thought. He'd formed a lasting friendship with them.

Jack pushed open the weathered wooden door to the pub, revealing its dark interior. The whole establishment wasn't more than twenty by thirty, including the bar that ran along the far end. As the door opened, conversation came to an abrupt halt. The eclectic gathering of natives, misplaced tourists, and a few permanent European locals turned to see who'd entered their domain. Tony Dunhill, standing behind the bar, broke the silence.

"Mother," he shouted to his wife, seated at the end of the bar, "pay the insurance premium, and call for the constable. I believe Jack Summers just darkened our door."

Mary Dunhill met him on a dead run in the middle of the room, arms wide open. Jack braced for the collision, and was able to maintain his balance as she engulfed him in a bear hug. It was only then that she noticed Sarah, standing behind Jack.

"Relax, Mr. Dunhill. I do believe someone's finally caught our Jack," Mary shouted over her shoulder to her husband as she smiled at Sarah.

"Welcome, my dear," Mary said. "Let me get you a proper seat at the bar. This slug can fend for himself. He's been here before."

They settled into the small bar crowd like old friends. Introductions were made all around, and the conversation flowed as easy as the liquor. No one mentioned Claire. Jack took the opportunity to pass Leon Black's photo around the group, in hopes that someone had seen him on the island. No one had, but Dunhill took a copy of it and assured Jack that he'd be the first to know if Black showed his face.

As they stood to go, hours later, Mary pulled Jack aside, telling him that he'd found a real keeper in Sarah. Jack started to protest that their relationship was "business" in nature, but Mary just smiled.

"Keep telling yourself that, lad," Mary said, slapping him on the back as they left the pub, "and you'll prove yourself dumber than the drunk I kicked out of here years ago."

It was after midnight when Sarah and Jack finally reached their hotel. There was an awkward moment as they entered the empty suite, lights dimmed and the bed in the master bedroom turned back.

"Apparently they didn't take our request for two bedrooms seriously," Jack remarked, looking to his darkened room. "I think I'll have a nightcap, Sarah. Care for one?"

She hesitated, but then said, "I should probably turn in, Jack. Thanks for a wonderful night."

She turned and pulling the door closed behind her, was gone.

"Nice going Summers!" Jack cursed to himself. Probably scared the shit out of her! This is a lady you need to take some time with, he thought.

During his wild days before meeting Claire, Jack hadn't taken any woman seriously. They were there to have fun with; not to be treated as you would a close friend, or even worse, understood. Claire had opened a whole new world to him. She'd taught him the magic of a good woman. They weren't really like men at all. She'd shown him that if you took the time, and made the effort, their depth of understanding of the human side of any situation was unparalleled in the male circles he inhabited.

After Claire's death, Jack had shut himself off to the world of women. He'd dated and slept with some, but never opened himself as he did with

Claire. He'd seen that same magic in Sarah when they first met, but hadn't recognized it fully until that night.

As Jack poured himself a large glass of Grand Marnier from the half bottle Dunhill shoved in his arms as he left the pub that night, Sarah was showering again. He could hear the water running, and involuntarily pictured her naked in the adjoining room. He moved to the balcony off the living room, glass in hand. Sipping the sweet orange liquor, he savored its familiar burn.

He left the French doors to the suite open behind him. The night had cooled, and a sweet breeze blew across the balcony. Three floors below, he could see the hotel's still lighted common pool shimmering in the shadows of several Queen palms.

Lost in his own analysis of the last twenty-four hours, ever the lawyer recalling details, he didn't hear her until she stepped onto the terrace with him. Reflexes, honed by hundreds of hours of training, caused him to spin, easing into a defensive stance. She was standing in the moonlight in front of him, clad in red silk pajamas. Her green eyes sparkled as she reached for his hand, pulling him toward her. They kissed, long and deep. Jack felt the arch of her back as her pelvis moved against him.

The night seemed to spin away from them. It crossed his mind for an instant that he was breaching a line with steps that couldn't be retraced. But, moving with her onto the floor of the living area, and later into her bed, he harbored no doubt that he'd made the right choice. Their hunger for each other consumed the balance of the night until, just before dawn, they slept.

A few miles to the east, Leon Black slept soundly for the first time in years. Ensconced in his room at Frigate Bay, he rested with the knowledge that the last person he thought could connect him with his scam in Las Vegas lie dead in a police morgue, now a permanently silenced witness. With Jesse dead, he saw no other connection that would lead anyone to Leon Black, wealthy investor and new resident of the West Indies. A man could still live a long time like a king on four million dollars in this part of the world. And Leon considered himself just the man to do it.

Several thousand miles to the west, Sam Marchesi received a report from Jim Eccles' security people that they'd monitored a phone conversation at Jack's office, early that same day. Summers had instructed his secretary to make reservations for himself, and another person, at the City Hotel in St. Kitts. In a fashion all too common to the service industry in Las Vegas, the message had taken nearly twenty hours to reach Marchesi. He placed an immediate call to certain associates in Miami. One of their representatives would be on the morning flight to the small island the next morning.

Jack, a habitual early riser, woke as the light of the tropical sun filtered into the Queen's Suite. Sarah lay next to him, sleeping quietly. The sight of her naked, partially covered by the bedding, caused an instantaneous stir in his groin. He brushed the soft underside of her breast, causing her to move, but not waken.

There was much to do, and Jack quietly left her to sleep as he moved to the second bedroom. He showered quickly and dressed, on his way to the reception desk thirty minutes later. He wore the only suit he owned that could pass for tropical. It was a cream colored, light weight linen, two-piece that he'd acquired several years before on a Bar Association trip to Miami. He found the night clerk still on duty in the lobby, and asked to see any fax transmissions directed to Jack Summers.

The clerk returned a few minutes later with a concise, three page dossier on Leon Black. Mac's system had been amazingly efficient. Leon's life story was sketched out in single spaced detail, with everything from social security number, driving records, and credit history, to the names and addresses of living relatives and some friends who'd acted as references for him in the past. It was just what Jack hoped for.

He gathered some fresh coffee and rolls from a small cart in the lobby, and, tucking the report into the coat of his suit, returned to their room. When he opened the door, Sarah was standing in the doorway to the bedroom, her white robe wrapped around her.

"I thought you'd left me," she said, a hurt look on her face.

"Sorry, Sarah," he replied. "You were sleeping so soundly, I didn't want to wake you. I've got some hot coffee and fresh rolls here. I'd like to catch the first boat to Nevis if we can."

"Jack," Sarah said softly, her piercing green eyes freezing his in place. "I think we should talk about last night. That's not something I would normally do..."

Jack interrupted her. "I want to talk about last night. Hopefully, over many more nights that will each struggle to compare with it. But, now is not the time. We've come a long way to get you, and several others, out of a real problem back in Vegas. Our window of opportunity will be relatively short."

She offered no resistance, and turned to the task of getting dressed. Jack arranged for their cab driver to pick them up in front of the lobby at eight o'clock. That would allow them to reach the first ferry, the Queen Caribe, in time to depart for Nevis. They made it with minutes to spare. Sarah had dressed casually, in a loose skirt topped with a tightly-fitted blouse, tied together at her mid-section. With little time to prepare, she'd pulled her hair back into a pony-tail, still wet from the morning's shower.

She held Jack's hand as they stepped on to the ferry, a token reminder of the intimacy they'd shared. With the prevailing wind in their face, the crossing to Nevis took about forty-five minutes.

They disembarked at Charleston, capital city of the island. Looking up on the hillside, Jack pointed out to Sarah the decaying replica of the birth place of Alexander Hamilton, first United States Secretary of the Treasury, and signer of the Declaration of Independence. Their cab driver had claimed to be a direct descendant of the famous American, and they shared a laugh together over the thought of it, walking up the cobblestone street towards the building that housed "Caribbean Holdings, Ltd."

Chapter Twenty Six

Leon woke to the sound of the maid knocking incessantly on the door to his room. After shouting her away, he lay back in the king-sized bed, and began planning the rest of his life. He ordered room service, a continental breakfast and coffee, and moved to the balcony off his room. It was a spectacular day; sun shining, with a light breeze from the south. Nevis rose from the horizon across the water, and he could see the eight o'clock ferry, the Queen Caribe, making its way towards the sister island.

He thought of the island girl at Caribbean Holdings, Coral, and decided to call her. The company wouldn't be opening until nine, but that would give him time to relax and enjoy his breakfast. Maybe he'd meet her that night for drinks at the Four Seasons Resort on Nevis. It was a spectacular property, and occasional vacation home to movie stars and other dignitaries. After all, Leon thought to himself, I'm a sort of dignitary now. Who knows where the night may lead?

As Leon nibbled on the remains of a croissant, the morning flight of American Airlines left Miami for San Juan, Puerto Rico. On board was a large, black man. Dressed casually, his powerful shoulders overlapped the seats on either side of him. He'd been employed by Florida associates of Sam Marchesi for years. Receiving a phone call late the previous evening, he'd packed a small case and reserved his flight. His instructions were to find Jack Summers and his traveling companion. He was told to maintain surveillance until they led him to a man fitting the DeMartes imposter's description. He had only a general description, no picture, but was told that Summers would be staying at the City Hotel in Basseterre. With the lay-over connection in Puerto Rico, he would arrive in St. Kitts by three o'clock that afternoon.

Jack and Sarah entered the offices of Caribbean Holdings, Limited, shortly after it opened at nine. Their walk up from the pier was an easy one. The narrow streets of Charleston were lined with small shops, spreading like so many spider webs to catch the passing tourists. A pleasant looking native girl greeted them as they approached her desk.

"Good morning. How may I be of assistance on this beautiful day?" she asked.

"I'm hoping that you can help me locate a friend of mine," Jack answered. "He's recently settled either here, or on St. Kitts. My wife and I are on holiday, and would like to surprise him. Unfortunately, we don't know where he's staying. He did, however tell us that he'd been doing some investing with you folks. We thought maybe you'd have a local address on him."

With that, Jack gave her his most ingratiating smile, and held his breath. The girl hesitated for a moment, as if weighing the propriety of giving them any information about a client of the company. A nice couple she thought; there could be no harm in hooking them up with a friend of theirs.

"What's your friend's name?" she inquired.

Jack could see the look of recognition in her eyes when he gave her Leon's name. As she was about to answer, she was interrupted by a tall gentleman who'd walked up behind her.

"I'm Ernest Drover, managing director for the company. How may I help you?"

Jack repeated his story to Drover, who listened, expressionless. He then asked Jack and Sarah to join him in his office. Summers knew the drill before he even heard Drover's apologetic refusal of their request for any information about the company's clients.

Of course Drover would "love to assist them," he'd said, "but, unfortunately, all information about the clients of Caribbean Holdings is held in the strictest of confidence."

Jack even tried to tempt him by suggesting that their friend had highly recommended the company, and that they might also be interested in transferring a substantial amount of their own funds to Caribbean. It was to no avail. Drover remained adamant that he could divulge no information, nor could he even acknowledge that Leon Black was indeed a customer.

Jack thanked him, trying to disguise his own disappointment. Sarah had remained quiet throughout his conversation with Drover. And, as Jack shook hands with the manager, thanking him again for his time, she stepped away briefly to converse with the receptionist.

Back on the street, Jack said, "Looks like we'll have to stake out the office. Maybe Black will come back." It would be a long shot.

"Maybe not," Sarah said softly, unable to contain a broad smile.

She handed him a piece of note paper, folded once. Opening it, Jack saw in flowing script, "Leon Black, Frigate Bay Resort, Ste. 320, St. Kitts." It was obvious that the receptionist, away from the prying eyes of the company's pompous manager, didn't share his need for secrecy when it came to people like Jack and Sarah.

"She told me he just called her," Sarah said. "They're meeting for drinks tonight at the Four Seasons resort about a mile from here, up the coast. She's invited us to join them!"

Jack pulled Sarah close, kissing her full on the lips. "You're a magician!" he exclaimed.

"Just one of my many talents," she replied, blushing.

Jack grabbed her hand, and they were off. Retracing their route down the hill to the ferry dock, they were just able to catch the ten o'clock boat back to St. Kitts. By eleven, they were passing through the Treasury Building, a small structure at the end of the pier that served as port of entry to the island. Jack recognized one of the guards posted there, a native they'd met the night before at Jack & Mary's pub.

"No sign of him yet," the guard said as Jack approached him. "Dunhill asked me to keep a lookout for the guy in the picture you showed us last night. I'll call your hotel if I see him."

"We may already have a line on him, but thanks," Jack responded, shaking the guard's hand. "Your help is greatly appreciated. He may slip by us."

"Nothing slips by me. This is all I do all day, and I do it well." He tipped his helmet to Sarah, as a sort of salute, and added, "You've got a lovely glow about you this morning, Miss Sarah. If you don't mind me saying so."

For the second time that morning, Sarah blushed deeply.

Jack thanked him again, and pulled Sarah toward a grouping of taxis near the entrance to the building. As the aging cab wound its way through the hills southeast of Basseterre, Summers explained what he hoped to accomplish to Sarah. She listened attentively, asking no questions. He asked her to verify Black's identity if they found him at the address they'd been given, and then leave him alone to discuss resolution of their problem with Black. She agreed, not understanding how Jack would convince Black to part with his newly found fortune.

The Frigate Bay Club, a resort a few miles from the capital, sat overlooking its own inlet and sand beach on the way to the island's newly developing southeastern peninsula. The Club's cottage suites stair-stepped up the side of a hill, with each room sporting its own open air veranda facing the sea. When they arrived, Jack instructed the cab driver to wait for them, handing him several bills sufficient to insure his compliance.

They approached the double doors to suite 320 and, with Sarah standing to one side, Jack knocked. After a few minutes, he could hear Black's voice from inside telling him to "go away, and make up the room later."

"It's the hotel manager," Jack said. "We've got a minor problem with your passport, Mr. Black. I need to speak with you for a moment."

Jack could hear movement from inside the suite, and finally, after what seemed like an eternity, he heard the door's bolt slide back and the door opened. Jack's first thought was that Black looked younger than the photos he'd seen on the copies of his identification that Jesse gave Sarah. Several inches shorter than Jack, with salt and pepper hair, he was dressed in one of the hotel's white cotton robes.

Black stared at Summers, who looked decidedly not like the manager of a Caribbean resort, and took a step back into the suite. As he did so, Jack moved into the room's perimeter, motioning with one hand for Sarah to step within view. She did so, and from over his shoulder he heard her whisper "it's him."

All color drained from Black's face as he caught sight of Sarah. Jack thought for a moment that he'd either faint, or start puking his guts out. Instead, he retreated farther into the suite, as if doing so would somehow make him disappear before their eyes. Jack followed him into the room, and turned, smiling to Sarah. He closed the doors behind him, and was alone with the elusive Leon Black.

When he turned back to face him, Jack caught a glimpse of Black swinging one of the small lamps from a night stand at him. Reflexively, rather than moving back to avoid the blow as an untrained fighter might, Summers stepped towards Black. This maneuver would cause his assailant to overshoot his mark, and at the same time allowed Jack to divert the strike with a rising block to the inside of Black's arm.

As the focused force of his defensive move collided with the uncontrolled arch of Leon's assault, the lamp launched from his hand, smashing into pieces against the wall behind Jack. Using the defensive strike to shift his weight, Summers spun counter clock-wise against his attacker, and brought an elbow into the side of Leon's jaw. He dropped like a bag of marbles to the floor of the suite.

When Leon regained consciousness a few minutes later, he found that Jack had moved him to one of the suite's over-stuffed chairs. His ears were ringing as he tried to orient himself. Summers was seated opposite him on a large Rattan couch.

"Pardon the intrusion, Mr. Black," Jack said amiably. "Or is it 'Mr. DeMartes'?"

Eyes shifting wildly around the room, a trapped animal, all Leon could muster was a quick denial of what on earth Jack was talking about. He thought of again taking the offensive, rising to his feet in outrage at Jack's attack, but sank back into the chair as Summers rose to face him. Jack again took his seat.

"Listen very carefully, Leon," Jack said. "What I'm about to say, and what you will then do, could save your life."

The controlled tone of Jack's voice left no doubt that he was deadly serious. Black, with no apparent options at the moment, sat back to hear what he had to say. The side of his head was pounding where he'd been hit, and his eyes still watered heavily. Jack knew that there's an art to taking an unexpected blow, but Leon clearly hadn't mastered it. For the next several minutes, without interruption from Leon, Jack laid out what he knew about Black's scam in Las Vegas.

He told Leon that he was an attorney, representing the interests of AmCon Title. As a result of Leon's ruse, Jack's clients stood to lose a great deal of money and would be put in jeopardy by the State of Nevada of losing its license to do business.

"Sounds like you've got a real problem there, mister. But hell will freeze over before any court in this part of the world gets its hands on that money. That, of course, assumes you are right about me," Leon interjected.

Jack listened to Leon quietly. When he'd finished, Jack began again. He pointed out that the stolen money actually belonged to a group backed by Sam Marchesi, a well known crime figure in Las Vegas. He asked Leon if he knew that his former associate, Jesse, had already been murdered along with Roger Temple in Las Vegas. The look on Leon's face told Jack that he already knew this.

"Look, Leon," Jack said quietly, "I think your scheme would have worked beautifully if the money had belonged to anyone but Marchesi's group. It's bad luck, really. But now you've got to be reasonable. I only want the money. If I can return it promptly, my clients will be absolved of their troubles, and I'll be a happy guy. I didn't come here to do violence to you, and I apologize for our little altercation. But I can promise you that the next group of people to visit you on this will want to hurt you in the worst way. They'll get their money, and you'll die a very nasty, slow death. And what's worse, my clients will still have to face a pile of legal problems at home. We don't want that, do we?"

Leon found himself almost becoming empathetic to Jack's problem as he listened to the persuasive man sitting across from him. He was very convincing.

"What if I just disappear?" Leon said after a minute.

Jack reached inside his coat, and Leon recoiled at the movement. When he pulled the three page dossier from his pocket, Leon visibly relaxed. "What I have here is your life story," Jack said. "No, it's not the fairy tale you created in Vegas. This is Leon Black, and how to find him. Your idea for stealing the money in Las Vegas was creative. However, your execution of the getaway was sloppy. I found you rather easily. If you don't cooperate with me, a copy of this will reach the wrong people within the hour.

I can imagine, with all of Marchesi's contacts around the world, that he'll have no problem tracking you down. For the moment, Ms. Dunn and I are the only people still living who can connect Leon Black to his counterpart in the Anasazi deal. Daryl McKenna doesn't know your true identity, and he's no where to be found. I suspect he may never be if Marchesi catches up to him."

Leon considered Jack's statement. Jack could sense the wheels turning in his head, a trapped rat frantically looking for an out. Then he spoke.

"What do I get if I cooperate. I can't leave empty handed."

"I agree," Jack responded, leaning forward in his chair, almost as a financial counselor would.

"You should have approximately four point two million in your account at Caribbean Holdings, I'm guessing," Jack continued. "I will need to verify that by seeing your account book. I'm prepared to leave you with, say, fifty thousand, on which to run away and hide. With a big enough head-start, and of course my promise that this dossier will be destroyed, you should be able to extricate yourself from this mess rather handily."

He could see the surprise in Leon's eyes when Jack mentioned his depository account.

"That's not enough!" Leon protested. "I'll need twice that amount to disappear. Besides, I had some expenses. There's only four million one left."

"You drive a hard bargain, Mr. Black," Jack said, smiling. "Here's what we'll do."

Jack told Leon that after verifying the balance of his account, Leon would call Caribbean Holdings and instruct Mr. Drover to liquidate it into negotiable bearer bonds, in one hundred thousand dollar denominations. He and Jack would be at Drover's office by two o'clock, assuming they caught the one o'clock ferry. Leon would then receive one of the bonds, and be free to disappear. Jack would take the remaining funds back to Vegas, and negotiate a settlement of all claims against his clients.

"What assurance do I have that you won't turn me in, once you've got the money?" Leon asked, still desperately trying to calculate any other options he might have at that point.

"You have my word on it," Summers responded, with a look that told Leon not to consider questioning his word.

After another few minutes of attempts to think his way out of his predicament, Leon agreed. Better to take something away safely, than to gamble that Summers was bluffing. He didn't seem the type. Leon dialed the number for Caribbean Holdings, and spoke briefly with Ernest Drover. Jack could tell from the one-sided conversation he was privy to, that Drover wasn't all that happy about losing such a recent large deposit. In the end, however, he agreed that Leon could pick up the bonds at three that afternoon.

While Jack conducted his negotiations with Leon, Sarah waited in the resort's open air lobby. She couldn't figure out how he would convince Black to turn over the stolen funds, but had absolute confidence that he would. She knew she could fall in love with Jack, and maybe already had. She found herself thinking about what kind of a father he'd make for Adam, and what their lives together would be like.

The night with him had been like nothing she'd ever imagined. She squirmed in the lobby chair she occupied and blushed again. With Adam in her thoughts, she looked at her watch to calculate what time it would be in Las Vegas. She wanted to call, but didn't want to wake him, given the time change. I'll call tonight, she thought, and let her thoughts drift back to Jack.

Jack waited as Black dressed, and they walked together to find Sarah waiting in the lobby of his hotel.

"Hello, Ms. Dunn," Leon said smiling, as he and Jack crossed the lobby to where Sarah was seated. "It's a pleasure to see you again."

Sarah didn't know how to respond to this man who'd turned her world upside down in the last few days, so she said nothing. Jack directed the small group to the waiting cab, and in minutes they were on their way back to the city dock.

Jack sent Sarah back to their hotel to wait, while he and Leon caught the water taxi back to Nevis. After collecting the bearer bonds at Caribbean Holdings, enduring yet more protest from Ernest Drover, they were on their way back to St. Kitts on the four o'clock ferry. Leon had ignored the receptionist, Coral, not bothering to cancel their date at the Four Seasons later that evening. Jack gave her a smile on the way out of the office, mouthing the words "thank you" out of her boss' line of sight.

Se la vie, thought Leon.

At the Treasury Building back in St. Kitts, Leon made a desperate attempt to escape with the large envelope containing over four million dollars in bonds. As he and Jack were exiting the building, Leon broke away, approaching one of the guards, and claiming that Summers had "stolen his files on the ferry." To Leon's absolute astonishment, the guard simply tipped his helmet to Jack as he quickly joined the frantic Leon.

"That seems very unlikely, I'm afraid," the guard replied. "We're quite familiar with Mr. Summers. I don't believe he's capable of such a disgraceful act. I do, however, think that you should join me for a strip search in customs. You're obviously irrational, and who knows what you may be trying to smuggle onto our island." Smiling at Jack, the guard took Leon by the arm, leading him back into the interior of the building. Jack waved, and left the building to join Sarah at the hotel, bonds in hand.

The black man from Miami was waiting near the cab stand. Jack noticed him, a sixth sense causing him to quickly evaluate the huge stranger who paid a little too much attention to him as he hailed a taxi. He was ready to approach him, when the stranger turned and disappeared into the Treasury Building.

Sarah pulled open the door to the Queen's Suite as Jack fumbled with his key.

"I'm so glad you're back," she said, wrapping her arms around him. "I was worried."

"Nothing to worry about," Jack replied. "We've got the goods, and we'll be out of here on the morning flight." The thought of another night together flashed across both their faces.

"I told the hotel's assistant manager that you'd gone to Nevis, but would be back soon," Sarah said as she moved towards the room's small bar. "He said he needed to check on some reservations you'd made. I hope it wasn't a surprise." Jack froze in his tracks.

"What did this 'manager' look like?" he asked innocently.

"He was a large black man," she said. "It's funny though, he didn't sound like he's from here. Not like the others, anyway."

Without reacting, he went to the phone and attempted to get them on the late flight out to San Juan. It was booked. The earliest flight off the island would be their scheduled one at eight in the morning. There'll be little sleep tonight, he thought, and all for the wrong reasons.

"What's the matter, Jack?" Sarah queried. "Don't you want another night in this paradise?" Her feelings were obviously bruised.

"No, Sarah, it's not that," he replied. "I just wanted to see if we could move our departure up. If it were possible, we'd be back in Vegas by early afternoon, and have a chance at putting the legal mess behind us tomorrow. But it looks like it will have to wait. Let's have a drink. I think we should dine in our room, if you don't mind."

"That suits me perfectly," she said smiling. "Will you be taking advantage of me again tonight?" she asked playfully.

Jack smiled, tossing the four million dollar envelope onto the couch like so much junk mail, and taking her in his arms.

"I'll make the drinks," he said. "Why don't you slip into something very casual while I make a few phone calls?"

She was off to the bedroom, and he poured two strong drinks. He dialed his office, connecting after a few minutes with his secretary. They went briefly through his phone messages, and he gave her instructions on whom to call back, relaying status on pending cases. One name surprised him. It was a call from Dominic Belcastro, and he wanted to see Jack as soon as possible.

Jack had known the Belcastro family for years back in Chicago. Dominic, or "Dean" as he was commonly known, was one of six sons born to Angelina and Raymond Belcastro. On more occasions than Jack liked to recall, he'd made a late night journey to the Cook County detention center to extricate one or more of the older Belcastro boys from the long arm of the law. Dean had still been a youngster when Jack left Chicago, probably twelve or thirteen. But even at that age, Jack remembered the hard look in the boy's eyes. A look of trouble, searching for a place to land. Apparently he'd landed in Las Vegas.

Surprised when he heard that the call back number wasn't that of the Clark County jail, Jack wondered what Dean could want after all these years. He still received a Christmas card each year from Dean's mother. Jack mused that if you looked up "long suffering" in the dictionary, surely you'd see a picture of Angelina Belcastro.

Just as soon as Jack had hung up the phone, it rang. It was Tony Dunhill, from the pub.

"Jack, it's Dunhill," he said. "Are you alright?"

"Yes, I'm fine," Jack answered. "Why?"

"I just heard that the man you went to Nevis with this morning was found on the rocks below his cottage at Frigate Bay," Dunhill said. "Pretty banged up, I hear. His neck was broken. Tulli says the magistrate is still trying to determine if the fall broke it, or if it was broken, then he fell." Tulli was the guard from the Treasury Building. "He also said he noticed a large, black stranger who struck out after your man when Tulli had finished giving him the search of his life this morning. I'd keep an eye on my tail if I were you."

"Thanks for the heads up," Jack said. "We're out of here on the first flight in the morning. I'll call you when I can spend more time here."

"Gator," as he was known in Miami, had arrived back at the City Hotel an hour before Dunhill's call to Jack. He'd been able to extract much helpful information from Leon, before snapping his neck and tossing his lifeless body over the balcony of his suite at Frigate Bay. Once back, Gator dialed the Las Vegas number he'd been given. He didn't know, and didn't care, who was on the other end. He relayed to his listener that Black had been located and eliminated. He also relayed that the lawyer was now in possession of the funds they'd been looking for. He listened carefully to instructions from the man on the other end of the line, and then settled back in his room to wait.

Chapter Twenty Seven

Marchesi slapped his hand on the desk with a force that made his empty coffee cup dance and topple. Charlie jumped at the cracking sound Sam's blow made and shifted in his chair. He'd been summoned to another meeting at Marchesi's office.

When he arrived, he was surprised to find John Kirshbaum seated on the couch at one side of the room, and Jim Eccles seated in one of the chairs opposite Sam at his desk. Bruno stood in a corner of the room, facing the door. Also on the couch was a younger man; Charlie wasn't familiar with him. Sam had just finished listening to someone on the phone and hung up.

"What's the matter, Sam?" Charlie asked, as much to try and cover up his reaction to Sam's fury, as to find out what was wrong.

"I'll tell you 'what's the matter'. I can't seem to get anything done right without doing it myself," Sam replied, leaning forward in his chair. "It looks like this guy Summers has got our money now. The scammer, Leon Black was his name, is out of the picture, permanently."

"That's great," interjected Kirshbaum. "He'll bring the funds back here, and we can straighten this whole mess out." When he spoke, everyone else in the room turned in his direction, with a look like he'd just farted aloud. He was obviously out of some loop that hadn't been explained to him.

Sam had checked out Kirshbaum's background before calling him. He knew that he was a former Chicago cop, and had been on the company's payroll for years before retiring to Vegas. Sam's associates in Las Vegas had employed him at one of their casinos for several years. The word on Kirshbaum was that he was a "stand up guy." He'd play ball and do what he was told. Sam brought him into the meeting because he didn't want Kirshbaum to go off half-cocked on his own trying to get his three quarters of million out of this deal. Also, he thought he could use Kirshbaum if they needed to apply some pressure in circumstances such as seemed to have now arisen. Given the proper motivation, such as having a chance at getting his money out of the deal, Sam knew he'd do what he was told.

"I'm afraid that's not exactly what we had in mind, John," Sam said, allowing the room to relax. "You see, we kind of wanted to get the money, and the land, and the title company, all in one big package. If we do, I guarantee your end of it. If this lawyer brings the money back, we've got a real mess on our hands. We've taken certain corrective steps already, and don't feel like we should settle for just getting the dough back."

"What can we do then?" Kirshbaum asked, when no one else stepped in with a comment.

"You and Bruno go over to the broad's apartment building and find her kid. Jimbo's guys have been watching the place, and the kid didn't leave with Summers and the girl. He's got to be with one of the neighbors. You dust off one of your old cop badges, and go door to door until you find the kid. When you've got him, take him over to the junk yard. He'll be just the insurance policy we'll need to make sure Summers comes to us with the dough. He's already had it converted to negotiable bonds, so that makes it even easier. He gives them to us, and the little boy makes it home safe and sound."

"What if he goes to the police?" Eccles asked.

"He don't seem like the type to me," Sam responded. "He'd have gone to the cops after Bruno tried to snatch him in Reno. No, this guy don't trust the cops any more than I do. As a matter of fact, seeing how he's handled himself so far in this deal, I'd like to have him working for me." There was nervous laughter around the room. No one was sure if Sam was joking or not.

Turning to Dean, Sam commented, "You stay here with me, kid. I might need you to run some errands."

Bruno and Kirshbaum left first, followed closely thereafter by Jim Eccles. When they'd gone, Sam focused his attention on Charlie and Dean.

"This Summers guy and the broad gotta go after this business is concluded," he said. "I ain't so worried about him as I am the broad. She'll be upset that we took her kid. It's too bad really, but it's just business. I don't want any loose ends on this deal, so we gotta make it look like they had a little accident. Charlie, you get the other broad, Ashley what's-her-name, to Bruno and Dean. They'll take care of the rest. Tell her to meet you at your office.

Dean, once this lady with Summers gets back, I want you to pick her up and take her to the kid. Leave a message for Summers that we'll trade the lady and her kid for the bonds. No cops, no bullshit, or they disappear permanently. If I read this guy correctly, he'll come. Then you and Bruno can arrange for a little car wreck for the three of them. Bruno's got a little score to settle with Summers. I don't think he's been able to get laid since he got back from Reno. You guys okay with this?"

It wasn't a question, but a statement of fact. Both Dean and Charlie nodded. There really wasn't any choice.

When John Kirshbaum and Bruno arrived at Sarah's apartment complex, they checked in with the two men who'd been parked there, keeping the place under surveillance.

"Any sign of the kid?" Bruno asked the driver of the van.

"No sign of any of them since the lawyer and the girl left. He's got to be somewhere in the building," the driver responded.

Kirshbaum and Bruno then proceeded to go door to door in Sarah's apartment building, starting with the ground floor, and working their way up. Kirshbaum did most of the talking. He'd brought an old police badge and identification with him. It was something he'd done a thousand times as a beat cop and then a detective. Canvassing a neighborhood was routine. Most people were very cooperative. No one ever took a close look at John's identification, and everyone was eager to help out in the search for a missing child. If they happened to hear later that Adam had been kidnapped, they'd all assume that it happened before Bruno and Kirshbaum came on the scene. On their fourth apartment on the second floor, they hit pay dirt. It was Bruno who knocked on the door, having watched the repeated action of Kirshbaum.

"Open up, it's the police," Bruno shouted. "We're looking for Adam Dunn."

Not exactly how he would have worded it, Kirshbaum thought. You just can't get the thug out of some guys. They could hear movement inside the apartment of Helen James. Finally they heard a response.

"What's the matter?" Helen James asked. "Is Sarah alright?"

Kirshbaum responded that the boy's father had been killed, and Ms. Dunn wanted the boy picked up. As the old nurse slid back the deadbolt, Bruno stepped into the doorway. Her eyes bounced up Bruno's large torso as she swung the door open. She took a step back into the room, now fully awake, as Adam rounded the corner from her bedroom, teddy bear in hand.

Kirshbaum followed Bruno into the apartment quickly, and pulled the door shut behind him flashing his badge in Helen's face. Still backing away from Bruno's threatening form, Helen took Adam by the hand, and moved to a nearby couch.

"I'll need to call his mother, detective," Helen said to Kirshbaum.

"Of course, ma'am," Kirshbaum responded cordially. "Why don't you gather up the boy's belongings for us first. Then you can call Mrs. Dunn."

"What was your name, again, detective?" Helen asked, still uncomfortable with his massive partner.

"It's Johnson, ma'am," Kirshbaum lied, smiling. "We've had quite a morning trying to locate the boy." This seemed to put Helen at ease, and she rose from the couch and headed for the bedroom.

"It will just take a minute to get his things," she said. "Then I'll call Sarah. He is my responsibility."

"Of course, ma'am," John interjected. "Better safe than sorry." As Helen turned towards the bedroom, Kirshbaum nodded to Bruno. "My partner will help you with his stuff."

Helen James' life, one dedicated to helping others as a nurse for thirty years, ended without ceremony. As she entered the bedroom, Bruno on her heels, she had no time to react when his powerful arm encircled her neck. Her last earthly sensation was a strong smell of garlic on Bruno's breath. Her cervical spine snapped like a twig when he grasped her head with his free hand, and gave it a jerk sideways. Mercifully, she died in an instant. There was no cry for help, and Bruno effortlessly eased her lifeless body to the floor. In the other room, Kirshbaum smiled at Adam.

"We're gonna go see your mommy. Do you want to do that?" John said amiably.

Adam just nodded his head, sleep still half-cradling the small boy. A moment later, Bruno appeared at the bedroom door. Taking charge, Kirshbaum told him to take the boy out to the car. He'd stay behind and take care of making the apartment look like it had been burglarized. He'd been to enough crime scenes in his career to make it look convincing.

They waved to the surveillance van as Kirshbaum and Bruno drove away from Sarah's apartment, Adam safely tucked in the back seat. With the trust of a child, he hadn't even asked about Helen James.

"I need to talk to Jack Summers," the man's voice said to Jack's secretary on the phone. "It's important. My name's Dominic Belcastro. Tell him it's life or death."

"Mr. Summers is out of town at the moment," she responded. "I'll be happy to convey your message and make an appointment when he returns." Jack's secretary was used to hearing the urgency in people's voices when they called for her boss. "Where can we reach you?"

"Have him call my cell phone," Dean said, giving her the number. Before she could ask another question, the secretary heard the line go dead.

Dean was in a phone booth on Koval Avenue, a block east of the Strip. The metal enclosure was stifling, and even at that early hour, hot to the touch. Sweat beaded at Dean's forehead and trickled down the center of his back. Dean cursed his luck, wondering if he was doing the right thing. After all, if Summers had gotten himself cross-wise with a made guy like Marchesi, should it be his problem?

On the other hand, Summers had always been there to help his brothers out of some tough spots back home. Now, he was gonna get whacked, and Dean would have to be a part of it. His Catholic upbringing settled on him like a bad cold. He couldn't do it. He'd whacked a few guys himself, back in Chicago. But they deserved it. Summers didn't. Besides, this Bruno character gave him the willies. He didn't just do his job when it came to killing somebody. He enjoyed it. The problem was, how could he get out of this mess? Summers would think of something.

This Anasazi thing's spinning out of control, Charlie thought to himself as he pulled on to Industrial Avenue in his Porsche. The rear tires on the small sports car squealed as he up-shifted, and he backed off the accelerator.

"People are dropping like flies in this mess," Charlie said aloud. "First, McKenna and his wife. Then, Roger Temple and some guy who lived with him. Now, Sam wants to grab a kid, his mother and a fucking well known lawyer, for Christ's sake!"

To top it off, Charlie'd been told to lure Ashley into a trap that would end in her untimely demise. It was too much! But what alternative did he have? Sam Marchesi wasn't the kind of guy you said no to. He'd just have to go along with it, or he'd be next on the list. As he turned west on to Sahara Avenue, Charlie reached for his cell phone, dialing a local florist. There'd be three dozen roses delivered to Ashley later that morning with a note that simply said "I'm sorry!"

Sam eased back in his oversized leather desk chair. If he could get his hands on those bonds, the Anasazi deal might just work out like he'd planned, he chuckled to himself. Patek Investments would still be in first position on its Deed of Trust, since it hadn't been paid in full, and could foreclose on the property. They could then resell it, or finish development of the subdivision, at their leisure. Sam's subcontractors would be paid on their mechanics liens, and Sundown Mortgage would be the injured party in a lawsuit alleging negligence on the part of AmCon Title in allowing Patek to remain ahead of it when the refinancing loan was made.

The loss, even after any participation in the foreclosure, would be large enough to force AmCon Title into a position where it would have to either go bankrupt, or turn its operations over to Sundown. Sam would get the property, the title company, and the money.

It wasn't what he'd told Patek, but it was perfect! Since Sam controlled Sundown, he'd get the title company for himself! The key to it now, was getting the bonds from Summers. Sam hadn't lived all his many years by under estimating his adversaries. He knew that Summers was a man to be careful with. But, he also knew that he'd be flawed, and that his Achilles heel would be the woman, Sarah, and her kid.

Chapter Twenty Eight

When Sarah emerged from the bedroom, she was barefoot, and wearing a pale green Calvin Klein cotton T-shirt, over white denim shorts. Her naturally curly auburn hair hung loosely over her shoulders. Jack sat in an over-stuffed rattan lounge chair on the veranda, just outside the living room of their suite, facing the port of Basseterre. From there, you could see the lights of the small town coming on as darkness settled on the island. An assortment of small fishing boats, sailboats, and a few larger yachts, their running lights on, bobbed on anchors in the harbor. The day's last rays of sunlight gave them the appearance of toys, floating on a sparkling bed of multi-colored blue gems. The evening's breeze, an ever-present reminder that you were on a tropical island, had blown out the last vestiges of the day's heat.

Sarah walked up behind him, and saying nothing, began to massage the back of his neck. He caught the scent of her perfume in the air, and moved to stand.

"Sit still," she whispered, leaning to his ear. "You've had a tough day and deserve a little pampering."

He didn't resist. It had been a tough, but rewarding day. They'd been on the island for a little more than a day, and already he had the money he'd come for in his possession. As he sat waiting for Sarah to change clothes, he'd been going over in his mind the next steps necessary to extricate his clients from their current legal woes.

Her touch pulled him away from the world of negotiations and contracts, and into one that focused solely on the pleasure of her slender fingers working the base of his skull. Having heard the news of Black's untimely demise, Jack knew that someone would come calling on him.

But for now, they were safe behind the locked doors of their suite, and he allowed himself a moment's indulgence.

Sarah was the first woman he'd been with since Claire who'd made him drop his inner guard while they made love. Usually, except for the lost minutes bracketing his climax, Jack found himself wondering if the women he'd bedded would be worth a life time commitment, or if he needed to plan a graceful disengagement as quickly as possible. In most instances, his thoughts centered on how to keep a relationship at arms length. Each one was subconsciously compared in Jack's mind with Claire. And until Sarah, each disappointed in the end.

Jack was scanning a wine list that was a part of the room service book in their suite.

"I see they've got a nice Ferrari Caranno Chardonnay on their wine list. It's one of my favorites, and unusual to find it in this part of the world," Jack said, leaning into Sarah's hands, his eyes closed. "I was thinking we might order their sea bass with some salad, and maybe a few shrimp for appetizers."

"Umm, it sounds heavenly," she responded softly. "I don't know much about wine, but I'll trust your judgment."

"It's a California white wine," he said. "I think you'll like it. It's smooth, not too sweet, and without the bitter after-taste you find in many Chardonnays. And, it's a good compliment to seafood."

Summers was somewhat of an amateur wine expert, and kept a fully stocked wine cellar at home. Sarah moved her hands to his chest, and he caught them, pulling her around to his lap. Their eyes locked, each hesitating to ignite again the passion that had consumed the previous night. Jack leaned forward, kissing her chastely on the forehead.

"I may need all my strength tonight," he said, smiling playfully. "We should have our dinner, since we haven't eaten anything but the morning's rolls today."

"That's an excellent suggestion, Mr. Summers," Sarah replied, standing up from his lap, and moving to the balcony. "I think you'll definitely need all your strength tonight."

He watched her standing there for a moment, curled tresses bouncing on the night breeze; long, tanned legs defiant against the rail. It took all of his considerable self control to suppress an urge to grab her then and skip their dinner.

Two hours later, they'd finished their meal at a small table in the suite. The sea bass was passable, and the shrimp, fresh and delicious.

Most of the wine was consumed with dinner, and Jack refilled Sarah's glass, emptying the bottle.

"You won't have to ply me with alcohol, Jack," Sarah said softly, smiling over the brim of her raised glass.

"That wasn't my intention, I can assure you, Ms. Dunn," Jack replied, returning her smile.

They spent the next several hours exchanging questions and answers about each other. Conversation was easy, and the evening seemed to spill out around them, like the remnants of the wine onto the carpet when Sarah bumped her glass. Both knew they'd found a promise of something in each other, and they moved cautiously, but without the usual uncertainty of new lovers.

Sarah listened attentively as Jack recounted his Midwestern upbringing, and then more detail on his days in the Navy. When he came to the subject of Claire, Sarah could see the pain that still lay behind his eyes as he spoke. It was obvious that she'd been someone very special in his life, and still was, even years after her death. She wondered if it were possible for him to feel that way about her, given some time.

Sarah filled in the details of her past for him. Much of the outline of her life they'd covered in his office at their first meeting. And though it had been only a few weeks, it seemed like they'd known each other for years. Jack saw the intensity of her love for her son, Adam, when she talked about his birth and their life together. It was obvious that she was a devoted mother to the boy, and Summers found himself drawn even more to the beautiful, caring woman seated across the table from him.

By midnight, they'd exhausted themselves with the conversation, and Sarah stood, holding her hand out to him.

"It's time you took me to bed," she said softly.

Taking her hand, Jack told her that he'd shut the place down and join her in a minute. When she left the room, he double checked the deadbolt on the door to the suite, and braced one of the table chairs under the doorknob. If anyone's coming through there, they'll need to make a lot of noise, he mused.

He thought briefly of locking the glass door to the veranda, but the cool air felt good, and it would be an unlikely climb to their suite from the outside. They were at least four stories up from the swimming pool area that lay below. Each staggered balcony would be an unlikely leap from the one below it. Jack turned out the remaining lights of the living room and entered the master bedroom.

Sarah had removed her shorts and was lying on the pillow top bedspread. One small lamp lit the room, bathing her in a soft glow.

"I just tried to call Adam," she said. "There's no answer."

"Maybe they went to the store or something," Jack replied lamely. He glanced at his watch, calculating the time differential. "You can try again later, if you like, but we'll be home by mid-afternoon tomorrow."

"No, I'm sure he's alright with Helen," Sarah responded. "Why don't you come over here and return the favor of that massage I gave you earlier?"

Jack smiled, and said, "That would be my distinct honor and pleasure. Where would you like me to start?"

Sarah sat up and removed her cotton shirt. At that moment, for the first time since he'd buried her, Jack put away thoughts of Claire. Looking down at Sarah in the dim light as he removed his clothes, Jack felt as though he'd come home finally from a long and arduous journey.

Hours later, Jack awoke with a start. He'd felt, rather than heard something. He looked at the small clock on the night stand. It said four forty-five. It would be daylight in a little over an hour. Lying motionless, eyes wide open and adjusting rapidly to his surroundings, he held his breath, and listened to the silence of the suite. The only audible sound was the rise and fall of Sarah's rhythmic breathing.

Lloyd Budreaux, "Gator" as he was known to most, had been awake most of the night. He was a night person, and it suited his work. He'd been raised in south central Florida, one of seven children of a father who smuggled drugs and a mother who spent most of her time sampling her husband's products. In the road atlas of the mega-million dollar drug trade of south central Florida, Gator's father was just a bus stop. Pilots would swing wide over the swamp where Gator lived, and bundles of hallucinogens would drop from the sky. Gator's dad and, later most of his boys, would hightail it out to the drop zone and gather them in. Marijuana, cocaine, and a laundry list of other controlled substances splashed down in Gator's backyard. From there, they'd be trucked out to find their way into the cool sets of Ft. Lauderdale and South Beach.

By the time Gator reached thirteen, the local school authorities had given up on trying to educate him. He was already six foot four, on his way to six eight. He'd topped out at about two hundred ninety pounds, and most of it was muscle. They let him play some semi-pro football for a short time, until, during one rain soaked game he nearly killed a running back on the opposing team. In the process of subduing him, several players on Gator's own team were seriously injured. That incident brought him to the attention of some associates of Sam Marchesi, in Miami. He'd taken care of business for them ever since.

Now he called Miami home, and enjoyed his work. Gator had already killed seven men with his bare hands by the time he got the word to take care of Jack and Sarah, and was kind of looking forward to doing his first female. Especially so, since he'd met her the previous afternoon in their suite. He'd take care of business, and get him some poontang in the process.

After talking to Sarah, under the guise of being an employee of the hotel, Gator bribed the desk clerk to move him from his present room, to the one just above the Queen's Suite. He sat for hours in the dark, listening to the muffled sound of Jack and Sarah making love in the room below him. He dressed, head to toe, in black. His skin was naturally the color of coal, like you might find in the back streets of Haiti, or Trinidad. In the dark of the room, what you'd see of Gator would be the whites of his eyes, and if he smiled, his teeth.

Jack slipped out from the sheet covering him and Sarah without a sound. Donning his shorts and pants, he covered the short distance to the bedroom door and stopped to listen. Again, there was no sound other than Sarah's breathing. He twisted the lock on the door, hoping the click it made when the bolt slid clear wouldn't wake her. As the lock disengaged, he looked over his shoulder. She hadn't moved. He slowly pulled open the door to the bedroom, and again held his breath. His eyes, adjusting to the moonlight that filled the common area of the suite, scanned the room's perimeter.

As he'd done so many times in service with the Navy Seals, he let his mind go blank and his senses extend out to the interior of the room. Even the slightest movement would trigger a response from him. But there was none. He looked to the balcony, bathed in moonlight, but nothing was out of place.

Jack stepped into the shadows to the side of the bedroom door and waited. He was ready for anything, but nothing happened. After several minutes, he decided that what woke him was a bad case of nerves rather than any threat in the suite. Walking slowly to the bar area, he grabbed a pack of Merit Lights and lit one. He'd been trying, off and on, to quit the cigarettes since Claire died. She'd insisted that he quit when they were married, but during the lost days following her death, he'd been hooked again.

Taking a long pull on the cigarette, inhaling deeply, Jack studied the door to the balcony. He was sure that it hadn't been open quite that wide when they went to bed. Maybe the moonlight was playing tricks on him, he thought. He'd taken one step in the direction of the door when Gator, who was standing in a darkened corner of the room, beyond the reach of the moonlight with his eyes closed, blinked.

Jack caught the split second reflection of light on the whites of his eyes, and stepped into a classic defensive position. As Gator exploded from the corner, Jack spun to his left and launched a side kick at his assailant. It was one of his most powerful offensive moves, and he could routinely snap ten inches of boards with it at karate demonstrations. His right heel caught the charging Gator in the chest, and Jack heard the sound of snapping ribs as the large man reversed direction, air exiting his lungs with a muffled "oomph."

The blow would have taken any normal man to the ground, but Gator merely staggered for a second and resumed his attack. Trained to deliver multiple blows in succession, Summers launched a descending kick aimed at his attacker's knee joint. Properly delivered, such a strike would snap the joint. But the big man had cat-like reflexes. Sensing the impact, he turned, and the hardened edge of Jack's foot caught Gator in the thigh muscle, and deflected away. Impact with his attacker's thigh felt like hitting a bag of bricks. Jack had by this time realized that the intruder was not armed. This man entered a darkened room with the confidence of someone who could kill with his bare hands.

Recoiling into a defensive position once again, Jack knew that his only advantage lay in keeping distance between himself and the giant black man who, despite two normally devastating blows, showed no sign of retreat or debilitating injury. Against an untrained fighter, Jack's experienced reflexes would make it seem as though his opponent moved in slow motion.

Not so with Gator. As Jack launched a reverse crescent kick at Gator's head, spinning his leg in a wide arc, the hardened edge of his heel leading the strike, the big man dropped quickly, ducking the move. This gave him an unexpected angle at Jack's lower body, and Gator leapt forward, knocking him to the floor.

Like a starving crab, Gator was on Jack in an instant. Hitting the floor, Jack executed a backward roll to get away, but his attacker clamped a huge hand on one ankle, pulling himself up towards Jack's throat. His grip was vice-like, and Summers instinctively knew he must counter attack.

As Gator scrambled to get on top of the now squirming Summers, he left his face exposed. Jack swung both his hands, palms open, with a violent snap, against Gator's ears. The speed and force of the blow caused both of Gators' eardrums to burst, and he hesitated, stunned with shock. Jack took advantage of the moment's hesitation, and with Gator now recoiled in pain, he drove both of his thumbs into the white orbs of the black man's face. One eyeball popped, and Gator screamed like a wounded bull, rolling away in the dark.

Not knowing how much damage he'd inflicted in the dark, and not wanting another close encounter with the large man who had incredibly managed to get to his feet, Jack retreated once again into a defensive stance. At that moment, the door to the bedroom swung open.

Sarah stood there, naked but for a bed sheet wrapped at her waist, starring in horror at the two combatants. Summers and Gator both turned in her direction, and Jack knew his attacker would go for her. Injured as he was, it would be his only means of gaining an advantage. The distance between Gator and Sarah would allow him to reach her before Jack could intervene. He took one step in her direction, and the room exploded with light, as Sarah flipped the wall switch. Sarah screamed.

Jack could see now the effect his attacks had had on the intruder. The man was a giant, even larger than he'd seemed in the dark. There was blood oozing from his left eye socket, and the eyeball was gone. You could see blood trails from both ears. The eye that remained intact, was a fiery red. The sudden infusion of bright light blinded Gator's injured eye for a moment, and Jack took advantage.

Changing the orientation of his body to allow a strike with his more powerful right side, he executed a sliding side kick that caught the stumbling Gator in the exposed area of his Adam's apple. It was Jack's strongest move, one which he'd practiced countless times on the heavy bag at home. The impact lifted Gator's two hundred ninety pound frame several inches off the floor, crushing his windpipe. He staggered backward, onto the balcony, grabbing at his throat.

Jack didn't hesitate. He immediately repeated the same attack, this time aiming the blow at Gator's solar plexus. As the side of Jack's foot impacted the big man's mid-section, his body was again airborne. He stumbled backwards through the open glass door, hitting the balcony's railing, and with his remaining eye locked on Summers, he tumbled over. Before Jack reached the edge of the balcony, Gator had bounced once on a railing two floors down, and landed in a twisted heap on the concrete swimming pool deck below.

When Jack turned back towards the suite's interior, Sarah was standing in the doorway, a look of mixed shock and horror on her face. He stepped towards her, and she recoiled from his outstretched arms.

"Sarah, I'm sorry you had to see that," he said quietly.

"He was going to kill us for the money, wasn't he?" she said, her voice broken with the sobs she fought back.

"I'm afraid he was," Jack replied, again moving to hold her. This time she let him, a flood of tears now flowing down her face. "There's some very bad people involved in this deal. Even worse than I expected."

He took her back into the suite, closing the door behind him. They stood for several minutes, Jack's arms wrapped tightly around Sarah as she wept at the reality of violent death. After a few minutes, she began to shake, and Jack feared she'd go into shock.

"I want you to go into the bedroom and take a hot shower," Jack said. "I'll straighten up in here, and we'll get packed to leave. We don't want to get bogged down dealing with the local police if we can avoid it."

"I want to call Adam," she said, an urgency in her voice.

"It's still the middle of the night, Sarah," he said.

"I know, but I need to call now," she insisted.

Jack could see there was no use in arguing. He let her dial Helen's number in Las Vegas, and they waited for an answer. After what seemed like an eternity, she hung up the receiver.

"There's no answer," she said simply.

The look in her eyes was that of a trapped animal. She turned to Summers with a sickening look of guilt on her face. It said she was a mother who'd left her young child in danger so that she could go off and have fun with a man she hardly knew.

Jack felt a knot in his stomach as he realized that any future he might have with Sarah would hinge on the events of the next twenty-four hours. He needed to get them into a safe, public place as quickly as possible. He had no idea if the night's intruder was alone on the island. The airport would be their safe haven. In the meantime, he would call Mac, and have him check on Sarah's neighbor and Adam.

By that time, Helen James was already dead.

Jack dialed Mac's home number. After several rings, he answered, fumbling with the phone.

"Hello," Mac answered.

"Mac, it's Summers. I know it's the middle of the night there, but I need your help. I'm leaving St. Kitts in a few hours, and should be back in Vegas by this afternoon. I need two things. First, I need one of your guys to go check out the apartment of Helen James. She lives in the same complex on the east side as Sarah." Jack turned to Sarah, and getting Helen's address, conveyed it to Mac.

"Next, I've run into a little more muscle on this case than I anticipated. If you know of someone at the FBI's local office with the organized crime unit who you can trust, I need a meeting with him later today. Tell him I think I can deliver Sam Marchesi."

Mac let out a low whistle on the other end.

"You've decided to step up to the major leagues, huh partner?" Mac said, now fully awake.

"I suspect I'm going to have no choice," Jack responded.

"You know you're going to have to give me several strokes every time we tee it up for the rest of your natural life, don't you?" Mac commented.

"It should be worth it, Mac," he said, smiling at Sarah. She was sitting on a bar stool near the phone, listening to one side of the conversation, tears rolling down her face. Jack said a quick "thanks" to Mac, and hung up.

They packed quickly, and were on their way to the airport in a cab by six thirty. Jack was relieved to depart the hotel. No one had discovered Gator's body at poolside yet. He didn't want to be delayed when the police came calling. A sudden rash of bodies flying off resort balconies would be bad for the tourist business, and the local magistrate would want the matter put to bed immediately. That meant questioning everyone in the hotel. Jack and Sarah would already be airborne for San Juan when they came knocking at the Queen's Suite.

Jack slipped the envelope containing the negotiable bearer bonds into a file in his briefcase. It contained miscellaneous legal documents and forms from several old cases. The vanilla envelope would hopefully look like just part of the same materials when they went through customs.

Chapter Twenty Nine

When Sarah and Jack changed planes in Houston, he called Mac. The news wasn't reassuring. One of Mac's employees had gone to Helen James' apartment, as instructed. Since no one answered at two o'clock in the morning, he reported it to Mac, promising to check again when a resident manager would be available to open Helen's apartment, if needed. Mac still had no word. Calling the apartment directly had elicited no response. Jack was worried, but he tried not to let Sarah know how much.

"We'll be there in a couple of hours, Sarah," he said. "You can go directly to Helen's and talk to Adam."

"If something's happened to Adam…," Sarah said, not finishing the thought out loud. She looked ill. They hardly spoke on the flights back, Sarah lost in her own world, and Summers planning his strategy when the got back to Vegas.

Their plane from Houston came in from the southeast, across Hoover Dam and a sliver of the Grand Canyon. Jack looked out at the desert landscape, such a complete contrast to the lush islands they'd left hours behind. Nearing mid-summer, Las Vegas would be dry and sizzling when they landed.

After talking to Mac, Jack called the cell phone number his secretary gave him for Dean Belcastro. Dean told Jack that he needed to talk to him, face to face, as soon as possible. He said it was about Sam Marchesi, and involved Summers and the woman he was with. Jack arranged to meet him as soon as he dropped off Sarah. He then called his secretary and gave detailed instructions on several documents he wanted typed. He would need a Release of All Claims form to be signed by Jim Eccles on behalf of Sundown Mortgage, together with a reconveyance of Sundown's Deed of

Trust on the Anasazi property. With Sundown's interest taken care of, the remaining claims of Patek Investments, and the mechanics lien holders, would become manageable.

When they landed in Las Vegas, Jack took Sarah to a cab and told the driver her address.

"Don't worry, Sarah," he said, kissing her on the cheek, and helping her into the backseat. "I'm sure Adam's fine. I'll call you as soon as I've finished up some stuff at the office."

She managed an uncertain smile, and without another word, pulled away in the cab, headed east towards her apartment in Henderson. Jack retrieved his car, and in twenty minutes, walked through the door of his office.

"People are looking for you, boss," his secretary said as he stopped at her desk and gathered up the documents she'd prepared for him. "Belcastro's in your office."

Summers smiled at his long suffering secretary. She'd been with him over eight years, and by Las Vegas standards, was one of the best.

"What's this all about, Dean?" Jack said, entering the door to his private office.

The young man seated in one of the client chairs by his desk stood to greet him. "It's been a long time. How's your mother?"

"She's doing fine, but you and I got a big problem," Dean replied.

Over the next thirty minutes, Dean related how he'd come to work in Las Vegas at the suggestion of some guys back in Chicago. Jack didn't ask who they were. Dean said he'd been recruited to work with Sam Marchesi's bodyguard. It turned out that the guy is some kind of "psycho", and had done some wet work in Chicago several years back.

He told Jack that Marchesi had ordered a hit on two people named McKenna. Dean left out much of the detail as he described how he and Bruno grabbed the couple in California, and took them to a remote cabin where Bruno killed them, burying the bodies in the desert. Jack took notes, and confirmed that Dean could find the grave if needed.

Dean then described the hits on Roger Temple and the young guy named Jesse. Finally, he recounted the recent meeting at which Marchesi sent Kirshbaum and Bruno to grab Adam. He told him that Jack, Sarah and the kid would get whacked as soon as they got the money back that Jack was supposed to have found on some guy in the Caribbean.

"Do they have the boy now?" Jack asked anxiously.

"Yeah, they got him out at an old scrap yard," he replied. "They're supposed to grab the woman as soon as she gets back home."

Jack grabbed the phone on his desk and dialed Sarah's number. There was no answer.

As Sarah's cab pulled up to the parking lot of her apartment, she saw several police cars, some with overhead lights still flashing, positioned outside her building. An overwhelming feeling of dread hit her like a mallet. Running towards the small crowd that gathered at the yellow tape police used to cordon off the entrance to the building, she grabbed a neighbor that she recognized.

"What's happened?" she demanded.

"Ms. James, in 204, was found dead by the manager this morning. Looks like a robbery," the neighbor replied.

Stunned in silence for a moment, Sarah finally managed to ask, "My son, Adam, where is he?"

"I don't know," the neighbor said. "Isn't he with you?"

Just then, a powerful hand grasped Sarah's arm, pulling her to the side.

"Your son's just fine, Mrs. Dunn," the man said. "And he'll continue to be fine if you keep your mouth shut and come with me. Otherwise, you'll never see him again in one piece."

The speaker guided her to a dark colored van, its windows painted over, parked across the lot. The side door slid open, and she was met by another man, who immediately pulled her into the back of the van, slipping a cloth hood over her head. Sarah's hands were jerked roughly behind her, and bound by what felt like a plastic strip.

Summers cursed himself as he slammed the phone down. How could he have been so stupid! There was only one thing he could do now to get Sarah and Adam out safely. He picked up the phone and dialed Mac's number. While waiting for an answer, he asked Dean if he knew the location of the scrap yard. Dean said he'd never been there, but was supposed to take Marchesi there later, to meet Bruno.

"Mac, it's Jack," he said as soon as Mac picked up the phone. "Tell your guy at organized crime that I can hand him Marchesi on a multiple murder wrap. When I pinpoint the location where he can be picked up, I'll call. In the meantime, I need a blanket immunity for one of my clients who will hand him over. That means State and Federal, and I'm talking California and Nevada. He'll also need entry into the witness protection program."

"Whoa, slow down partner," Mac replied. "That's a tall order, and there's lots of prosecutor strings to be pulled to get that kind of a deal into cement."

"I know what it takes," Jack shot back. "If they want Marchesi bad enough, they can get it done. My guy's name is 'Belcastro, Dominic Belcastro'. I've known his family for years. If there's any leak on this, his head will be on us. So only reliable people, okay?"

"How strong is this guy's information?" Mac asked.

"The strongest," Jack said. "He heard the direct orders, and he was present at the killings, but didn't participate."

"How much time do you have to get this?" Mac asked.

"I need it in writing in two hours," Jack replied. "And I need you to meet me at the main office of Sundown Mortgage in one hour. You investigated a robbery at their place before you retired, didn't you?"

"Yeah, I dealt with some guy named Eccles, I think," Mac said.

"Perfect," Jack replied. "Meet me there in an hour. And Mac, dress like you're still in the Bureau."

Mac had wanted to nail Marchesi for years when he was still with the Bureau. He would have met the devil himself if there was a chance that he'd finally get it done. It didn't matter that he wasn't active in the FBI anymore. It was in his blood. He still had good friends at the local office, and one in particular that he could trust.

"I'll see you there," Mac said. Jack hung up the phone and looked across the desk at Dean.

"You have one chance only of surviving this, Dean. You've got to roll over on Marchesi and go into Federal witness protection."

"And what if I don't? I ain't no rat!" Dean shouted.

"I just took the liberty of eliminating your options," Jack said. "The FBI has your name, and soon enough, so will Marchesi. Whether you testify or not won't matter, believe me. Marchesi won't take the chance. You've seen him in action. He eliminates all possible witnesses. Your only chance is to cooperate."

Dean squirmed in his chair. He'd come looking to help Summers out of a jam, and for the sake of saving Sarah, Jack had, from Dean's viewpoint, thrown him to the wolves. A minute of silence passed when Jack wasn't sure whether Dean would bolt for the door or not.

Finally, a look of acceptance crossed his face. Jack told him to go back to Marchesi and follow directions. Summers was sure that he'd be contacted soon by Marchesi, or someone working for him, and that they would lead him to Adam and Sarah.

In the meantime, he had one shot at saving his client, AmCon Title, from the firestorm. When Dean left Jack's office, Jack retrieved the envelope from his briefcase and pulled out the bonds. Counting out thirty-five, and returning them to the Caribbean Holdings envelope, he placed the remaining six in a separate envelope.

Just a little insurance, he thought to himself.

Charlie Patek sat in his office on West Sahara, looking at the phone. He'd just hung up from a short conversation with Sam. Marchesi wanted

Charlie to get Ashley over to Charlie's office around ten that night. Sam said that he needed a sit down with Charlie. Marchesi would take care of Ashley from there.

Charlie was a hustler, not a murderer. This was new territory for him, and he didn't like driving blind. In all of the scams he'd pulled in the past, he always felt in control of the situation. Now, he didn't know where this whole deal was headed, and he didn't like it. If it was so easy for Sam to make all these people disappear, what would stop him from doing the same to good old Charlie, he wondered.

For the first time in his life, Charlie knew what it must feel like to be the mark, and Marchesi was calling all the shots. But, he couldn't see how he could change the direction of events at this point. If he crossed Marchesi, he'd have to deal with Bruno. Charlie shuddered involuntarily again at the thought, and picked up the phone once again. Ashley answered at her home number.

"Hello."

"Ashley, baby. It's Charlie. Don't hang up, sweetheart. I'm so sorry about what happened. I don't know what got into me. I've been under a lot of pressure. You know I'm crazy about you."

There was a moment of silence before Ashley responded, "I'm going to have you thrown in jail, you bastard."

"No, honey," Charlie interjected. "I want to make everything right with you. I lost my head the other day. I wasn't myself. You've got to give me another chance."

There was no immediate response, so Charlie threw out the bait. "I'm going to clear up this Anasazi Properties mess for you. I've got a release of my security interest waiting right here for you at the office. I'll release our first lien, and you're in the clear with Sundown Mortgage."

There was still no response, so Charlie, knowing Ashley as he did, played his last card. "I can't have the woman I'm going to spend the rest of my life with being hassled by anyone," he said. It was the trump card he'd been holding back. Charlie knew that Ashley was looking for a sugar daddy to settle in with. It was an offer she couldn't refuse.

"Is that your version of a proposal?" she asked, after another moment's hesitation.

"Yes, ma'am, it is," Charlie said. "I don't want to lose you. I've realized how much you mean to me since the other day. I must have been trying to break away by hurting you, but now I know how much I need you."

"Oh, Charlie," Ashley said. "You son-of-a-bitch! What's taken you so long?"

Charlie told her to meet him at his office that night. He had a big surprise for her. He said he'd have all the paperwork ready to clear up Patek

Investments' first lien on the Anasazi Properties deal, and that there was something big and sparkling that he wanted to give her. She agreed to meet him at ten o'clock. Charlie rocked back in the over stuffed leather chair behind his desk and smiled. Still haven't lost your touch, he thought to himself.

In the living room of her house, Ashley sat crying on the couch. She'd waited so long for the right guy to support her. Charlie certainly fit the bill. Sure, he'd knocked her around a little. But what guy didn't do that? And, after all, it was the only time it'd happened.

"Mrs. Charlie Patek," she whispered. It had a nice ring to it. She could hang up the daily escrow grind, and help Charlie build his already immensely profitable business, she mused as she headed for the shower. Then, as she entered her bathroom, dropping the robe from her shoulders, reality once again slapped her across the face. She caught a glimpse of her reflection in the mirror. Her cheek bone was blackened, and red marks rose at her throat. Both bare shoulders were badly bruised, and her large breasts and back bore the welts of the whipping Charlie had given her.

She'd marry Charlie, alright. And when the time was right, she'd cut off his balls in divorce court.

Sarah had been in the back of the van for what she guessed was about a half hour when it came to an abrupt halt, sliding on what sounded like gravel. She'd been forced to lay on the floor, and with her arms behind her back, her shoulder muscles knotted in pain. The hood covering her head made it difficult to breathe, but her sole focus was on getting to Adam. Her emotions had taken a roller coaster ride from the night before with Jack. That now seemed an eternity away.

The back door of the van came open, and Sarah was jerked out to a standing position. Her legs nearly gave way, as she tried to stand on her own. Grasping her arm, someone moved her along the gravel, and onto what felt like a cement surface. The temperature, stifling hot in the van, now felt cool as she heard a door slam behind her.

The room reeked of oil and gasoline, like an old garage. A few steps later, her captor slammed her down into a straight-backed chair. She called out for Adam, but got no response except a blow to the still covered side of her face. Her ears ringing from the impact, she passed out.

Chapter Thirty

Jack got the call he was waiting for shortly after Dean left his office. His secretary buzzed the intercom, announcing that "Sam Marchesi is on the phone." Taking a deep breath to calm himself, he picked up the receiver.

"Good afternoon, Mr. Marchesi," Jack said pleasantly. "What can I do for you?"

"You can cut the crap for starters, Summers," Marchesi growled. "I've got a couple of packages that belong to you. They look extremely perishable. I'd say if you don't pick them up by eight o'clock, they'll be so spoiled that you won't want them. Be sure and bring that money you owe me when you come to collect them."

Marchesi gave Jack an address in North Las Vegas, and hung up. Jack had less than four hours to make his plan work. He opened a file drawer and pulled a stack of blank corporate share certificates out. They were preprinted, official looking, and about the same size as the negotiable bonds. He slipped these in the envelope with the six bonds he'd separated earlier. Jack dialed Bill Roxburgh's direct line at AmCon Title.

"Bill Roxburgh," he answered.

"Bill, it's Jack Summers. I've got good news. I recovered a large chunk of the money that Leon Black embezzled from Anasazi Properties. I'm on my way to Sundown Mortgage to meet with Eccles and get a release of their security interest in the project. That will just leave us with the remainder of Charlie Patek's loan, the Kirshbaum loan, and the mechanics liens on the property. I believe the project's easily worth more than enough to pay those off, so you'll be off the hook. There may be a few other minor problems, but I think I can work those out. You need to keep this to yourself for now.

It's crucial to my negotiations that no one else knows what I'm doing. Sarah should be back to work in a day or so. I just need your authority to proceed as I've outlined."

"That's fantastic news Jack," Roxburgh said. "You're a miracle worker! You do whatever you think is best."

Thirty minutes later, he met Mac in the parking lot of the offices of Sundown Mortgage. Mac approached him with a smile, and dressed as requested in the plain, dark suit with white shirt and tie that was the uniform of the FBI.

"I'll never be able to repay you for your help, Mac," Jack said, shaking his friend's hand.

"Don't worry, buddy. I'll think of something the next time we tee it up," Mac replied, a broad smile on his face. "Seriously, sounds like you're playing with fire. You sure you're up to this?" He knew Jack's background well. The word of caution was given to reassure himself as much as to warn his friend.

"I guess we'll find out," Jack said. "What do you hear from your friends at the Bureau?"

"I hear that you can have a job there tomorrow if you can hand them Marchesi. Not that you'd want one," Mac said. "They've got the witness protection and immunity deals in the works. We should be able to meet with them at the Bureau office when we leave here. Incidentally, what are we doing here, anyway?"

"We're getting rid of one of the vultures trying to steal my client's company," Jack said.

"My guy just called," Mac said. "He went back to Sarah's apartment, and there's cops all over the place. The neighbor she left her kid with got killed in an apparent robbery. No sign of the boy. What aren't you telling me?"

"Marchesi's got the boy and Sarah," Jack replied without emotion. Mac had seen a similar look in his friend's eyes only once. Jack had, a couple years earlier, needed to make a ten foot putt to win one of the local amateur tournaments. There'd been no sign of doubt in his eyes, just a deadly calm. That look had now returned, with a vengeance. He wondered how well he really knew his friend, and what he wouldn't do to achieve his goals if needed. He made the putt...dead solid perfect.

"You need to call the police," Mac blurted out, knowing Jack's reply before he heard it.

"Neither one of us knows who to trust in the local police department," Jack said. "I can't risk it. I'll bring your FBI guys in when the time's right. Right now, I need to get Eccles and his partners, other than Marchesi, out of the equation. You won't really need to say much. Just act like you're still with the Bureau."

"I can do that, alright," Mac replied, "but if you don't bring in the FBI, I will."

"Right after this meeting, I promise," Jack said. "I'll go to the local office as soon as I finish my business here. I want you to hang with this guy like a second skin after I leave. I don't want him making any phone calls to Marchesi."

With that, Summers led the way into the offices of Sundown Mortgage. It was nearly five o'clock, and Mac and he were met by a blonde, smiling receptionist who looked like she'd probably been a dancer somewhere before the gravity gods started playing with the essential tools of her trade.

"We'd like to see Mr. Eccles," Jack said pleasantly. Though he smiled, the tone of his voice let her know he was in no mood for any attempted brush-off. "Tell him it's Jack Summers and Mr. McCormick. He'll remember Mr. McCormick from the FBI."

Jack was careful not to represent that Mac was still "with" the Bureau, but he knew the distinction would be lost on the blonde. Impersonating a federal officer was still a crime.

"Just a moment, please," she said, returning Jack's smile.

With that, she rose from her desk and departed towards a private office located behind her. As she walked away, both Mac and Jack's eyes were involuntarily drawn to the blonde's spectacular legs and backside. Their faces reflected a look of not bad for her age. A minute later, Eccles emerged from the office, with the receptionist trailing behind. He turned towards her as they reached the reception desk.

"You can call it a day Crystal," Eccles said, never taking his eyes off of his two visitors. "What can I do for you gentlemen? I hope there's not some problem with our accounts."

"No," Jack interjected, not allowing Mac a chance to answer. "Mr. McCormick is a friend. I've recovered the bulk of your money from the imposter, DeMartes, and I asked Mac to drive over with me since it's a lot of money."

Eccles had just gotten off the phone with Marchesi, and he knew that they had both Sarah and Adam at the salvage yard. Marchesi told him that Summers would be bringing the money there later that night. Now, it looked like Summers was bringing the FBI into the deal, and things were going south in a hurry. He escorted them into his private office as Crystal began the process of gathering her things to leave. Mac couldn't resist one more look over his shoulder as they walked away from her. She turned, unexpectedly, catching him appreciating her backside, and smiled.

"How much of the funds have you recovered?" Eccles asked Jack as they entered the office.

"I have three point five million here in negotiable bearer bonds," Jack answered without hesitation. "I also have a Release of All Claims for your signature. I'm prepared to turn these funds over to you in exchange for your agreement, as well as a reconveyance of your company's interest in the property."

Eccles had taken a seat behind his desk. Now he was on his feet again. "My company's not going to take that kind of loss!" he shouted. "We've got five million in this deal. I can't and won't agree."

Jack turned to Mac, who was seated in the chair next to him. "I wonder if you might excuse us for a few minutes," he said to Mac. Mac nodded, and without saying a word, left in the direction of the comely receptionist, hoping to catch another look before she left the building. Jack then turned his attention to Eccles, who was still standing behind his desk, the veins in his neck bulging, face reddening.

"Sit down, Mr. Eccles," Jack said, as if to a young student who'd just disrupted the class. Eccles hesitated momentarily, and then dropped into his seat. Jack let silence hang on the room until Mac closed the door behind him. Then, leaning back in the leather chair in front of Eccles' desk, he laid out his proposal.

"You and I have much in common, Jim. Can I call you Jim? We both have clients who depend on us to cut their losses in a bad situation. What we have here is a very bad situation. Your company made an ill advised loan to an imposter, one who I believe you personally should have checked out a little more carefully. If you keep your present security position and sell the property, I estimate that you'll lose, conservatively, more than half of your loan by the time you get done fighting me in court.

My client will take this money and pay off everyone else involved. We'll buy Patek Investment's position, Kirshbaum's note, and pay off the mechanics liens at a discounted rate. You'll be the only one I'm fighting with, and I can promise that we'll do our best to see that our security comes out on top. Realistically, you may end up losing your whole investment."

Jack paused to let Eccles consider his threat. A metered clicking from the grandfather clock in the corner of Eccles office was the only sound. As Eccles frantically considered what had been proposed, Jack continued.

"On the other hand," he continued, "you can accept my offer now, and be out of the deal with a manageable loss. We both know that you have others to answer to than Marchesi, who will soon be in federal custody for murder and kidnapping."

"I'll need to consult with my investors before I commit," Eccles replied, bartering for a chance to call Marchesi.

"No, I don't think that would be wise," Jack responded. "You see, my friend out there seems convinced that you are somehow connected to the kidnapping portion of Mr. Marchesi's problem. I've told him that this seems unlikely, and that as a businessman you'd accept my offer. I'm afraid, given the present circumstances, any other course of action would indicate that I'm wrong about you. The FBI may think you are refusing my offer because you and your co-conspirators in the kidnapping have plans for this money, other than legitimately settling our differences. In any event, you and I both know that your own lawyers would take a third of the five million dollars to get you whole on your ill-advised loan."

"I don't know anything about any kidnapping!" Eccles protested, again rising to his feet.

"Of course. That's just what I told Mr. McCormick," Jack replied calmly. He waited for Eccles to sit before continuing. "But what better way to demonstrate your lack of involvement? Let's settle our differences in this matter, here and now, like gentlemen."

Jack opened his briefcase, and pulled out the Release and Reconveyance forms. He set them on the desk in front of Eccles, turning the case so that the stack of bonds was visible. Jim Eccles frantically weighed his options. If he crossed Marchesi, he'd be dead within the week. On the other hand, if he took the three and a half million that Summers was proposing, and added to it the up front points, or two hundred fifty thousand, he'd collected at the closing of the loan, Sundown would be out just about a million dollars, or twenty percent. It was, in fact, a reasonable loss, given the circumstances. And, if Marchesi was on his way to prison, the loss could be blamed on him when Jim met with the other investors. Besides, with the FBI in the next room, he didn't see how he had any real choice. If he didn't agree, he was certain that he'd be arrested on the spot.

Jack looked around the room as Eccles pondered his proposal. The office was large, decorated tastefully in earth tones and leather. It had a woman's touch, and Jack wondered in passing who'd done the work. He just couldn't picture the lizard sitting in front of him knowing any woman with such good taste. Eccles must have paid a small fortune to have the place decorated, he mused.

"Alright, it's a deal," Eccles said after a long pause. He grabbed the documents that Jack had laid out on the desk, taking his time to read them in detail.

While Eccles reviewed the Release and Reconveyance, Jack walked to the door of the office. Opening it, he saw that Mac was involved in an animated conversation with the blonde receptionist. It looked like Mac was in the middle of some serious negotiations of his own. They both turned toward the office door as Jack motioned for them to enter.

"I assume that your secretary is a notary public who can attest your signature on the Deed of Reconveyance," Jack said in the direction of Eccles.

Eccles grunted his assent, and Jack asked the blonde to get her notary seal and witness her boss' signature on the documents. When the formalities were completed, he told Eccles that Mac would be staying with him for a couple of hours. Eccles began to protest, but Mac interrupted.

"It's really for your own protection, and in your best interests, Mr. Eccles. I strongly suggest that you agree. It would confirm your lack of involvement with Marchesi and his problems tonight." There was no room for disagreement in the tone of Mac's voice. Jack was impressed. Again agreeing reluctantly, Eccles took his time counting the thirty-five bonds and placing them, together with his copies of Jack's documents in a wall safe behind one of the pictures in his office.

Jack left the office with the blonde, leaving Mac and Eccles to kill a few hours waiting for a phone call that Jack promised to make when the deal went down with Marchesi. He promised Mac that he was on his way to the FBI field office and walked the blonde out into the oppressive heat of the parking lot.

It was nearly six o'clock, and there would more than three hours of daylight left at that time of year in Las Vegas. The temperature was still above one hundred fifteen, and he was thankful for the air conditioner in his car. The two-seater XK8 Jaguar that he'd driven for several years would cool down before he'd covered a block on his way downtown.

Sam Marchesi lumbered through the side door of the metal building that served as office and work area for the scrap yard. The room was large enough to hold several vehicles, and was typically used to strip stolen cars. It was air conditioned by two large, aging window units built into the side of the corrugated metal building. The rumbling hum of their McGraw-Edison compressors was the only sound in the building as Sam entered.

Near the center of the room, a female was strapped into an old wooden straight-backed chair, held tight by one inch plastic strips at her wrists and ankles. She was clad only in a bra and summer shorts. Her head listed to one side, but she was clearly still alive.

"Where's the kid?" Sam demanded to the assembled group.

"He's in the office," Bruno replied immediately.

The office was a ten by ten dry-walled enclosure that housed a small desk and a few filing cabinets. It was purely for show. This business had no need for record keeping.

"The lawyer will be here at eight," Sam said. "Wipe the blood off the broad's face, and leave her alone. I don't want any more damage done until I get the money."

Dean Belcastro walked to a sink in the corner and, wetting a rag, proceeded to wipe Sarah's face. A large bruise had started to form below her left eye where Bruno hit her when they brought her in.

Sarah had been unconscious for almost an hour before waking in the chair. The bag that had covered her head had been removed, as well as her blouse and shoes. White plastic strips dug into her wrists and ankles binding her to a chair. She'd called out for Adam, but was instantly silenced by a blow to her solar plexus.

Bruno had stood behind her, rubbing his groin into the back of her head. He'd ripped off her blouse, fondling her breasts, and promising her the "fuck of her life" once their business was finished. Since then she'd remained quiet, only occasionally looking around the room. She couldn't see her son, but she'd heard him call out from the office.

"Don't fuck this deal up for me, boys," Sam barked.

Bruno took a seat near Sarah, rubbing his hand up and down the side of her bare arm. Dean Belcastro leaned against a tool bench several yards away. Another man, one of those who picked up Sarah at her apartment, sat on the same bench, several feet away, playing with one of the ratchet wrenches that lay there.

"Check on the kid," Sam said in Dean's direction. "I want him alive and kicking when Summers shows up."

"What difference will it make?" Bruno asked. "We're just going to ice him anyway."

"We need to make sure he brought the money, genius," Sam replied with a sigh.

It's a good thing he's useful for something other than his brains, Sam thought to himself.

"I'm leaving here in a few minutes," Sam continued. "I've got some other details to take care of across town. When Summers gets here, make sure he's got our money. Then get rid of him, the girl and the kid. Dean, you bring the money to my office while these guys clean up this mess."

Sarah couldn't believe what she'd heard. They were going to kill Adam, herself and Jack! She started to struggle against her bindings, and the effort was rewarded by Bruno's fist to the left side of her face. She saw a blinding flash of light and once again lost consciousness.

"Take it easy, Bruno," Sam yelled. "You can do whatever you want with our guests after we get the dough. Until then, we want them looking all pretty for Summers. And don't underestimate that son-of-a-bitch. I get a bad feeling about him. You don't want him busting your balls again, do you, Bruno?"

Bruno shifted in his chair involuntarily at the memory of his encounter with Summers in the Reno garage. It was pay-back time tonight.

Dean loosened the electrical cord that held Adam to a chair in the office. He whispered in Adam's ear to "stay cool" and he'd be alright. Adam had been crying for a long time after they first brought him to the garage. Now he sat quietly, in a state of shock.

Chapter Thirty One

Cross town traffic was heavy as Jack swung his sports car on to the I-15 heading north towards downtown. It was past six o'clock, and to his right the mega-resorts of the Strip shimmered in the late afternoon sun. After all the years he'd spent in Las Vegas, he still marveled at the sight. The sidewalks would be speckled with groups of tourists at this hour. Slow moving tours of Orientals snapping pictures of everything in sight, and families craning their necks at the volcano in front of The Mirage. The tail end of rush hour edged north past the tower of the Stratosphere. Jack had heard a rumor that one of the support struts on the tower had been built at an unexpected angle, when it was too late to change it.

He exited at the Charleston off ramp, heading east. The field office of the FBI was located just east of Las Vegas Boulevard on Charleston. He was heading for a meeting with Tom Foley, Mac's contact in the organized crime unit. At six-thirty, Jack pulled into the parking lot. Inside, he identified himself and was asked to take a seat. A minute later, a tall man in his early thirties walked into the reception area and extended his hand to Jack.

He stood about six foot three, and his broad shoulders tapered to a waist that Jack knew from experience required a lot of exercise to maintain. He had close-cropped blond hair, and wore a gray suit over white shirt and plain tie that marked the uniform of most field officers. He looked directly into Jack's eyes as he approached. Jack made a living on his gut feeling about people. This was a man to be trusted.

"Mr. Summers, I'm Tom Foley," the man said, extending his hand. "If you'll join me in the office, I think I've got everything ready that Mac and you talked about."

Jack followed Foley into a private conference room. The suite of offices was strictly government issue, which Jack always found to be mildly depressing. Even the newer Federal Court buildings had a sterile look about them, done in grays and pastels. There was a long wooden table in the center of the room. It looked to be solid mahogany, and would have cost a small fortune in the private sector. Probably cost Uncle Sam two fortunes, Jack thought to himself.

Seated at the table were two men and a woman. The first man was older, probably mid-fifties, and was introduced to Jack as the Las Vegas' Special Agent in Charge. Seated next to him was a much younger man, probably late twenties, who Foley said was the Assistant Attorney General assigned to the case.

Finally, sitting opposite the two men, was a young woman, Jack thought not older than twenty-five. She was introduced as a Deputy County Attorney representing Clark County and the State of Nevada. Summers was familiar with most of the attorneys in that office, but had never met the young lady at the table. She had long, straight blonde hair, and wore a pin-striped business suit with a skirt that climbed up to mid-thigh on what appeared to be a pair of great legs. The movie, Legally Blonde, flashed in his head. Jack shook hands with each, before addressing the group.

"Who represents the State of California in this?" Jack asked, turning to Foley.

"I have a signed copy of their immunity agreement that was faxed to us just now. The original will follow by overnight delivery," Foley answered. "Now, tell us what you've got, and why Belcastro should be immune from prosecution."

Jack knew it was another make or break moment in his plans, and he said, "My client, Dominic Belcastro, is in a position to directly implicate Sam Marchesi in four premeditated murders. Mr. Belcastro was employed by Marchesi on the recommendation of certain friends of his in Chicago. The evidence will show that this employment embroiled him in a situation that resulted in these murders without his direct participation.

He is still in Marchesi's employ now, so his position, if known to Marchesi, would prove fatal. In exchange for his cooperation and testimony, if required, I want complete immunity from prosecution for him at the Federal level, as well as in both Nevada and California."

Jack sat back in his chair, situated next to the blonde, and evaluated the impact of his offer on the group. The older man spoke first.

"Who are we talking about on these murders?"

"A couple was executed on Marchesi's orders a few days ago in California," Jack replied. "I believe their last name was McKenna. My client can lead you to their grave in the desert just east of the Air Force base on I-15.

The other two were men. Jesse Dunn and Roger Temple. They were found in an apartment on the east side of town a couple of days ago. They were also killed on Marchesi's direct orders. My client is prepared to testify as to the details.

The icing on the cake will be a tape recording of Marchesi's direct participation in the planning and execution of the kidnapping of two Las Vegas residents, Sarah Dunn and her son, Adam. That kidnapping is on-going as we speak."

With Jack's last comment, the assembled group was on its feet.

"What do you mean, it's on-going?" the assistant attorney general blurted for the group.

Jack let them re-take their seats before continuing.

"Just what I said. Sarah Dunn and her son have been kidnapped and are being held for ransom by Marchesi and his people. My client should be with them, and I've instructed him to tape all conversation with a small recorder I gave him earlier today. By now, he should have gathered some very interesting comments from Marchesi that I think will make our offer irresistible. I only have one additional demand."

"What would that be?" the young, blonde prosecutor asked.

"I want everyone's agreement that, unless absolutely necessary, you will not use Ms. Dunn's or her son's testimony against Marchesi," he said. "You must agree to go after him on the murders first. If, and only if, that proves to be insufficient for a conviction, then you can use Ms. Dunn and her son. You see, they are also my clients at this point."

"Is your man going to be a credible witness?" Foley interjected.

"I've known him since he was a small boy," Jack answered. "Prior to this, as far as I know, he's only been involved with the law on petty crimes in Chicago. Besides, the fact that he can show you the bodies in the desert should support his credibility. Anyway, that's the deal, take it or leave it."

Again Jack rocked back in his chair, waiting for a reaction. He felt a trickle of sweat roll down the nape of his neck, as a minute passed.

"Speaking for the federal government, and the State of California, I'll take the deal. I have our paperwork here," the assistant district attorney said as he shoved a stack of paperwork in Jack's direction.

"That just leaves the State of Nevada," Jack said, smiling in the direction of the blonde. Her face had gone chalk white, and Jack laid his hand on her arm.

"It's the smart thing to do, Ma'am," Jack whispered to her. "This will be a big feather in your cap at the office. I know the District Attorney would agree. Unfortunately, we don't have time to track him down on a Friday night in Las Vegas. You need to make the call right now."

Another moment passed when Jack felt sure she would throw up on him before she could speak. Finally, visibly gathering her strength, she responded.

"Thanks for the reassurance, Mr. Summers," she said, making Jack feel ancient.

"I'm perfectly capable of deciding this issue on my own and have the inherent power to do so. I agree that we should accept the deal." Jack had been properly rebuked for condescending to her.

"But," she continued, "if you have knowledge of a crime in progress in my jurisdiction, I suggest that you give us the details immediately. I didn't bring an immunity agreement with your name on it today."

The men, collectively holding their breath as she spoke, broke out in laughter, with a new appreciation for the young lady at the table.

"I'm prepared to do that, ma'am. I'd just like to get the ground rules set first," Jack replied.

"Let's hear them, then," she responded, assuming control of the group. "But you can call my mother 'ma'am' if you like. My name is Sonia Wade. You can call me 'Sonia'."

Jack noticed for the first time the sparkle in her cobalt blue eyes, and knew this was a woman to be reckoned with. He continued.

"I have funds in my briefcase, in the form of negotiable bearer instruments, that Marchesi wants in exchange for Ms. Dunn and her son," Jack said. "I have no illusions that if he suspects that I have brought the authorities into this then they will disappear without a trace. You and I both know that he can do this." There was a general nod of assent around the table. "I propose that Mr. Foley put an electronic bug in my briefcase that will allow you to monitor my progress in delivering these funds. You will have your task force, which, for the sake of security, I suggest be comprised of FBI agents only, positioned to enter the building where they're being held on my signal."

The agent in charge was first to speak. "I can't put you in that kind of danger, Mr. Summers."

Before Jack could respond, Foley interceded, saying, "I'm informed by a reliable source that Mr. Summers can sufficiently take care of himself. I believe the risk is justified. If he's on the inside, he can position the hostages for us before we enter. It makes the take-down ultimately much more secure. Besides, the bug may add valuable evidence to the kidnapping charge later, if needed."

There was a general discussion of logistics, with Sonia Wade agreeing to limit the local police's participation to traffic control of the area. It was a risk Jack didn't want to take, given the odds that someone might tip Marchesi to the added activity, but he didn't see another choice.

While the others made phone calls to line up the field team, Jack went over the immunity agreements for Dean, line by line. When he was satisfied, he signed for himself and Dean. Belcastro would need to sign again later personally, but it was enough under the circumstances to convince a Court if the authorities tried to renege on the deal.

Jack found himself alone with Sonia as the others left to handle further details of the strike team's night. Foley took Jack's briefcase with him to have the bug installed. Before entering the building, Jack had removed all but one of the bonds from the case. The remaining five were tucked under the front seat of his car. As Jack turned back from watching Foley exit, he caught the leggy beauty eyeing his backside. She blushed and looked quickly away. He reflexively looked to her left hand, noting the absence of a ring.

"So, how long have you been with the prosecutor's office?" he said, filling the awkward silence.

"Just a year, Mr. Summers," she replied with a smile.

"It's 'Jack'," he replied, returning the smile. "Mr. Summers was my grandfather."

She considered this for a moment, and lowering her voice, said, "Well, you don't look like any grandfathers I've ever seen."

Jack felt himself blush, and busied himself shuffling the paperwork in front of him. A few minutes later Foley returned with Jack's briefcase, a small transmitter having been installed in the lining. Sonia Wade said her good-byes, and excused herself. On the way out she stopped to tell Jack to call her when the deal was finished, and to wish him luck. When she'd gone, Foley spoke first.

"That one would keep your blood pressure up for a while. To be young and single again," he said to himself as much as to Jack.

"Let's get the ground rules set," Jack replied. "And I'm talking about Ms. Dunn and her son."

"Of course," replied Foley, still looking in the direction of Sonia's departure.

Jack spent the next twenty minutes going over the details of the rescue operation. He would enter the property alone. He explained to Foley that Belcastro had called it a "scrap yard," and gave the agent the address. Foley was familiar with the lay-out of the property, as he'd had Marchesi's operation under surveillance for months. The assistant district attorney was on his way to the Federal building to get the appropriate search and arrest warrants. He would meet them at the scrap yard.

The plan was that Jack would give a signal to Foley by saying, "It's hot in here," when he felt that Sarah and Adam were in a position to be reasonably protected. This would trigger an assault from two sides by the strike team. They agreed that it would be too risky for Jack to enter the building armed. He would undoubtedly be searched, in any event. With any luck, there would be a few minutes after Marchesi got the money, during which they would relax their guard. This would be the opportunity for Jack to give Foley the signal.

Jack knew there would be little chance of such a break if Marchesi looked closely at the briefcase, discovering that it contained only one bond worth one hundred thousand, rather than over four million dollars worth of bonds. He didn't share this thought with the agent across the table from him.

Jack glanced at his watch. It was nearly seven thirty. Time to head north to meet Marchesi.

As Jack walked to the parking lot on east Charleston, Sam Marchesi made his way back to his dark blue Mercedes in the parking area of the scrap yard and drove south. He was on his way to the North Las Vegas airport. He'd already made arrangements with his pilot to have the Citation jet fueled, and ready for a quick flight to Mexico.

Sam was fairly sure that Summers wouldn't try to cross him, but his years in the business gave him reason to trust his instincts. If Summers brought in the law, Sam would have options. There was no reason to be there when Summers showed up with the money. Bruno could handle that, with the help of the two guys he'd left with him. Better safe, than sorry, Sam thought.

He called John Kirshbaum from the car, and told him that to get his money he'd have to take care of Charlie Patek and Ashley Roh. Sam told him that Patek and Roh would be in his office on west Sahara for a meeting at ten. With any luck, Sam's plane would have departed for Puerto Vallarta by the time Charlie Patek met his maker. Too bad about Charlie, Sam thought, but he knew too much for his own good.

Kirshbaum didn't have any problem with his end of the deal.

Nothing like a good cop on the take, Sam mused to himself as his car pulled into the entrance to the airport.

The sun hovered just above the Spring mountain range to the west of the Las Vegas valley as Jack arrived at the address Marchesi had given him.

Chapter Thirty Two

The gate to the chain link fence surrounding Marchesi's scrap yard was open. From the street, all Jack could see was mound after mound of the shells of wrecked or stripped car bodies piled high. Toward the center of the lot, he could see the corrugated metal roof line of a building. Looking up the street, he noticed two gray vans with no markings. That would be a part of Foley's strike team. Inside each van would be six heavily armed FBI agents, dressed in body armor. Each would wear a sleeveless pull-over with large, highly visible "FBI" markings.

Jack gunned the engine of his Jaguar, spraying gravel as he drove into the lot. Seconds later, he pulled up in front of a metal building. A sign, bearing the faded logo of "Acme Scrap & Metal" swung cock-eyed above a gray metal door. Stepping from his car, Jack removed his suit coat and threw it in the front seat. He cleared his mind, deeply inhaling and forcing himself into a practiced calm.

The door to the building opened as he approached. He was expected. As he stepped into the entry way, a silver Citation jet airplane passed overhead, its contrail bending south. A second later, enveloped by the first brush of cooled air from the interior of the building, Jack felt the barrel of a hand gun press against the side of his head.

"Drop the case, and put your hands behind your head," a voice to Jack's left said.

He did as instructed. Though the interior of the building was lighted, Jack struggled to adjust his eyes from the outside blaze of light. As the interior came into focus, he saw Sarah tied to a chair in the center of the building. Adam was nowhere in sight.

Sarah's face was bruised, and she was wearing only a bra and the shorts she'd had on when he put her in a cab that morning, headed for her apartment. It seemed like a week had passed, instead of less than a day. When she saw Jack, she started to speak, but was cut short by a scream of pain as Bruno grabbed a handful of her dark hair and pulled back violently.

Jack scanned the room quickly. The entire interior couldn't be more than forty by fifty feet. It was empty, except for a few old car parts that littered the perimeter and a lone tool bench built against the far wall. The bench was scattered with various tools. Jack noticed a large power tool that appeared to be a pneumatic nail driver.

To his left, a makeshift office had been fashioned out of unpainted wall board. It looked to be about ten feet across, with a wooden door in the center. He assumed they would be holding Adam in there. Dean Belcastro stood guard by the doorway to the office, Glock automatic pistol hanging at his side in his right hand. There were only three men in the building, unless more would be found in the office.

The man who'd greeted Jack at the door shoved him forward, towards Sarah. As he moved closer, Jack could see the absolute terror in Sarah's eyes. She was crying soundlessly, tears streaming down her flawless cheeks. Jack forced his eyes away from her, looking to Bruno.

"We meet again," Bruno said with a snarl.

"I'm not aware that we've met before," Jack replied conversationally. "Where's Marchesi? He asked me to join him here for an exchange."

"I'm in charge of this meeting," Bruno hissed. "Where's the money?"

"It's in the case that your associate took from me," Jack said. "It's locked. Why don't you let me show you?"

Jack's hands were still behind his head, fingers interlocked. As he came to a halt in front of Sarah, he didn't look down at her. He wanted as little eye contact with her as possible until he made his move.

"Where's the boy?" Jack asked in a manner that might have suggested that he was only slightly interested.

"He's in here," Dean spoke up. "Do we have a deal?" It was a pre-arranged communication. And, when Jack quickly replied that they did, Dean knew he would get immunity from prosecution for cooperation. Bruno cut him off.

"Shut up, Dean. I'll do the talking here. The kid's alright, and you can see that your girlfriend is in tip top shape. I been checking her out for you," Bruno said with a sneer.

"Why don't you let me see the boy," Jack said calmly. "Then I'll open the case and show you your money."

Bruno nodded in Dean's direction, and he disappeared momentarily into the office. He returned seconds later with Adam at his side. The boy cried out at the sight of his mother tied in the center of the room.

"Alright, I'm satisfied," Jack said to Dean, motioning for him to take Adam back into the other room.

As Dean complied, Jack walked to the tool bench with the other man close behind. He still had his handgun pointed squarely at Jack's mid-section. Bruno's eyes never left Jack as he approached the bench. Jack gauged that there would be about ten feet between him and Bruno when he reached the bench. As he did, his guard set Jack's briefcase in front of him. The nail gun sat to his right. It was within reach, but Jack couldn't be certain that the extension cord it was attached to would have power. It could be a useful weapon, but only as a last resort.

Jack made a show of fumbling with the lock on his briefcase. He ignored Bruno's taunting chatter about being too nervous to open it. He took his time with the lock, fumbling with his keys. Bruno was losing patience, and took a step in Jack's direction when suddenly the case sprang open.

At that same moment, Jack dropped his keys in front of the man standing next to him. Reflexively, the man looked down. It was just enough time for Jack, his back to Bruno, to slip his old letter opener from the case, and palm it.

Jack turned, facing Bruno. The big man had taken another step closer, and a large fish boning knife appeared in his hand.

"Are the bonds in there?" he asked Jack's guard. The man glanced into Jack's case, seeing the stack of documents, topped by the single one hundred thousand dollar bond.

"Looks like they are," the man responded. "Want me to count them?"

"No," Bruno replied. "This fish is too scared to try and fuck with me. Aren't you counselor?"

Jack made no reply, but shifted his weight, moving a step closer to the man next to him who was now facing Bruno.

"Looks like our business is done. It's hot in here, isn't it?" Jack said, giving Foley the signal to come in.

Bruno looked perplexed at the incongruous comment, and stopped in his tracks. Then his eyes narrowed, the look of a predator about to strike.

"You're not going to have to worry about it, Counselor," Bruno growled. "You owe me some serious pain from our meeting in Reno, and this seems like a good time to collect. I think I'll cut your balls off and let your girlfriend hold onto them while I skin her alive. You shouldn't bleed to death before you get to see most of it. The last young pussy I got to carve was some pregnant bitch back in Chicago years ago. You should have heard her beg like a wounded puppy. Her husband was a meddling U.S. Attorney who was bothering my friends back there."

"What was her name?" Jack asked, his mind numbed by the incredible possibility that he was facing Claire's killer.

Bruno, taken back by the question, thought for only a second before saying "Claire something. Why do you care? You want the details, asshole?"

This comment apparently amused the man guarding Jack, as he laughed out loud.

Jack, who was now standing close enough to touch his guard, swung his arm up in the motion of a rising block directed at the man's gun hand. As he did, he exposed the razor edge of the knife in his hand, driving the barrel of the gun toward the ceiling, and severing the tendons in the man's wrist. The pistol discharged twice into the ceiling, and dropped from the man's disabled hand. In a continuous motion, Jack brought the knife back down into the man's solar plexus, and he exhaled audibly.

As his guard staggered back against the tool bench behind him, Jack delivered a forward punch to the man's jaw. The knife, its blade extending from Jack's palm, opened the guard's throat like a split melon.

Jack's assault had been so unexpected and had produced such a geyser of blood from the soon to be deceased guard, that Bruno stopped, facing Jack, a look of disbelief frozen on his face.

Jack weighed the distance between them again, and launched the balanced throwing knife with a flick of his wrist. Bruno flinched, trying to raise his arms in defense. He was too slow. The knife was imbedded to its handle in his Adam's apple. He staggered back, choking on his own blood, and swinging the blade in his hand wildly. He was still several feet from Sarah, but Jack took no chances. He executed a perfect sliding side kick at Bruno's hands, now frantically clutching the knife protruding from the front of his neck. The impact of Jack's strike drove his already imbedded knife through Bruno's neck, severing his cervical spine, and nearly decapitating him. He was dead before he hit the ground at Sarah's side, his eyes fixed open in amazement. Sarah screamed.

Jack looked to the office door, where Dean stood holding a crying Adam Dunn in his arms. At that moment the metal door to the building exploded open and a torrent of FBI agents poured in, automatic weapons drawn. Jack raised his hands immediately, and motioning to Dean, yelled, "He's with us!"

Foley was the first to reach Jack, his clothes covered in blood. Other agents moved to help Adam and Sarah, and to take Dean into custody. They would hold him until it was clear that he was what Jack represented.

"Are you hurt?" Foley asked as he scanned the blood covering Jack's shirt and suit pants.

"No," Jack replied. He was trying to get control of the adrenaline rush that had fueled his attack on Bruno and his associate. "The blood's all theirs."

"We're supposed to take care of the bad guys, Summers," Foley said as he surveyed the havoc that had been wrought in the less than thirty seconds that had elapsed since Jack's signal.

"Sorry, Tom," Jack replied. "I didn't think it was safe to wait."

"Safe!" Foley said. "I don't think you know the meaning of the word. Where's Marchesi?"

"I'm afraid he elected not to show up," Jack replied.

"He was here earlier," Dean said from across the room. Jack could see that he'd been handcuffed.

"Would you mind taking the cuffs off of my client," Jack said. "I think you can see that he's cooperated fully."

Foley acknowledged Jack's request, and directed the agent next to him to remove Dean's handcuffs.

Jack turned his attention back to Sarah, who'd been cut loose from her restraints. A blanket was wrapped around her, and she stood, holding her son in her arms as they both wept. They made only brief eye contact before she and Adam were escorted to a waiting ambulance.

Foley was on the phone to his team charged with surveillance of Marchesi's office, and got the word that he hadn't shown up there.

"Damn. The old fox's out of the coop again," Foley muttered.

He turned towards Jack, and the two men knew each others' thought without speaking. Marchesi would retaliate. An agent appeared with Jack's briefcase, and Foley told him to book it as evidence in case they needed to press the kidnapping charge.

"Sorry, Jack," Foley said, "but your briefcase will be tied up for a while."

Jack just shrugged, and said, "I've got more."

"You did a remarkable job here, from what we could hear," Foley commented. "Remind me not to piss you off."

Jack, looking down at Bruno's corpse and wondering if through an incredible twist of fate he'd just evened the score for Claire's murder, simply said he would need to change clothes before joining his client at the FBI field office. He told Foley he wanted to visit Sarah at the hospital, and would meet him in two hours. He verified that Sarah and Adam would be under federal protection until they located Marchesi. Foley agreed, and suggested the same for Jack, who was also a potential witness.

Jack declined, and Foley agreed saying "You can probably take better care of yourself than the FBI could."

With that, Jack drove home, his mind racing over the possibility that Bruno was Claire's murderer.

An hour later, Jack walked into University Medical Center on west Charleston, where Foley told him Sarah and Adam would be. He met Foley in the lobby, who, along with one of the staff physicians was discussing Adam's condition. He explained to Jack that Adam was suffering from a form of post traumatic stress syndrome, and had withdrawn, refusing to talk to anyone, including Sarah. She was naturally beside herself, and had been sedated. There would be no talking to either of them until the next morning, the doctor explained.

"Can I at least see her?" Jack asked.

He was led to a private room on the second floor, where a uniformed police officer, courtesy of Sonia Wade, stood guard outside the door. When Jack entered the room, Sarah was sleeping. She had on the usual hospital garb, a pin-stripped gown that covered her from knees to neck in the front.

Jack thought in passing that the gowns had been invented to humiliate the patients, and thereby keep them docile and cooperative. After all, who would really feel like causing much of a ruckus with their bare ass hanging out?

Sarah's breathing was deep and even. He held her hand gently and looked down at her battered face. The beautiful creature he'd met was in there somewhere, but this woman looked cold, like she'd brushed death and looked too long. Foley told him that she'd sustained two broken ribs, and bruises to her face, arms and back. Other than any possible psychological fall out, her prognosis was good.

The doctors were worried about Adam, however. He'd apparently withdrawn during his ordeal and was having a hard time coming back. His physician wouldn't let Foley interrogate him about the kidnapping until he showed more progress in dealing with the trauma. At least they hadn't abused him physically. Standing at Sarah's bed, Jack made a silent promise that he would make sure she and Adam stayed safe from Marchesi…whatever it took.

Foley was still in the hallway when Jack emerged from Sarah's room.

"We need to go to my office," Foley said. "Our guys are itching to question your client, and frankly, so am I," Foley said.

"I'd like one of your men on this door, Tom," Jack replied, referring to Sarah's room. "I'm sure there's little chance that the Metro guard won't do a good job, but I can't take it. You, of all people, should know how far Marchesi's influence can reach."

"Not a problem," Foley responded, and was on his cell phone calling for an agent.

Two hours later, Jack sat in Foley's office on east Charleston. The FBI team had just completed its preliminary interrogation of Jack's client,

Dominic "Dean" Belcastro. There would be more questions as they checked out his story, but not tonight. They were scheduled to drive to the gravesite of the McKennas at first light in the morning.

Jack was just starting to feel the let-down from his day-long adrenaline rush. He felt no remorse connected with the killing of Bruno and his helper. As far as Jack was concerned, they were vermin, and he'd feel worse about stepping on a cockroach. As Foley poured them a drink from a bottle of vodka kept in his desk, Jack asked the question that had been on both men's minds.

"So, where is Marchesi?"

"We have some early reports," Foley answered. "His private jet left the North Las Vegas airport at about the time we arrived at the junk yard. We haven't confirmed that he was on it, but I've had agents at all of his usual haunts here and can't find a trace. The plane's pilot didn't file a flight plan, but I just got word from our people that he checked in with Mexican authorities a couple of hours later. It looks like the plane went to Puerto Vallarta. Marchesi's got a villa, south of town, overlooking the Bay of Banderas. Unfortunately, even if he is there, I can't touch him unless the State Department gets the Mexican government to cooperate. That will take time."

"In the meantime, he's free to call the shots on retaliation against Sarah," Jack said, stating the obvious.

"I can get her into witness protection, along with Belcastro. You should probably think about it yourself," Foley responded.

"If you don't mind, I'll take care of Sarah and the boy for the next few days," Jack said. "When they're ready to leave the hospital, I'll move them to my house. You can put up your security there. By the way, what's the name of Marchesi's villa?"

"Villa Lucia," Foley replied.

"Do me a favor," Jack said. "Can I get a DNA sample from Marchesi's bodyguard? I think he may have been involved in the death of my wife in Chicago several years ago. I can give you the name of the forensic tech back there to send it to."

"What are you talking about?" Foley asked.

"My wife, Claire, was killed by someone who liked his work; much like the dead guy with the boning knife back at the garage," Jack replied. "I want to get a comparison of his DNA with the samples collected after Claire's murder."

"Let me know where to send it, and my office will follow up for you," Foley said, still trying to get his mind around the possible connection. He wondered if Jack could be in some type of shock himself.

Chapter Thirty Three

Dark clouds gathered over the valley, and it was starting to rain. Cloud bursts that hit Vegas without warning were legendary. In a matter of minutes, the sky would darken, and open up with a torrent that would flood the Strip in an hour. Large drops of water hit the heated pavement and sizzled. The combination of oil, seeping all day from the super heated asphalt, and the rain water, would turn the parking lot into the equivalent of an ice rink.

Sam had told Charlie he wanted a meeting and to be sure that Ashley was there. By now, Charlie thought, Sam should have collected the money from Summers. Was Sam thinking about a hit on Charlie? Hadn't he always kept their agreements? Hadn't the greasy son-of-a-bitch made a pile of cash from Charlie's efforts? Hell, he's got first and second security on the Anasazi property! Between his investment through Charlie's company, and his interest in Sundown Mortgage, the old man was more than secure. He should have gotten most of the Sundown money back and was in a position to take over both the construction project and the title company. Their plans were all coming together.

John Kirshbaum cursed as his shin hit the corner of an end table in Charlie's office like a hammer. He'd been temporarily blinded by the neon lights of Trini's Bar as Charlie pushed open a door in the back corner of the room. Kirshbaum had entered the building from the front, using a lock pick that he'd perfected as a cop in Chicago. Just as Marchesi had described it, the locking mechanism was a simple turnkey lock; child's play for anyone worth their salt in the breaking and entering business.

Once inside, he moved quietly across the reception room, taking a position opposite the open door to Charlie's office. From there, several feet back in the darkened reception area, he could see the outline of Charlie Patek sitting in a large chair behind his desk. Charlie called out, and it was clear that he couldn't see Kirshbaum. Taking a braced firing stance he'd learned those many years before in the police academy, he brought his pistol up with both hands, aiming at the center of the outline of Charlie's head. With his years of practice, he could hit a target the size of a quarter at that distance. Taking a deep breath, and then exhaling slowly, he squeezed the trigger.

At that instant, for some inexplicable reason, Patek ducked. Instead of the expected sound of the silenced bullet hitting Charlie's skull, he heard it strike the padded leather chair behind his intended target. Recovering quickly from the surprise, Kirshbaum fired again in the direction that Charlie now fled in the dark.

Kirshbaum was about to fire a third time when Charlie hit the door, and in an instant, was through, taking most of a curtain with him. As he hopped on one leg in the dark, rubbing his throbbing shin in pain, Kirshbaum heard the unmistakable blast of a twelve gauge shotgun explode beyond the door that Patek had used to escape. There was no sign of the bitch, Ashley.

Kirshbaum's inner voice of experience told him to cut and run back through the front door. It was obvious that he wasn't the only one after Patek that night. But, his greed got the better of him. Marchesi promised him the rest of his money if he got rid of Patek and Roh, and he was damn well sure gonna make that happen. He'd worked too long and hard to lose almost half of his savings to a con artist.

Kirshbaum felt his way to the corner of the room where Charlie exited. The door was once again closed, enveloping the room in darkness. His eyes again adjusted to the dim light, and he found the push bar that would open the exit door.

The man standing below the staircase behind Charlie's office had done odd jobs for Marchesi over the years. More than once he'd helped people, who were in the way of Sam's plans, to disappear in the desert. Tonight, he'd been told to follow John Kirshbaum to Charlie Patek's office. Once there, he was supposed to wait until Kirshbaum took care of Charlie and Ashley.

Sam's instructions were to get rid of Kirshbaum, taking him to a grave that would never be found. The man was reliable, a professional known in the trade as a cleaner. He was called in to clean up any loose ends that might threaten Marchesi. Sam wanted it to look like Kirshbaum killed Charlie, presumably in a fit of anger over losing his money, and then disappeared. Ashley would look like an unfortunate victim, in the wrong place at the wrong time. Sam's professional would make sure that the murder weapon, traceable to Kirshbaum, would be found near the scene.

Sam's man had followed John Kirshbaum that night, as instructed. He watched him park behind the building and walk toward the front entrance. He was waiting under the back staircase for the ex-cop to return after putting the hit on Patek and Roh. There'd been no sign of the broad. He was smoking a cigarette, watching the storm clouds roll in. Large droplets of rain were just starting to bang on the metal staircase he was standing under when he heard a door above him open.

The metal door sounded like a gunshot as it swung wide, hitting the side of the building. Sam's man had a thirty-eight caliber pistol tucked in his belt, and a sawed-off twelve gauge shotgun wrapped in a coat that he held in his hands. The coat looked a little strange, given that even with the rain, the temperature was still well over a hundred that night. But then he always worked with two guns. Tonight was no exception. He'd use the pistol if he could, but there was no substitute for firepower that could hit a moving target.

Ashley'd been drinking for several hours after the call from Charlie. She was still trying to come to grips with the fact that Patek finally agreed to marry her. He'd told her that they'd clear up the Anasazi mess. The more she drank, the better the deal sounded. She'd be off the hook with her employer, and would finally be getting what she'd worked for her whole life…a rich husband.

Stumbling from the kitchen, where Charlie had administered her recent beating, she moved to the bedroom. She selected a pair of shorts and a cut-off T-shirt that was two sizes too small. Might as well go with the horses that brought you, she thought to herself, sliding the shirt over her bare breasts.

She applied a heavy make-up base to her face, covering, as best she could, the bruise Charlie'd given her. On the way back through the kitchen, she made herself another rum and Coke in a plastic glass, and headed for the door. She would be almost an hour late by the time she arrived at the building that housed Charlie's office, she mused, but then it might do the asshole good to wait. Talking to herself, she said, "He'd better get used to waiting on me."

By the time Ashley backed her car out of the driveway, her blood alcohol level would have tested at almost twice the legal limit.

Traffic was light as Ashley made her way west on the "215" towards Charlie's office. The air conditioner in her car had been on the fritz, and she powered down the driver's side window. The sun dropped below the mountains to the west, and dusk faded quickly into darkness. The lights of the Strip to the north blurred in Ashley's vision, and the heated night air whipped her black hair.

Just after eleven o'clock, Ashley turned off Sahara Avenue, and into the parking lot of Charlie's office. It was starting to rain, and she fumbled for the seldom used switch that would turn on her windshield wipers. Through her still open windows, rain beginning to pelt her shirt, she could hear the strains of a Jimmy Buffet song blaring across the lot from a new bar.

She decided to park at the rear of the building, and use the back stairs as a direct entrance to Charlie's office. Accelerating towards the bar, and fumbling for a button to power up the windows on her Camry, she heard her tires squeal, as she made a wide turn around the end of the building. The rum from her drinks had by this time saturated the lining of her stomach, and alcohol sped into her bloodstream.

Charlie, his head down and legs pumping to recover from stumbling on the wet asphalt, never saw Ashley's car. The glare of her headlights would be his last sense impression. The front bumper of the Toyota caught Charlie in mid-section, and he was catapulted, head first, into her windshield. In Ashley's defense, she probably wouldn't have seen Charlie in time to avoid the collision, even if she hadn't been drunk.

The rain had, in seconds, become a torrent. Charlie's skull exploded like a ripe pumpkin when it hit the glass, and Ashley slammed on her brakes, losing control and smashing into a parked SUV.

Ashley shook her head, trying to clear it. She wasn't quite sure what had happened. Blood trickled down her face where she'd hit the steering wheel. She could taste the salt, and rubbed her face. She lowered her hand, covered in blood, and screamed.

Seconds earlier, Sam's cleaner had heard the rear door of Charlie's office open for a second time. Struggling with his coat, he'd fired the shotgun from his hip in the direction of Charlie's retreating figure. The sound of the blast would coincide with the screech of Ashley's squealing tires rounding the corner of the building.

As the exit door above him filled with the outline of John Kirshbaum, gun in hand, the assassin turned and dropped to one knee, firing with his pistol. The sound of Ashley's collision with Charlie covered the sharp report of the man's gun, and Kirshbaum, a healthy portion of the left side of his face torn away by the .38 caliber's impact, dropped to his knees and expired.

Turning back in the direction of Trini's, the cleaner could see people streaming from the bar, drawn into the rain by the sound of the collision. Time to go, he thought to himself, wondering how Marchesi would react to the news that their best laid plans had gone awry.

He made his way to his car, holding his coat over his head and covering the shotgun. He then joined the gathering crowd around Ashley's car. He could hear police sirens drawing closer. The driver of the Toyota hadn't moved from her seat. Blood covered a portion of her face, but she fit the description of Ashley Roh as Marchesi had described her. With the police soon to arrive, there would be no getting to her that night.

Marchesi's cleaner backed out of his parking spot, and pulled away as Las Vegas Metro units arrived on the scene.

A cop from the first black and white helped Ashley from her car, and into the patrol unit. Charlie's corpse lay, face down, near the rear of her car, blood spreading from his head like a virus out of control. A few minutes later, the first ambulance unit arrived at the scene, followed by an unmarked police car. A plainclothes detective was taking charge of the scene, waiting for the duty sergeant to arrive. Ashley told the cop who helped her from her car that "he ran out in front of me" before breaking down in tears.

An accident investigation team would soon be there to confirm what happened. In the meantime, the first officer to reach Ashley reported to the detective that the driver reeked of booze. Given Ashley's current state, they would follow the ambulance that would take her to University Medical Center and secure a blood sample to be tested for alcohol content. Once there, she would likely be placed under arrest for suspicion of driving under the influence, and perhaps, motor vehicle homicide.

No one would think to investigate the body of John Kirshbaum lying in a pool of his own blood at the top of the stairs near the exit from Charlie's office. Though a few patrons of Trini's could see the body lying in the dark as they left the parking lot, they'd all assumed it was just one of the many homeless people who populate Vegas. They could be found sleeping in dark stairwells throughout the city that night, seeking shelter from the rain. It would be the next day before a call came into Metro reporting Kirshbaum's body. By that time, the county coroner would be pondering over an array of buckshot he'd found in the right shoulder blade of an accident victim from the night before.

A week later, detective Jack Smith, homicide division, made the connection between Charlie and Kirshbaum. It would lead him to a complete investigation of the records of Patek Investments. The one thing Charlie had always feared, now made no difference to him.

Chapter Thirty Four

Three weeks passed since Sarah and Adam left the hospital. She'd resisted only briefly when Jack suggested that she and Adam move in with him. The boy had recovered well, and watching him wreak havoc around a house designed for a bachelor, Jack knew he'd be fine. He wasn't so sure about Sarah.

They'd been at Jack's home for two weeks, living in the upstairs guest quarters when she came to him in the middle of the night. He'd put no pressure on her, and most nights when he returned from work, they'd sit quietly watching Adam play with some of the toys that were streaming in from Mac and Foley.

She'd taken Adam to bed after dinner, and Jack assumed that they were down for the night. He was sitting at a small desk in the alcove next to his bedroom, working on a contract for one of the many clients he'd been neglecting, when she appeared at the door. She was wearing a silk robe, covered in a rose print.

"Want some distraction?" she asked.

It was just what Jack didn't need. He'd stopped taking new business when they'd left for the West Indies and was still dancing around his existing case load on a daily basis to spend more time with Sarah. He was already getting the evil eye from his secretary every time he walked in the office.

"You bet I do!" he replied. "What's up?"

"Adam is asleep," she said. "I thought maybe you and I could spend some alone time together."

"There's nothing I'd like more," Jack said, smiling and dropping the contract he'd been working on.

Sarah walked slowly towards him. The only light on in the master suite was a small desk lamp he'd been using to read. She stopped a few feet short of his chair, letting the robe slide off of her shoulders. Jack caught his breath at the sight of her and stood to embrace her. She'd never looked more radiant to him; her dark, auburn hair glowing in the dim light of the desk lamp. They held each other quietly in a wordless exchange. After a minute, she led him by the hand into his bedroom and, without a word, undressed him.

Jack made love to Sarah that night with an intensity that would be with him the rest of his life. She responded in kind, their bodies moving together in the lovers' dance until just before dawn. Then she was gone. She said nothing about their encounter the next day, and Jack respected her silence. He knew that Sarah was still struggling with all that had happened to her and hoped that she could work it out, given time.

He spent the next week negotiating a settlement of the mechanics liens on the Anasazi Properties development. The subcontractors took sixty cents on the dollar. The single one hundred thousand dollar bond that was in Federal custody in his briefcase, after being documented and photographed, had been released to Bill Roxburgh at Jack's request. It would be just enough to cover Jack's statement for services rendered to AmCon Title in the Anasazi Properties mess. Roxburgh was happy to pay.

Now, three weeks removed from the events at the scrap yard, Jack sat by his pool sipping coffee. He'd sworn himself off the stuff some months before, but this morning, he needed it. Mac and his girlfriend had been over for dinner the night before. Mac had hammered him on the golf course that afternoon. He just couldn't seem to marshal the concentration he needed to play well since Sarah and Adam took up residence with him.

He had a feeling of impending doom, like the other shoe was about to drop.

After golf, Jack had fired up the Weber and grilled steaks that he'd marinated in a wine and garlic sauce. Indirect cooking rendered a pile of filets that you could cut with a fork.

After dinner, Jack and Mac found themselves alone on his patio overlooking the night skyline of Las Vegas, and sipping on a couple of glasses of Grand Marnier. Sarah and Mac's current girlfriend were inside, dealing with the aftermath of dinner, and Adam had been retired to the upstairs bedroom.

"Not much progress on the extradition of Marchesi from Mexico," Mac said.

"Yeah," Jack responded, "no surprise to me. Marchesi's developed some very influential allies in the Mexican government through his years of paying gratuities in the drug trade."

"I'd say the chances of getting him legally are pretty slim to none at this point," Mac said, stating the obvious.

"He's still pretty much in control of business in Vegas, isn't he?" Jack asked.

Hesitating only briefly, Mac replied affirmatively. Sarah, Adam and Jack, for that matter, would not be safe until Marchesi had been removed from power.

At Jack's request, Mac had been able to get his hands on photographs, from several angles, of the villa where Marchesi now took refuge. He handed the envelope containing the pictures to Jack as they sat alone, looking at the skyline.

"If you're going to visit this place, you'll need help," Mac told him. "From what I hear, it's guarded like Fort Knox. My advice is don't do it. Let Sarah and her son go off into the Federal witness protection program somewhere. Foley will arrange it. I know you're too stubborn to consider it yourself, but at least they'll be safe."

"I don't want them to have to live that way," Jack responded, and took a moment to tuck the photographs away in a drawer by the grill. "Besides, I didn't say I was going to do anything on my own."

They were joined by the ladies a minute later, and the conversation about Marchesi ended. The rest of the evening was dedicated to drinking several more bottles of wine from Jack's collection, and the morning brought with it a hammering in his head.

Hangovers were rare for Jack, and, as he sipped the hot coffee Sarah had ground and brewed, he accepted his punishment.

"How are you feeling?" Sarah asked, as she appeared behind him on the patio. At eight o'clock in the morning, the summer sun was already starting to heat the patio deck. It would be another clear day across the valley.

"I'm just fine," Jack lied. "Maybe just a touch of a hangover."

Sarah stood behind him, rubbing his neck and shoulders. She wore a black bikini, covered by a gray sweat shirt, with a blue "Navy" logo, Jack had given her. The temperature would again rise well above a hundred, and they were planning on recuperating at poolside all day.

"We need to talk," Sarah whispered, and Jack knew he'd just heard the other shoe hit the deck.

Turning towards her in his chair, Jack smiled.

"Sure, what's up?"

"I'm in love with you, Jack," Sarah replied, and pulling one of the other lounge chairs close to his, sat down. Their eyes locked in a moment of silence, her words hanging over them.

"Sarah," Jack started to respond, when she cut him off.

"Don't say anything, Jack," she said. "Most of all, don't tell me that you love me too. It will just make what I have to say more difficult. I've given my situation a lot of thought. I want to raise my son back in Nebraska. We've all been through a lot, and I think it's for the best, at least for now. You've built a new life for yourself here, and I'm not going to ask you to change that for us. I think it's best if we take some time apart."

"Sweetheart, let me say something," Jack interjected, taking her hand in his.

"No, Jack, please don't," she said, interrupting again. "If you care for me and Adam, and I know in my heart that you do, you'll let me do this. I need help getting out of my apartment lease. Adam and I will be entering the federal witness protection program back there. Foley has arranged it, and that's more than he said I could tell you."

"When would you leave?" Jack asked, the cloud of his hangover instantly gone.

"Tonight," she replied. "I've already started packing, and would like to be on the road when it gets dark."

That son-of-a-bitch, Jack thought. Mac had surely known from Foley of Sarah's plans last night, and didn't say anything. Sarah could see the wheels spinning in Jack's head.

"Don't be mad at Mac," she said. "I swore him to silence. He has friends back there who will keep an eye on us. I need to get Adam away from the violence of this town. I've seen you in action. You can obviously handle it. I can't."

"Sarah, I only did what I had to. Those men deserved what they got," Jack said, stating the obvious.

"I know you did, and they deserved it," she replied, a single tear making it's way down her cheek. "But it's a side of you that I don't know if I can handle. I need some time alone. There's been too much death. I wake with nightmares almost every night."

Jack had heard her cry out in the guest quarters on several occasions. Standing, Jack took her in his arms and kissed her.

"I don't want to lose you," he whispered quietly, not knowing what else to say.

"You never will," she vowed, tears now pouring down her face.

Sarah was scheduled to leave by ten o'clock that night. Jack had a few minutes alone with her just before they left. She came to him as the others finished up the loading and amused Adam in the yard.

She held him close in the entry way to his home, and spoke softly.

"I can never thank you for what you've done for Adam and me. I wish I could spend a lifetime trying, but I'm just not ready for it now. Maybe someday, I will be."

Jack pulled her close. There was no way he could say what he felt. No one since Claire had felt so right to him. From the moment they'd met, he knew she would be someone special in his life. But standing there, the eloquent trial lawyer was tongue-tied. He wanted her to stay, but knew it was best if she left.

Maybe someday his heart would be ready to replace Claire, but he wasn't sure that this was the day. Until he was sure, he couldn't ask Sarah to stay.

He led her by the hand into the living room, and retrieved a plain vanilla envelope from a small table. He handed it to her and answered the question on her face.

"This is security for Adam's future," he said. "You've earned it. There are two one hundred thousand dollar negotiable bearer bonds here, so don't let loose of the envelope. It's like cash, and a new start for you and, maybe, a college degree for Adam. There are no strings attached, and only you and I know about this. Let's keep it that way."

Sarah hesitated, not knowing what to do. Her instincts told her to refuse. But she trusted the look in Jack's eyes, and reading them, took the envelope. They kissed for the last time, long and deep, and she was gone.

Mac and an old friend from the FBI, retired for several years, appeared at Jack's door. They said he would take Sarah and Adam and drive through the night, taking a southern route across Arizona and New Mexico. Just past Las Vegas, New Mexico, they'd cut north and up through Kansas, probably making Liberal by morning.

Their guardian promised to check in with Mac every two hours during the trip, and he'd keep Summers advised. When Sarah got settled, they agreed to let Mac know. The fewer people who knew their exact location, the better. This included Jack.

Chapter Thirty Five

A week after Sarah left Las Vegas for Nebraska, Jack drove southwest on I-15 towards San Diego. It was four in the morning, and the lights of the Strip shimmered in his rearview mirror. He had the window cracked open on the driver's side of his sports car and was blowing smoke from a Merit Light into the dark of the desert night.

Glancing back, he could see, like a light saber stuck in a black pyramid, the beacon of the Luxor Hotel stabbing upward at passing airplanes en route to dump tourists into McCarran airport. He gunned the engine, and, with a satisfying rumble, the two-seater accelerated to ninety miles per hour. Flicking his cigarette butt through the open window, he set the cruise control and settled in for the four and a half hour drive to San Diego. He'd be there by breakfast time, and, with any luck, cross into Mexico at Tijuana on Highway 1 before noon.

He stopped for lunch in Ensenada. Careful to avoid anything that might cause him stomach problems later, he downed what looked to be two fairly fresh fish tacos. Set on fire by a green sauce that he used too liberally, he'd live with the after effects until just past Santo Domingo, where the Tums finally kicked in. It was there, near the eastern coast by the Sea of Cortez, that he stopped to rest.

Spotting a dirt road that led into the hills, he pulled the Jag onto the side of the gravel shoulder. He was well into the Baja California Sur region by then, and he cut the throaty rumble of the car's engine, casting him into pure silence. It was pitch black, and the night sky took him back to a planetarium he'd visited years before on a high school field trip.

He sat motionless for a moment, letting his eyes and ears adjust to their new environment. It was a far cry from the noise and lights of Las Vegas. He'd driven nearly a thousand miles with a few brief stops. Stretching his back he could feel knots of muscle that needed space bigger than a bucket seat. From beneath the driver's seat, he pulled his semi-automatic pistol and chambered a round. When he was satisfied that his night vision had reached its optimum, he opened the door and stepped out.

The hours behind the wheel left his knees shaky, and he staggered slightly as he stood. There were no other sounds of traffic, just the desert night air gusting through cactus groupings nearby. He knew that Mexico is a place where even the government sponsored advertisements warn you not to travel at night. The cool steel of the Glock, hanging in a soft grained leather shoulder holster at his side, gave him some comfort in the vastness of the night.

He was a trained professional. Jack had a mission to complete, and he had a lot of miles to go before he'd be in a position to complete it. Walking to the rear of his vehicle, he popped open the trunk. Inside, there lay two duffel bags. One contained a black wet suit used for diving in cold water, along with a serious looking diving knife. The blade of the knife curved up and away from the handle, and its opposite side was serrated, with a sharpened niche for cutting a diver loose from unexpected underwater netting or fishing lines. He kept the blade sharp enough to shave with. Next to the knife, sheathed in its case, lay a snorkeling mask, snorkel tube and swim fins.

The other bag contained a folded wool blanket, a few clothes, a twenty foot length of nylon cord with knots tied at two foot intervals, a small aluminum hook, and a case with the markings of an emergency medical kit. Jack checked each item carefully. There was no excuse for lack of preparation.

Re-locking the trunk, he took the blanket with him as he entered the car. The night was an odd mixture of sea air and the sharp, dusky smell of the desert. He was still several hundred miles north of his destination at LaPaz, a small port on the Sea of Cortez, but he needed sleep. Covering himself in the dark with the wool blanket, and reclining the bucket seat, he fell into a restless sleep with the hand gun nestled in his lap.

Four hours later, he was on Highway 1 again, headed south through Santa Rosalia, and on to LaPaz. It was almost noon when he pulled into the small driveway of his friend's adobe style home overlooking the bay. He'd come nearly a thousand miles since crossing the Mexican border, and had driven more than eighteen hours since leaving Las Vegas.

"You're a sight for sore eyes," the big man called out to him as he stretched his back next to the dirt covered sports car.

He'd known Alex James for many years. James was a former Navy man, and a sailor, through and through. After retiring from service, he'd bought a small sail boat and traversed the Pacific Ocean more than once on his own. Jack always claimed you could toss a basketball off of an ocean liner and, given proper coordinates as a starting point, Alex could sail to it from a thousand miles away.

Jack hugged James, slapping him on the back as men do. There was an unbroken, and unspoken, bond of friendship and loyalty between the two men. They would help each other, no questions asked. The big man helped Jack empty the contents of his trunk onto a sailboat, about forty feet in length, which was docked just below James' house.

Without much further conversation, Jack parked his car in a small garage near the house, and they boarded James' boat, setting the sail and heading southeast towards the mainland of Mexico.

Jack woke early the next morning, having slept through the previous afternoon and the night that followed. Alex James was at the helm as he emerged from the cabin.

"Thought maybe you died on me down there, Captain," Alex shouted over the whipping sound of the sail.

"You should be so lucky," Jack answered, raising his voice to be heard above the trade wind. "Where are we?"

"I figure we're about ten miles northwest of our target, give or take a couple of yards," the big man yelled with gusto. "I'm not all that accurate since I found a permanent land based home and a Mexican wife to keep me there. By the way, Captain, what are we fishing for?"

"Shark," Jack said without further comment.

"Always a favorite of mine," Alex responded. "Do I get to throw in a line, or will you be doing all the fishing?"

"I'm afraid you'll have to sit this one out, my friend. Can you park this piece of work about a half mile out from the coordinates I gave you?"

"In my sleep, Captain," he responded. "In my sleep."

The two men said nothing further until the boat lay at anchor a half mile off the southern shore of the Bay of Banderas and Puerto Vallarta, Mexico.

A moonless night came on fast, and Jack's calculations were, as always, on the nose. Alex James had sailed through the night across the Sea of Cortez and part of the Pacific Ocean. He was in serious need of rest and told his friend as much.

"That's fine," Jack said. "I'll be slipping over the side for a little fishing in another hour. Just leave the lights on, and I'll be back here before you know it. Why don't you write down the reverse coordinates for me, and I'll head us back home while you sleep. The worst that can happen is we'll end up in Tahiti."

As his friend retired below, Jack used a telescope his friend kept on board to survey the coastline. He could see the lights of Villa Lucia. The place was lit up like New Year's Eve, and he compared the layout to Mac's stack of photographs.

The main villa, flanked by two smaller structures which he guessed quartered the servants and some of the guards, consisted of four levels. The top level would spill out onto an access street on the inland side. This would be a party level with a large room opening onto an even larger veranda overlooking the bay. Directly below that would be the master sleeping quarters, housing the shark he was after. The two lower levels would contain sleeping quarters for guests and kitchen facilities. From the bottom of the lowest level a sand beach ran sharply down to a boat dock sandwiched between two outcroppings of rock.

He watched the villa carefully for an hour. There were only two guards tending the ocean side of the villa. If an assault were to come, it was clear that they expected it from the inland side.

Two hours after the sun dropped into the Pacific in the west, Jack slipped over the ocean side of the sailboat. Covered totally in black, he would appear as a ripple on the surface should anyone from the shore be looking. He was in superb shape, and the swim to shore, moving with the tide, went easily.

Pausing under the cover of the rocks near the villa's dock, he took a minute to fix the details of his ascent in his mind. One of the two guards was seated on the uppermost deck, automatic weapon slung casually across his lap. A maid from inside had just brought him some food, and, having finished it, he appeared to be nodding off. The guard at shore level was patrolling back and forth on the perimeter of the house.

From his position in the rocks, Jack could see that his guess as to the height of the levels of the house had been a good one. He checked the illuminated dial of his dive watch, calculating that it would be roughly four in the morning. If ever he needed to light a cigarette, now was the time. He took a deep breath and suppressed the urge, vowing once again to quit the cancer sticks when he got home.

Moving with practiced skill, he covered the open sand between himself and the side of the villa. Under the sound of the ocean lapping continuously on the shoreline, his sprint would be undetectable.

Gaining control of his breathing, Jack calmed himself. From the bag that he'd brought with him, he removed a small medical case. In an instant, he had a piece of cloth, soaked in chloroform, waiting as the guard on the lower level neared the edge of the house. The guard stopped briefly, just short of the shadows where the Jack stood, and turned to retrace his steps in the opposite direction. Jack got a strong whiff of the cigarette the guard was smoking and knew his first target was close. He stepped forward without a sound, and grasping a nerve near the base of the guard's neck, partially immobilized him. At the same time, he covered the guard's mouth and nose with the chloroform soaked rag, quickly rendering him unconscious.

Holding the guard's limp body, Jack held his breath and, as he had done in the hotel in St. Kitts, let his senses stretch out into the night. There was no change in the pattern of the sounds around him. No one heard his attack.

He carefully moved the guard onto one of the lounge chairs on the lower patio, placing his automatic weapon, its ammunition clip removed, next to him on the ground. It would appear that he'd simply fallen asleep there. Waking several hours later as the effects of the anesthesia wore off, even the guard wouldn't be certain that he hadn't.

Jack moved to the end of the villa opposite where the guard on the top level was sitting and, retrieving the knotted rope he'd brought with him, he secured a three inch aluminum hook to the end. He'd wrapped the hook in tape to deaden any sound its metal surface might make when thrown. With practiced skill, he threw the hooked end of the rope to the railing on the balcony above him. In seconds he'd scaled the wall, pulling himself hand over hand up the rope, and crouched in the shadows listening.

Again, there was no change in the pattern of the night. When he was sure that no one was aware of his presence, he repeated the process, climbing to the level of the villa that would hold the master bedroom suite.

Standing motionless for several minutes in the shadows of the Villa, Jack listened to the sounds of the ocean surf pounding below. He closed his eyes, letting his ears search the darkness around him, but found that the pounding of his own pulse seemed louder than the crashing surf below.

Jack strained to hear any sound from the guard who remained on the level above him. There was none.

Sliding glass doors were open to his left, and sheer white curtains billowed in and out with a tropical breeze. It was time to do what he'd come for. He could hear, a counterpoint to the flap of the curtains, the rhythmic sounds of snoring coming from inside the bedroom. Taking a deep breath, diving knife in hand, he entered the dark room and stood motionless against the wall. At the far side of the room was a king-sized bed. Its sole occupant was the source of the snoring. He moved without hesitation across the room, knowing at any moment someone could enter. If discovered, he'd never see Sarah again.

Moving to the side of the large bed, Jack looked down at the old man sleeping. It struck him as odd that Marchesi could sleep so peacefully. How many men had he murdered? But, wasn't Jack there to do the same thing? Was it only the murderer's own perception that distinguishes between heinous and hero?

Shaking his head to clear it, Jack knew what he must do to protect Sarah, even if it was what would drive her away from him. Taking the syringe he'd brought in his medical kit, he slid back the plunger filling it with air. With his free hand, he retrieved the drug soaked cloth from inside his wet suit and placed it over the old man's mouth and nose. He was incredibly strong for his age, and as his eyes opened, he struggled to move.

Summers was younger and stronger. The old man's efforts to move only caused him to inhale the anesthesia more deeply. In a moment, his body relaxed and he lay peacefully once again. Jack turned his target's head to the side and deftly located the artery he was looking for.

"Goodbye, Mr. Marchesi," Jack said softly, and injected the needle into the old man's artery.

The reaction was violent and immediate. When the air bubble that had been injected into the old man's artery hit his brain, it caused a chain reaction which would result in a massive stroke.

By ten o'clock that morning, the upstairs maid discovered Sam Marchesi's body. The official explanation from the Mexican physician who examined him would be that he died of natural causes. He'd apparently suffered a stroke while sleeping and, his lungs failing, he'd suffocated. No one could say otherwise, and the tiny needle hole on the side of his neck went unnoticed in a part of the world where insect bites are common.

The shore level guard woke with a slight headache the night before, but finding nothing amiss, simply thought he must have fallen asleep. He wasn't about to report his siesta to anyone at the villa.

Chapter Thirty Six

A couple of weeks after Sam Marchesi went to his final reward, Jack Summers sat working in his office. His secretary announced that "Tom Foley, with the FBI" was at the front desk.

"Show him in, please," Jack said, standing to greet the FBI agent. "How have you been, Tom? Any news on Marchesi?"

"We just heard from the Mexican government that he died," Foley answered. "Apparently he had a stroke in his Villa at Puerto Vallarta."

"Well, I guess that ends your efforts to bring him to trial," Jack said. "Probably takes me and Ms. Dunn off the hook as witnesses, don't you think?"

"I'd say it does," Foley replied. "No reason for anyone to worry about a trial, so I guess no one's got a reason to be concerned about your testimony."

"It's too bad he couldn't be brought to justice, as they say," Jack quipped. "But sometimes things just work out for the best."

Foley walked to the door of Jack's office and turned back, saying, "I just stopped by to tell you the news in person, and to give you this. It's the DNA results from Chicago. Looks like Bruno was your wife's killer. I'm sorry."

"Thank you," Jack said simply, dropping into his chair. "I guess I'm not surprised."

After an awkward pause, Foley said, "Fate has a strange way of evening the score, I guess."

"Yeah. I guess it does," Jack replied.

"Probably doesn't help though, does it?" Foley asked.

Jack paused before answering, his conflicting emotions waging a battle that he knew would never let him rest. "Yes, it sort of does," he answered finally, and Foley caught a look in Jack's eyes that made him shiver involuntarily. "Revenge truly is a dish best served cold."

"Well, I guess I'd better get back to work," Foley said, turning to leave. "Oh, I almost forgot." Foley held out a piece of paper with a phone number on it.

"You can reach Sarah here," he said. "By the way, I heard a rumor that you were in Mexico recently?"

"Yeah. I figured it was a good time to lay low and relax. I went fishing with a buddy of mine off of Cabo San Lucas," Jack answered.

"How was the fishing?" Foley asked, a wry smile on his face.

Jack, dialing the number in Omaha and looking up at the FBI agent, said, "Never better."

Printed in the United States
138816LV00006B/5/P

9 780595 535088